I0603403

The Calibre of Justice

Book 2 of the Tony Signorotto series

Phil Copsey

in case of emergency press
We are proud to acknowledge the Traditional Owners of country
throughout Australia and to recognise their continuing
connection to land, waters, and culture.
We pay our respects to their Elders past, present, and emerging.
We support recognition, reconciliation, and reparation.

The Calibre of Justice

Book 2 of the Tony Signorotto series

Phil Copsey

in case of emergency press
http://www.icoe.com.au
Travancore, Victoria
Australia

Published by **in case of emergency press** 2021
Copyright © Phil Copsey 2021

ISBN 978-0-6485571-6-6

This book is dedicated to the thin blue line.

Phil Copsey

Table of contents

Chapter One

The image that stared back from the full-length mirror in the station change room wasn't all that different to the one that he had seen on a daily basis over the previous ten years or more. Except for one glaring difference. Today was the first time his navy-blue police shirt was attached with the chevron emblazoned epaulets of a Senior Sergeant of the Victoria Police Force. Previously there had only been the three V shaped stripes depicting the rank of Sergeant. Displayed now on his broad shoulders was the combination of the three stripes integrated with the laurel wreath and Queen's crown emblem.

As the newly promoted Senior Sergeant, Tony Signorotto opened the change room door. Lined up on either side of the corridor leading to his office was the entire morning shift consisting of twelve members. Even the patrol crew had made a point of being there.

The round of applause started slowly but gathered momentum as the now red faced Signorotto walked between his troops. His popularity and leadership had never been in dispute. It had been earned through years of working alongside members past and present. Those who had transferred to other areas for promotion or just a change from the hard slog of working the United Nations of Carlton.

Tony never shirked the issues of the day. If ever a person needed 'back up' on a job, they only had to take a step backwards and they were rewarded with the wall of navy blue in the solid form of Sergeant Tony Signorotto.

"Thanks guys. It means a lot to me to have your support," he said to the men and women around him.

Tony suddenly spotted two young female Constables standing at the back, kitted out in their yellow ballistic vests and 9mm Smith and Wesson pistols strapped to their thighs.

"What are you two doing here?" he asked the nearer one.

"Boss! We just came in to say congratulations, that's all I!"

"Well Constable Schaeffer, I think the public would prefer it if you were in your vehicle and out on the street. Taxes remember? Taxes. We all pay taxes so people like you can protect the public. You can't do that in here."

Smiles disappeared and stone-cold silence hung heavily in the air.

Trying to hide a grin, Tony spoke again.

"However, on this occasion I am willing to shout coffee and cake for the station this morning," he said as he pulled a fifty dollar note from his wallet.

The smiles and laughter took over the corridor as Schaeffer ran past him, snatching the note from his hand.

"About time boss," she said smiling up at him. "Back soon."

"That's for the coffee and cake you two," he shouted to the back of both girls as they hurried to the door. "I want to see some change thanks. No buying yourselves lunch at Angelo's Deli of Delights on my money."

After much hand shaking and telling people to get back to work, he walked into the Senior Sergeant's office and sat down in the leather office chair behind what was known to all and sundry as 'the mahogany fox hole.'

The previous Senior Sergeant had been promoted to Inspector and re-assigned to a back room in the corridors of power at Police Headquarters in Flinders Street.

Tony had never really thought about promotion until his great friend and newly promoted Superintendent, Phil Stone, had encouraged him to do so.

Signorotto and Stone, as Sergeant and Inspector, had been through good times and bad at the old bluestone building. Fights with mafia relatives of Signorotto's had nearly been the end of Tony, but with the unwavering support of Stone, the station had survived. Freshly installed into the new Carlton Police Station at the corner of Grattan Street and Rathdowne Street, he could see himself in a much wider role and had the additional responsibility of being father to beautiful Gracie Signorotto, now aged just two. Life was good, he thought to himself as he bellowed out the door to anyone who would listen. "Call that car crew and tell them to hurry up with the coffees!"

A voice shot back from the muster room, "What did your last slave die of?"

Holding in a smile he yelled back, "Mutiny will be punished by death!"

With a sigh, Senior Sergeant Tony Signorotto, Officer in Charge of the Carlton Police Station, switched on his computer and began to scroll through the many emails that had been left dormant for weeks since the office had been empty.

"Hope it stays as quiet as this," he said to himself under his breath.

Chapter Two

Sitting at his desk in the middle of the 'bullring' at the Melbourne C.I.U. office, Max Tyler was still finding it hard to comprehend.

A few months ago, he had been patrolling the streets of Carlton as a uniformed officer when he had received a radio call summonsing him to Police Headquarters. Upon asking who he had to report to he was given the name Superintendent Phil Stone. Stone had been his Inspector at Carlton, and they had a history. A good history. It was only two years previously that Stone had approved his secondment to a temporary plain clothes assignment to work alongside Tony Signorotto. The job was never destined to be simple, as it involved local Carlton mafia, which was headed by Tony's uncle, the now 'retired 'mafia boss, Benny Illarietti. The situation had dragged in Tony's then girlfriend, Susie Doherty, his young cousin Sav Illarietti and had ended with the still unsolved disappearance of a local drug supplier and mafia 'wannabee,' Mickey Midolini. At the completion of the investigation, Max had been singled out for praise by both Stone and Signorotto. He was a raw recruit but had been blooded very quickly and survived in the world of vice, drugs and crime.

Police headquarters in Flinders Street was certainly different from the Carlton Police Station. There were officers walking in and out of every nook and cranny. Locked doors that you needed card readers for and work areas teeming with public support officers. To the uninitiated it was a maze.

Max was eventually guided towards a very modern office that was almost bigger than the Carlton flat he rented with a couple of other young coppers. Knocking on the open door, the familiar voice of Phil Stone called out.

"Come in Max, come in."

Max opened the door and saw the now Superintendent Stone sitting at a round worktable surrounded by bookshelves full of blue four post binders. Whoever had the contract for those navy coloured binders with the department was undoubtedly very rich and probably very retired, Max thought.

"Morning sir," Max said. "How did you know it was me knocking?"

Phil Stone burst out laughing. "Remember that time at the old police station when you walked into my office as a rookie without knocking? You got such a mouthful from me that I knew you'd never do it again."

A rather embarrassed Max replied. "Not wrong boss. Never have made that mistake again."

"Sit down son. I've got a pretty busy schedule today, but I think I have an offer you can't refuse."

Taking a seat at the table, he listened as Phil Stone offered him six months secondment to the Melbourne Criminal Investigation Unit. He was stunned.

"Max. This isn't being offered because you were just one of my lads at the old shop. This relates directly to your good track record and the investigative skills you showed when working with Tony a while back. I waited to make this offer because I wanted to see if your work rate and ability to catch crooks had stayed the same since that job. I know it has because I've been checking on you regularly."

"Thanks boss, love to, but won't some of the regular detectives think I'm a bit wet behind the ears to do C.I.U. work?"

"Just think of it as six months work experience. I'm the Superintendent of the Division and even though the C.I.U. doesn't come under my jurisdiction, a very good friend of mine is the Detective Superintendent in charge and he is always looking for talent to add to his teams. He knows your history and wants you. How about it? Up for a bit of action?"

"Boss, I don't even own a suit."

Stone laughed. "Well don't buy a good one. Get two cheap ones. You won't always be stuck behind a desk in this city."

"I'll jump at it boss. When do I start?"

"Next roster son. You'd better get shopping."

Chapter Three

The luxurious Maserati was parked directly under the white glare of the streetlamp in Argyle Place, North Carlton. That should have been enough to warn off any potential car thieves. Especially two desperados like Lou Carbone and Angelo Morelli.

Lou Carbone was a product of a Broadmeadow's upbringing by parents who thought the Government owed them a living and subsequently hadn't worked a day in their lives. One generation was like the next in the Carbone household. Even their neighbours called it the 'handout house.' The northern Melbourne suburb had been the breeding ground for run of the mill car thieves since the day the Ford factory in nearby Campbellfield had opened in 1959. Most of the residents were glad of the opportunity for full time work. Not the Carbone family. The only interest they had in cars was jacking them.

Angelo Morelli wasn't much different. He was dragged up in the adjoining suburb of Coolaroo. Same place, different location. They hadn't really attended Broadmeadows High School together, they had just wandered through it on occasions. Usually to steal anything that wasn't nailed down. On this occasion they were well out of their comfort zone in looking for a car to heist. This was downtown Carlton, not downtrodden Broadmeadows. Added to this, it wasn't just downtown Carlton but right next to Argyle Square which was in turn directly next to the famous Lygon Street.

Lygon Street on a Saturday night in spring meant quite a few things in Carlton.

The first was the famous Melbourne strip of restaurants would be packed with families and tourists from anywhere and everywhere around the globe. It was the outdoor eating mecca of Melbourne since the first spaghetti restaurants had opened years before. Generations of Italians had plied their restaurant skills over the years. Places such as Donnini's, Papa Gino's and Villa Romana were institutions. Even if you had no Italian blood coursing through your veins you still felt a little bit Italian while sitting at a table covered with a red and white checked tablecloth. This was the street where people greeted each other in loud voices, big hugs and kisses on both cheeks. And that was just the men saying hello. All the regulars to Lygon Street knew there were certain types of vehicles in the vicinity on a night like this. The first being the loud and proud Ducati motorcycle. Red in colour, they would cruise the strip from Victoria Street in the south to Johnston Street in the north, back and forth. Ridden by singlet clad young macho Italians. The riders would lose count of the laps they did on their 'café racers', duly named because they cruised from café to café looking to impress any long-legged young chick that would look their way. Ducatis and Motto Guzzis weaved in and out of the night-time traffic as if they were racing around the Via dei Fori, with absolutely no care given. The riders would greet each other in even louder noises than their steeds at each red light. It was a Lygon Street tradition and in general it was all very harmless. Harmless, but very loud.

Next on the list were the young Princes of Carlton whose aim was to impress. Their chariots of choice for the night cruise were either Ferraris in their signature racing red. If it wasn't the Italian Stallion it was the Lamborghini, the Raging Bull in the latest colour of yellow.

The boys had to flex their muscles early in the night because most of the racing thoroughbreds were hire cars. The drivers didn't have the time or the inclination to park for long. One scratch and a couple of weeks wages from your nine to five job was shot to pieces.

The third but deadliest of the species was the Maserati. This had become the modern-day sports headquarters of the drug dealing, pistol carrying criminals who had slithered into the inner suburbs over the previous two years after the forced retirement of local mafia Don, Benny Illarietti. The Maserati had no need to cruise. They were there for a different show. They were showing off the proceeds of their various enterprises. Drug deals, vice deals, firearm deals. All money deals. There was no longer a king pin of the Carlton crime scene, just an ongoing fight over who was the biggest, fattest, low-life rat.

If Leo Carbone and Angelo Morelli had known the Maserati factor of Carlton, the last thing they would have done was try to steal the matte grey, 2018 Maserati Gran Turismo that belonged to the biggest rat in town, one Alessio 'Big Al' Lombardi.

One thing that Big Al loved was his Maserati. Sex and drugs were his loves too, but cars and guns were first and second in line. Through drug and firearm dealing he had quickly graduated from what he considered to be Australian and Japanese rubbish up to the top of the range Italian masterpiece. Every young punk in town drove Ferraris and Lamborghinis, but the Maserati had made a big comeback in the previous years after he and his compatriots had started buying them with their laundered money.

Sidling up to the driver's window of the Italian beast, Leo nodded to Angelo and spoke quietly. "Keep an eye out. I'll be in this rocket ship real quick."

As he started to slip a flat edged tool down beside the window, he turned to glance back at Angelo, but couldn't understand why a huge, black T-shirted thug was standing there instead.

Leo looked down at the thug's feet, the last thing he saw before his head exploded into a kaleidoscope of bright lights was the body of Angelo lying prone at the feet of the ape.

Chapter Four

Leo's eyes opened slowly. There was no other way to avoid more pain coursing through his skull. His headache reminded him of an erupting volcano, rivers of blood flowing like red hot lava — and lots of it.

The last thing he remembered was the apparition that was now taking shape on the outside of his aching eyeballs. A big, black-clad Italian ape whose form seemed to fill the entire room. Leo was glad of one thing. He didn't think ape man had seen him open his slowly focussing eyes.

Moving his eyeballs slowly across the semi-darkened room, he took in the sight of Angelo's prone figure at his feet. Just beyond, protruding from underneath the front of a large wooden desk, were a very expensive pair of burgundy coloured Oxford shoes.

Strangely, the first thought that crossed his clouded mind was that no one who wore those shoes would kick him.

The shoes disappeared from under the desk and then reappeared inches away from his face.

"Turn him onto his side," a deep voice ordered.

He was picked up bodily by ape-man and dumped again onto the carpeted floor on his left side. Staring at the highly polished shoes, he saw one of them travel backwards and then accelerate towards him until it exploded into his solar plexus with the power of a Mike Tyson punch. So much for his judgement regarding the wearer of the shoes. As he struggled to breathe, the same deep voice resonated over him.

"You fucking piece of shit. It's lucky I'm letting you and your friend live. You want to enter the world of Big Al Lombardi and touch something he owns? You are lucky to be still breathing."

Leo looked up at the red-faced figure standing over him and mouthed the word 'sorry' to it. The figure spoke again.

"After going through your wallet, my man here could only find connections to you out Broadmeadows way. He could not find a passport allowing your type of gutter crawling scum to travel to my beautiful home of Carlton. Your name is Leo Carbone, you piece of dog shit?"

Leo gulped some much-needed air, spluttering the word, "Yes."

"My associate has saved you and your dumb ass friend here, young Leo. Everyone around Carlton knows there is only one matte grey Mazza around here and that is mine. No one copies Big Al Lombardi if they know what's good for their health. Now you really only have to think about one thing and that is this. How do we repay the generosity of Mr. Lombardi? You are both my guests for the time being so think long and hard Leo. When I come back tomorrow, I will expect your answer together with your deepest respect, understanding, and above all, your eternal gratitude for the air you are still sucking in. Capiche?"

Chapter Five

Tony Signorotto was feeling trapped. Not only trapped but isolated. As a Sergeant downstairs in the heart of the station he never had these feelings. The inquiry counter was always a hive of activity. Every surrounding police station was the same. Carlton, Collingwood, Fitzroy and Richmond police stations buzzed twenty-four seven.

Being a Sergeant at one of these stations was a combination of being boss, mentor, father figure, complaints department and much more. You were never bored, and it was never dull. Guiding young police around the pitfalls of inexperience had given Tony a day long adrenalin kick. He was now finding the upstairs downstairs difference in policing very foreign to him.

As a Senior Sergeant, Tony knew it was his responsibility to do the monthly returns to Divisional Headquarters for property, prosecution briefs, rostering and many more mundane items. The trouble was he was finding it very hard to make time to get downstairs to the 'engine room' to see how the ship was running. Not that he had any problems with the Sergeants or the troops. He knew he had to adjust quickly from being the downstairs Sergeant to the upstairs Senior Sergeant. In layman's terms it was like transferring from being the foreman on the shop floor to general manager in an office. The first one knew exactly what was going on and the second had to ask someone what was going on. And he hated having to ask.

Phil Stone had told him this would happen if he got the promotion to Senior Sergeant. It was all part of the game. Tony had always stood shoulder to shoulder with his boys and girls in blue. Always! Now he had to take a back seat and let the engine room be run by other people. He was now responsible on a Divisional level, not just a station level.

Tony stopped checking the monthly property forms on his computer, slumped back in his chair and ran a hand over tired eyes. He could have sworn his eyes had turned square, but was determined to keep going on these returns simply because he couldn't keep risking himself on the street. Nowadays, the streets were for the new breed of police. The risk taking had to end. He had his wife, Susie and Gracie to think about. Like it or not, he was a nine to five cop from now on. Maybe the odd afternoon shifts now and then. If coming home safe after every shift meant hours over the computer counting the beans, then so be it.

As he was putting his aching fingers back on the keyboard, the sound of light laughter drifted into his office from the corridor. It wasn't his secretary Veronica's laughter. She had a laugh that would shatter glass. He was intrigued to hear the voices as he walked around from behind the pile of forms, binders and books that were covering his desk and looked into the passageway. He could make out the back of a young, suited man who was leaning far too casually against the fading yellow painted wall near the office next door. There was something familiar about him.

A blonde uniformed policewoman stepped suddenly out from behind the figure. The penny dropped. Putting on his serious Officer in Charge face, he challenged the pair.

"Constable Schaeffer. Are you upstairs on official business or are you just chatting up the hired help?"

Constable Chloe Schaeffer's face took on a shocked look, realising it was the Senior Sergeant addressing her. At the same time, the 'hired help' turned towards Tony.

"Well, well. If it isn't Senior Detective Maxwell Tyler himself. Come all the way down from headquarters to share your immense knowledge of Carlton and crime amongst the plebs, have you?" Tony inquired.

Max Tyler began to speak but was cut off immediately by Tony.

"Constable Schaeffer, I happen to know this man's reputation— as do many young ladies from one end of Lygon Street to the other. Maxwell, how are the Santino girls these days?"

Dom Santino and his family were a Lygon Street institution and many police send-offs, weddings, births and even a few divorces had been well and truly celebrated at his famous restaurant. It was the place where Tony had proposed to Susie.

"Ah, they're all good thanks boss," Max replied in a slightly embarrassed voice.

"Well, if you've come here to see me, step into my office. Constable Schaeffer you have approximately ten seconds to text Maxwell your phone number. After that, get back downstairs and resume what you're getting paid to do. Catching crooks and keeping the suburb of Carlton safe."

A chastened Constable Chloe Schaeffer was busily tapping on her mobile phone as she started down the stairs—but not without a very nice smile back in the direction of the young detective first.

Max Tyler stepped into the office to see a grinning Tony Signorotto.

"Shit boss. At least you could have called me Max, not Maxwell. Got no chance with her now."

"I remember our much loved and now retired Senior Constable Norton, the keeper of our watch-house, calling you Maxwell on several occasions when you got your abilities mixed up with your capabilities."

Max Tyler looked down at the lit-up screen of his phone. He beamed, put the phone away and smiled at Tony.

Tony raised his eyes to the paint-cracked ceiling. "That was a quick roster swap. You be bloody careful with that girl. She's going to be a good copper. Oh, and by the way, do you recognise the name Schaeffer?"

Realisation dawned on Max's face. "She's not a relation to John Schaeffer from Internal Affairs, is she?"

"That's Assistant Commissioner John Schaeffer to you Maxwell, and yes, she is the daughter of said Assistant Commissioner. The only daughter."

Max threw his mobile phone onto the table at the same time as slumping into a chair opposite Tony. "Well then," he said with resignation. "Let's move on to why I came to see you, boss."

"To what do I owe the pleasure, Max?"

"A rumour boss. A nasty rumour which we all hope at the C.I.U. isn't true," Max said. "It looks like we're about to have a firearms problem somewhere in the Division."

Chapter Six

Tony listened thoughtfully to his young colleague's report before he spoke.

"Max. We have six firearms shops in Carlton. You know that. No more, no less than when you were stationed here. Can you narrow it down a bit?"

"Boss, I would if I could. As I said, it's just a story that started up at the Magistrates Court last week."

"If this is factual Max, we will have to warn the gun store owners. Christ, all these shops stock everything from antique firearms to the latest military hardware. I'm going to have to get my daytime patrols to word them up and check their security set ups and all their C.C.T.V. gear."

Max leant on the front of Tony's desk. "Boss, as I said, it all started between two bikies waiting in the cells at the Magistrates Court. It was overheard by one of the Prison Officers who was checking the cells opposite them. These two clowns were waiting to go up in the lift to the court. One is from the Black Rats and the other from the Carnivores. The Prison Officer was an old retired Highway Patrol veteran who reckons he knows you from way back. Bob Chesterfield. The Carnivores run the Hume highway from Melbourne to Sydney and that was his patrol area. Once he heard the words 'nine millimetres' he hit the switch."

"Bob Chesterfield! One hard-nosed ex-copper, Max. Taught me a thing or two years ago that helped me survive my early days. Must catch up with him now that I know where he works. Anyway. Was it word for word what Bob overheard?"

"Boss, I know they have closed the cells here at the new station, but for over a year now all Prison Officers have been wearing a camera and a microphone. Not just for their own safety. Allegations are always made against them from some would-be hero who wants to get off a charge or two. It was great that he switched his microphone on so quickly. He caught everything these idiots argued about."

"Run through it for me again will you Max? Bikies and gun talk send a shiver up my spine."

These two clowns had both been charged with assault and affray— the result of an all-in brawl up at the Meadow Inn hotel in Broadmeadows. There's an ongoing turf war between the Black Rats and the Carnivores. When they were getting them out of their cells for their preliminary hearings, the Carnivore spoke to the Black Rat. It's all on the transcript from the recording."

"I've got the transcript right here," Max said as he handed Tony the record of the conversation on paper. Tony continued reading from the transcript.

"*Couple of weeks fuckwit and us Black Rats will have all the firepower we need. You won't be called the Carnivores anymore because our new nine mils will blow you all away. You'll be the fucking pop guns.*"

"*You've got no money. You fucking Black Rats are shit. Where are you going to find the cash for nine mil shooters?*"

"*Who needs money dirtbag? We've got the Man to organize it. The Carlton Man. Midnight shopping you fool. Cash and carry. One stop local withdrawal from his patch. No one argues with the King of Carlton.*"

"Bloody hell," Tony replied, flipping through the typed report. "We both know who refers to himself as the King of Carlton. That lowlife Al Lombardi. I thought he might have gone to ground in the last couple of years since we fixed up Uncle Benny."

Tony stood and walked around to the front of his desk and faced Max.

"Mate, I'm running the show here now, so I'm not allowed out there on the front line as much as I'd like. I'll want every bit of information on this that you can get me. If that scum Lombardi thinks he is going to be the King of Carlton, then he'd better be prepared to come up against me—the Prince of Darkness!"

Seconds past before Tony spoke again.

"Come on, let's head up to Dom's and I'll buy you lunch."

Max's eyes lit up with a surprised look. "You buy lunch? Your shout? You wouldn't shout if a shark bit you."

"Don't be a smartarse Max. When was the last time Dom ever let me, or for that matter you, pay at his place? Besides, why do you think I made him little Gracie's Godfather?"

"How are Susie and Gracie? I've got to get a visit in soon. Been ages."

"They're both good, mate. By the way, did you notice the new Sergeants" position that was taken for here in the last Gazette?"

"Saw the name. Didn't recognise it though."

"Some new female from headquarters. Already a Sergeant but wants station experience to get her Senior Sergeants' apparently. Name is Kate McLaren. Don't know her. Gets here next week. Anyway, let's head up to Dom's and we'll make it a working lunch. Need a plan for de-throning the King. With my first gig as Senior Sergeant in Charge, I don't want to get caught with my pants down and my gun on the toilet floor when it comes to something like this."

Chapter Seven

"Nice grouping," the voice next to her said.

She turned and looked at the shooter standing in the booth to her right. Mid-thirties, black T-shirt, black jeans. Toned and muscled. She'd seen and met a lot worse men.

"Thanks. Have shot better though," she said, hitting the recall button with her left hand as she holstered her pistol smoothly into the right-hand thigh holster she wore over her blue jeans. The cardboard target came quickly back up the range to her with a mechanical whirring sound, coming to a stop directly in front of her booth. It had been set at the twenty-metre mark down range.

The centre of mass of the target had five holes punched tightly dead centre. One hole was slightly to the right and upwards a couple of millimetres.

He spoke again. "If you don't mind me asking, what's your weapon of choice you just holstered?"

She turned to face him and instinctively placed her right hand on the butt of her firearm. Always safety first.

"Sig 9 millimetre," she said referring to the jet-black Sig Sauer P229 semi-automatic pistol her hand was resting on.

"What about you?" she inquired as he turned, drew his pistol and put six shots straight through the centre of his target that was set at twenty-five metres.

Holstering his firearm, he turned towards her.

"Remington Recon Commander. We had our choice where I last worked."

"Where was that?" She said a little too quickly.

"Just finished a second deployment. R.A.R 3rd Commando Regiment. Afghanistan. Out now. Two tours were enough. Just keeping my eye in for my job now."

Raising her eyebrows slightly she replied. "What job needs that impressive skill set?" Pointing at the centre of the now returned target directly in front of him.

"Security guard," he replied.

She looked directly at his eyes, hoping for an indication of what sort of individual she was talking to. The only discernible thing she detected was a tiredness. Not the sort of tiredness from lack of sleep, just one from concentrating on a job or situation too long. Understandable, considering where he had been.

"Who do you work for?" She suddenly said.

He looked at her without speaking. Seconds went by.

"Sorry about being so inquisitive," she said. "Comes with the job. Victoria Police."

He smiled back and she suddenly heard herself saying.

"Coffee?" indicating the indoor café at the Melbourne Pistol Club.

Blushing slightly, he hesitated before speaking.

"Yeah. Thanks. That would be good."

Being both members of the pistol club they walked to the back of the range and checked in their weapons at two Safe Loading/Unloading Devices and then handed them to the Rangemaster for storing in the pistol club safe.

Walking towards the café, she put her right hand out and introduced herself.

"Kate McLaren."

He replied as he took the outstretched hand. "Tom Cole. Thanks for the invite."

Strange thing to say, Kate thought to herself as she sat down. A word immediately came to her mind regarding him. Loner. But why?

Chapter Eight

The coffee came too quickly for Kate. There was something about Tom that she liked besides what she saw in front of her. Something deeper.

"Sorry about the pistol question when you were about to shoot," Tom said, as his hands moved nervously between the now empty cup and a much folded and nearly destroyed paper napkin. "Force of habit on the line. We were always checking that we were tooled up."

"No problem at all," Kate replied. "Nice to see someone so good around firearms. Some of the people who come here couldn't shoot to save themselves. All ego and no talent. Just an expensive habit and talking point at their local bar. A security blanket for them."

Tom began to laugh lightly while looking at Kate through penetrating blue eyes, forcing her to catch her breath slightly.

"Hey, I'm just a security guard who spends his time between here, work and a six-year-old daughter who outmanoeuvres me better than the Taliban ever did."

Kate's optimism took an immediate nosedive on hearing the child part.

Damn. What's coming next? Why do I meet the good-looking married ones?

She decided to take the plunge with her next comment.

"What's your wife do for a job?"

A look of sadness passed over Tom's face.

"No. No wife. Well there was until a couple of years ago. Not anymore though."

Divorce I can handle. No strings though, Kate thought.

"Didn't work out with the army thing?"

"Nothing like that. I had to give up the uniform. My wife was killed outside a shopping centre by a hit-run drunk driver while

I was on deployment. She'd left Summer, our daughter, with a friend while she went shopping. The bastard that hit her was pissed. Your lot got him a couple of hours later hiding under his bed. He got six years and Summer and I got life. Simple as that."

Kate couldn't find words to say. She looked down at the table and realised she had her hand on top of his.

"Sorry. Didn't meant to upset you. Just the way it is. You just get hardened to it. Probably like your job. It's life and you just have to deal with it," he said, giving Kate a very unconvincing smile.

"I'm thirty-five and haven't been married to anything but the Police Force. I don't have any kids so I can only imagine what it must be like for you. How do you cope?"

"When you're busy everything is okay. It has to be. I'm lucky in some ways. Gorgeous little daughter, a nice house I can afford and a boss who looks after me."

"How do you go with your job if you're caught up somewhere? What about little Summer?"

"Funny you should say that. I have one of yours as a neighbour. A retired one who used to be at Carlton. Even has a Valour Award. Jill Norton. She and her husband treat Summer like one of their own grandkids. They take her and pick her up from school when I'm stuck. Be hard to survive without them. Summer doesn't have anyone else. No aunts or uncles on either side of the family. We are our own Team Cole."

Sad. Very sad. Kate thought.

"I'm actually transferring to Carlton next week," she said. "Hey, have you got time for a quick lunch?"

"Yeah, sure. If you want to? I have heaps of time before I pick up the little tornado from school," he said with a laugh.

She saw something in Tom that made her feel very at ease in his company.

"Told you a fair bit about myself. What about you?" He said as he waved to the counter for a menu.

"Not that interesting really. Been in the job thirteen years. Got promoted to Sergeant at D.24 and been there a couple of years.

Had to get out for my sanity. The calls that come in and all you can do is listen. You feel like jumping through the phone to help. I want some outside experience in the solving part. That's why I grabbed the chance when one of the Sergeants took up the Senior Sergeant's job. That left a rare vacancy and I was lucky enough to get picked."

Time passed and the conversation between them flowed back and forth.

Looking up at the café wall, she suddenly saw the time on the clock and realised they had been there over two hours.

"Hey, I'd better let you head off. If you're passing the station at all, why don't you drop in for a coffee? If it's the usual standard as all police stations, it won't be as good as here, but hopefully the company is up to scratch."

Tom looked directly at her. "The company here has been really great. Thanks so much. With a six-year-old in tow, there's usually only time for a takeaway and an ice cream. I don't want to drop in and find you on another shift. What if I just ring the station?"

"I think I trust you enough to give you my mobile number. You trust me with yours?"

Ten minutes later they were both saying goodbye to each other in the pistol club car park.

Climbing behind the wheel of her car, Kate thought she had never felt more comfortable about giving out her phone number.

Chapter Nine

Big Al Lombardi knew there was only one way to stay on top as the King of Crime in Carlton. That way was fear.

Not your average fear, but the type that, once instilled into people, was never to be forgotten.

The fear of a few broken bones only lasted as long as the healing process. The permanent way to make your enemies sit up and take notice was to do it with a gun. The feeling of the cold steel business end of a handgun placed between the eyes was something no one ever forgot.

Leo Carbone and Angelo Morelli were now sharing that feeling in spades with the four- inch barrels of two loaded and cocked .38 Smith and Wesson revolvers being held by Lombardi and pushed in each of their mouths.

Leo was too scared to swallow. Sweat was beading across his face as the two hoons pinned his arms behind him. What he saw and heard behind the revolver scared him just as much. The maniacal laughter and face of Alessio Lombardi.

"Which one will die first, boys?" Lombardi said as laughter boomed around the office of the King of Carlton.

Leo's mind was racing as he thought of the previous night where he and Angelo had spent shackled to each other and guarded in a downstairs basement. No food, no water. Time was a blur. He didn't know how long both of them had been there before they were dragged upstairs. The only thing he knew was the fact that he would do anything, anything at all, to get out of this. Why had they tried to steal a Maserati in Carlton? No good was ever going to come of it he thought as he closed his eyes waiting for his brain to explode into a thousand bits of blood and gore.

Suddenly the barrels were pulled viciously back out of their mouths without warning, causing one of Leo's front teeth to be badly chipped. The pain was excruciating but at least he could breathe. Sucking in some desperate breaths he realised he could hear Angelo sobbing. He swung his head to the left and saw his friend lying on the carpeted floor, head in hands, crying uncontrollably. It was like looking at a whipped and beaten dog.

"You, Mr Carbone, have taken to my little bit of fun with the right attitude," Lombardi said with a voice that sounded like gravel being crushed. "Your friend here does not seem to have the same attention span. The fortunate, or unfortunate part if you want to look at it that way, is that you will now both be working for me to re-pay my generosity for not taking your lives."

A flicker of hope registered in Leo's wired brain. At least he wasn't going to die just now. Most likely later, but not now. He knew he would be taking a big risk if he spoke, but a pistol whipping from one of Lombardi's heavies was a chance he would have to take. With a cracked voice going up and down with each word, he dared speak.

"Mr. Lombardi. Whatever it takes to make it up to you for being so dumb and disrespectful in ever thinking about stealing your car, we will do. We didn't know it was your car. Honest we didn't."

The shadow of a swinging arm began its descent towards Leo's head but was thwarted with a raised hand from Lombardi.

"Enough boys. Time for business. These two will do what they are told otherwise their families will suffer," Lombardi said.

Leo and Angelo were lifted bodily into two chairs at the front of Lombardi's desk with the two goons taking up positions directly behind them. Lombardi continued.

"Boys, you have been selected to assist myself and my associates with a little job. If it goes well I may, just may, offer you full time employment. If I don't get what I want out of it, you will be the first to receive the Lygon Street kiss."

Both Leo and Angelo stared at the brick-like face of Alessio Lombardi.

"Ah, of course," Lombardi said. "You two nobodies are just visitors to my headquarters here at Club Maximus in Carlton and don't have any idea about a Lygon Street kiss, do you?" With that, Big Al stood and after handing back the revolvers to his goons he removed a large black automatic pistol from his desk drawer and walked around to where Angelo was cowering in his chair. Racking the slide on the semi-auto he placed the muzzle behind Angelo's right ear. Holding it there for a few seconds, he enjoyed watching the little punk start to shake uncontrollably. Then he pulled the trigger. The ominous metallic snap of the hammer hitting nothing resounded around his office. Angelo buried his head further into his hands and sobbed.

"That my little friend is the dry Lygon Street kiss. A wet one…"

Lombardi went back to his chair and kept speaking.

"I have had my associates do some checking on both of you. You may claim to be residents of the northern suburbs, however I have it on good authority that you both owe quite a few favours and a lot of money to some people who would love to find you if only to break your bones very slowly. I presume that was your reasoning for trying to steal my beautiful Maserati, eh? Would that be a fair and reasonable assessment of your current financial situation? Speak up boys, you are among friends."

"We do owe a bit but not to people you would know. Nothing that would affect you, Mr Lombardi," Angelo said quietly.

"Nothing north of Brunswick affects me, Angelo. If I wanted to run my business further up Sydney Road, then I would without any hesitation."

Silence engulfed the room as Lombardi continued while looking Angelo directly in the eyes.

"You have very few connections and you will not be missed by anyone I assure you both."

Fear could be smelt on the opposite side of Lombardi's desk.

"I am a man of my word, boys. You will both be kept as guests at one of my houses while our plan takes shape. My friends here will take your phones."

Suddenly two of the largest Pacific Islanders either Leo or Angelo had ever set eyes on morphed out of the dark background of the office. The room was filled with wall to wall steroid munchers.

"Gents. Stand up and I will introduce you to my associates," Lombardi said.

Leo and Angelo stood quickly, but neither of them came up to shoulder height of the two Samoan giants that stood before them.

"Angelo and Leo, meet your minders. Loseffa Salessa, otherwise known as Joey and Feba Felagi who goes by the name of Feb."

"Angelo and Leo," Lombardi continued. "You are now on my payroll. You won't be paid money as such at the moment, but you will be looked after and want for nothing. Let me tell you though. Both of you are very low on the food chain so if there is any hesitation on your behalf to comply with any instructions, be it from myself or any of my boys here, then your contracts will be terminated. I think you know what I mean, eh? Ask no questions and be told no lies. You will live with Joey and Feb and devour every bit of information that I drip feed you about our upcoming mission. You will find out everything in due course. The choice is now up to you. Work for me and be looked after or, well, there is no or, is there? What's it to be?"

Leo rubbed his upper arm where one of the giants had been holding him. Taking a small step forward toward the King of Carlton, he put his right hand out in an attempt to shake the crime boss's hand.

"Sounds like a deal we can't refuse, eh Angelo?"

Lombardi looked at the outstretched hand. "Don't get your ambitions mixed up with reality Leo," he said, ignoring Leo's futile gesture. "Go with your new friends here and we will talk again soon. Enjoy my hospitality."

The two puppets were pushed roughly through a side door of Club Maximus by the two Samoan giants.

Chapter Ten

Sergeant Kate McLaren stepped nervously up to the back door of the Carlton Police Station. She had made sure she was in full operational uniform including her equipment belt complete with her nine-millimetre Smith and Wesson Police and Military pistol. She had never met Senior Sergeant Tony Signorotto before and had no pre-conceived ideas about her new boss.

Negotiating a corner inside the rear of the new and very modern building, she bumped into a Constable heading in the opposite direction.

"Sorry about that, Sarge," Constable Chloe Schaeffer said as she bent and picked up a folder of notes that she had knocked from Kate's hand.

"That's all right Chloe," Kate replied after quickly looking at Schaeffer's name badge. "Now that we have been unofficially introduced, I'm the new Sergeant here. Kate McLaren," she said, struggling to put her right hand out to shake and at the same time hold on to her box of files that she had brought with her.

"Ah, okay," Chloe replied with an engaging smile, "Constable Chloe Schaeffer, or Schaeffer if you have to yell at me, I suppose. Do you prefer Sergeant or Sarge?"

Kate was immediately impressed with the fact this young Constable was not about to call her by her first name.

"Sarge will do just fine, Chloe. Let me tell you, I'm not a big one for calling people by their surname so I'll probably never yell at you," she said smiling.

"So good to have another girl around here. Even it up a bit in the Sergeants' office, too," Chloe laughed. "They are all men but are pretty forgiving when one of us Probationary Constables stuffs up."

"Many Probationary Constables here, Chloe?"

"Six of us Sarge. If you stick with us, we can start a seven a side rugby team. What do you think?"

"We'll see about that later, Chloe. Don't know about rugby. I'm an Aussie rules person. Big Melbourne fan. What about you?" Kate said.

"No team really Sarge. Around here though it's safer to be a Carlton supporter. Senior Sergeant Signorotto is a big Blues fan."

"Well, that'll be the first argument he and I will have then. Now, where's our changeroom so I can unload some of this?"

"Follow me Sarge. Have got you a prime position in the locker room."

Have to keep this one on my side, Kate thought.

After a tour of her new station, Kate made her way upstairs and was pointed in the direction of the O.I.C's office, seeing immediately that this man had an open-door policy. Knocking gently on the wall, she waited for a response.

Tony Signorotto looked up from his desk and waved to Kate to come inside. Placing a hand over the phone receiver he was using, he spoke quietly.

"Sergeant McLaren. Great to have you on board. Got the Superintendent on the phone. Won't be long. Meet you in the mess room for a coffee in ten?"

Kate gave Tony a thumbs up sign in recognition of the request and received one straight back. She turned and headed downstairs.

Inside the spotlessly clean messroom, she saw an older woman in civilian clothes sitting at the table, coffee in one hand and a copy of the morning newspaper in front of her.

The woman looked up as Kate started to reach for the large tin of cheap coffee on the shelf.

"Don't touch that rubbish Sergeant."

Kate turned, but before she could speak, the civilian continued.

"Sorry. Didn't mean to startle you. Here. Have some real coffee. I bring my own when I visit this place. Most of the men here wouldn't know good coffee from floor sweepings," she said, reaching for the half full coffee plunger beside her on the table as the rich aroma of brewed Arabica coffee beans filled the air. Confused, Kate took a cup from the overhead shelf and sat down beside the woman.

"Ah, sorry. You are?" Kate said quietly, realising that this person had no identification on her that she could see.

"My apologies. Jill Norton. Retired Jill Norton. Used to work here. Well, used to work at the old Carlton station. Senior Constable. Ran the watch-house. Just popped in to see how Tony is running the place. Knowing him it will be all under control. You just dropping in?"

"No," Kate said as she put the cup to her mouth and tasted the delicious brew. "God that's good. Definitely not from the tea club money, that's for sure. I've just got the Sergeant's position here. Kate McLaren."

"That's great news. Said for years that there should be more females in this bear pit," Jill leant across with an outstretched hand. Kate reciprocated and a smile crossed between them.

Recognition crossed Kate's face. "Are you the same Jill Norton that has her name up on the Valour Award board at headquarters."

Jill Norton immediately looked uncomfortable.

"Yeah, a couple of years ago now. I'll leave that story for Tony to tell though. Just on my way back from shopping so I thought I'd pop in. With the boss having a name like Signorotto, a good coffee is always appreciated."

Both women were laughing quietly just as Tony walked into the mess room.

"Good to see two generations of women's policing having a chinwag."

"This isn't a tea club you dinosaur, Signorotto. Wait till I tell your lovely Susie you made that comment. Makes us sound like a couple of old gossips," Jill said winking at Kate.

With a broad grin Tony sat down next to Kate. Pointing at Jill, he spoke. "Couldn't control her at the old watch-house. Can't control her in here. If it wasn't for the coffee, I'd kick her onto the street."

Jill gave a dismissive snort. "Try me big fella. See how far you get. Saved your arse more times than I care to remember. Don't know why I kept at Susie to chase you. One of my poorer decisions."

The banter that was crossing between the two old colleagues was infectious.

If this is the way the staff get on here it will be a great place to work, Kate thought.

"Pour me a cup of Mocha Java Norton or I'll tell Kate how I had to cover you for years at the old place," Tony said as he moved closer and kissed Jill on both cheeks.

Pushing him away very gently, Jill spoke. "Cut that Italian crap. "You'll be giving Kate here very bad ideas."

Ignoring Jill, Tony turned his attention to his new Sergeant, putting his hand out and giving Kate a firm handshake.

"Great to have you here Kate. Welcome to Carlton. Great station with good crooks. By that I mean crooks that think they are good but get sorted out pretty quick by our team here."

Looking at him, Kate immediately felt at ease.

A real boss who obviously backs his troops.

Kate suddenly looked around and exclaimed. "Jill Norton. Of course. I've not only seen your name on that honour board, I heard it just recently."

"In nice terms, I hope," Jill said with a sly grin on her face.

"Your neighbour Tom Cole. Met him last week at the pistol club. Nice guy. Said you were his go to person in times of need with his little daughter Summer."

"Tom's a great bloke. Great father also. Such a tragedy with his wife being killed. Got to look after types like him. Returned Afghanistan vet and doesn't expect anything from anyone. After all the useless excuses for fathers I saw come through the cells at the old station it's an absolute pleasure to help him. Little Summer is a gorgeous kid too," Jill said.

"He said he might pop in here sometime if he's not working. Only if he's passing by though," Kate said quickly.

With a friendly raised eyebrow, Jill glanced over at Kate.

"Mmmm. Wonder why he'd want to stop in here for crap coffee? You must have made an impression," she said looking at Kate's ringless left hand.

Kate smiled as she glanced around the kitchen.

"Excuse me ladies but I think match making time is over. I've only just met our new Sergeant and have never laid eyes on this Tom Cole. Jill, you'd better tell him that if he pops in here for a cuppa, he needs to get past this Senior Sergeant first. Won't have any of my staff being harassed."

Jill Norton stood and gathered her shopping. "Lovely to meet you Kate and I hope to see you again soon. If not here, then next door at Tom's sometime. As for you Signorotto, if it wasn't for me you would have ended up a crusty old bachelor. Remember mate, it was me who guided you towards that lovely wife of yours. You might meet her someday Kate. Her name is Susie and why on earth she puts up with this dinosaur I don't know."

Jill moved towards Tony with a friendly grin and was about to give him a gentle clip over the ear when a voice screamed out from the direction of the front inquiry counter.

"You can't take my car off me. Give me my fucking keys back or I'll come over this counter and beat the shit out of both of you."

Kate immediately jumped up from her chair quickly followed by Tony. Both charged towards the inquiry counter shoulder to shoulder. As they ran into the counter area, they could see a youth standing on top of the counter screaming obscenities at Constable Schaeffer and her colleague.

"I said give me my fucking keys back bitch or else," the youth screamed as he stood clenching and unclenching his fists in front of his twitching body.

Kate had her full equipment belt on but quickly realised that using a can of capsicum spray in the enclosed area would affect everyone else besides the ranting character. She chose the next option. After releasing her extendable baton from her belt, she flicked it backwards in an upward motion over her right shoulder and brought it swinging down in an arc, collecting the youth heavily with the tip of the baton to the outside of his left knee. An ear-piercing scream echoed throughout the room and the offender fell heavily to the floor clutching at his now useless left leg. Tony immediately pounced on the crying heap and held him down as Schaeffer and her offsider quickly brought his hands behind him and handcuffed them.

Just as Tony was about to say something to Kate about her lightning quick action, she spoke first.

"Welcome to my police station son. You ever think about threatening one of my troops again and you'll get a hell of a lot more than a sore leg. Now stop crying you little piece of shit."

Turning immediately to her two young Constables, she continued.

"Pick him up and take him to an interview room. Son, I don't know what traffic offences you were facing before your little hissy fit, but I am personally going to charge you with assault, indecent language and trespass. The top of that counter belongs to us, not you. Now get his arse out of here."

Chloe Schaeffer and her offsider dragged the sobbing mess towards an interview room. As they passed Tony, she looked at him, smiled and spoke.

"Now that's my kind of Sergeant, boss!"

"You're not wrong there, Constable," Tony replied.

Chapter Eleven

The house was a fortress. There was no other way to describe it. Double storey, double brick, double iron gates, double guards and double Rottweilers.

Angelo wasn't complaining, although it was two weeks since he and Leo had been blindfolded and driven to the premises in a van by Joey and Feb. They had wanted for nothing since their arrival. They knew they might as well enjoy the hospitality of Big Al Lombardi while it lasted simply because, if it stopped, it didn't take a genius to figure out that they would be stopped also. Stopped permanently.

Angelo and Leo weren't big time gangsters. Far from it. The only thing they were good at was jacking cars. All except Maseratis it seemed. In the two weeks of their residence they had been given free run of the house which included an indoor heated pool. Neither of them could swim to save themselves. After all, Broadmeadows, where they grew up, wasn't exactly a beachside suburb. What they did enjoy however was the plentiful supply of booze and drugs as they saw the days through. It was a great life but they both knew it had to come to an end sometime.

On the first day when the relaxed lifestyle and the booze disappeared, both guests just waited around and occasionally talked to each other. No in-depth conversations, just questions and frightening answers about what would probably happen to them. Striking up a conversation with Joey and Feb was like trying to talk to the four-metre-high brick wall that surrounded their prison. An odd grunt or two was heard from their guards but that was all. Any banter about football, soccer or any form of sport fell on deaf ears.

"I get more sense out of the two Rottweilers," Angelo said to Leo late in the day. "Don't know about you mate, but I can't take much more of this. Can you?"

"No mate, I'm with you there.' Leo replied sullenly.

Walking back into the kitchen, Leo suddenly baulked because Angelo had quickly stopped in the doorway in front of them. Looking around Angelo he could see the reason. Sitting at the kitchen table with his two Samoan guards flanking him was a sight neither of them had missed over the last two weeks. It was the larger than life figure of Alessio Big Al Lombardi. The King of Carlton.

"The good times are over, boys," Lombardi said. "For now, anyway. If this job I am planning comes off, you will of course be able to continue in the lifestyle of the rich and famous. Just not in Australia."

A chill ran down Angelo's spine.

Whatever job it is, this bastard will never let us see daylight when it's over.

Lombardi continued. "From now until the job is done, you will be working for me. Forget about booze and anything else that might bring a smile to your faces. Both of you will be a part of history when this comes off."

Silence engulfed the kitchen for what seemed like an eternity until Angelo spoke with a whispering, respectful voice.

"Mr Lombardi. May I ask what we will be doing?"

Lombardi stood from the table causing both Angelo and Leo to take a step backwards. The presence of fear was palpable.

"Boys, boys," Lombardi said. "Don't be afraid. I have performed my own surveillance on you for a while now. I wanted to see if you would make a run for it or stay around to enjoy the benefits of working for me. You chose the latter. You haven't tried to contact anyone, so I presume my hospitality has met with your approval has it not?"

Both Angelo and Leo nodded simultaneously. Angelo had asked his question and wasn't about to press the King of Carlton for more. Unfortunately, Leo didn't possess the same sense of self-preservation when he opened his mouth and spoke.

"After all the girls and booze I've gone through that you have supplied Al, I think I'm a bit tired to even look at a phone or make a run for it."

As he finished his Pulitzer prized speech, Leo stepped forward and slapped Lombardi on his shoulder in what Angelo thought would be a life-ending gesture. A shadow seemed to pass across the face of the mobster.

You have probably just got both of us killed tonight you fucking idiot, Leo, Angelo thought.

After a long stare at Leo, Lombardi continued.

"Gentlemen. Neither of you will be leaving this house until I have fine-tuned my plans. There is no 'out' for this. Either you fall in line or you don't. The first choice is easily the best. Upon completion of the job you will both receive twenty thousand dollars and first-class one-way transport to any destination in the world of your choosing that doesn't have any extradition treaties with Australia. Upon arrival I will arrange employment which, after having completed this world class heist, will ensure your good-will with many contacts of mine. You will never want for anything. The only thing is that you will never come back to Australia again. You will however, live in luxury and have top of the range employment with some of the leading criminal figures in the world. The second choice for both of you isn't really a choice. You may walk out of here right now, but I guarantee that neither of you will see the sunrise. Just remember. This job will have risks. You won't be killed doing it but if you get caught you will wish you had. My reach is very long and Barwon State Prison will be no protection for you."

Angelo's mind was racing. He had heard and digested what Lombardi had said and had no intention of swimming against the tide at the moment. If it came to be that he ended up living somewhere overseas then so be it. A luxury lifestyle even in crime was better than breaking into cars in Melbourne. Looking at Leo, he could see that not everything had sunk into that small brain of his. The money had been heard loud and clear but the 'no return' policy had not registered with him.

With dollar signs shinning in his eyes, Leo's head just started to bob like a cork on a wave. "With you so far Mr. L. What's the job?"

Lombardi clenched and unclenched his right fist as he stared at Leo. His right hand went behind his back and under his suit jacket. It stayed there, much to the relief of Angelo, who was almost on the verge of hyper-ventilating.

"I take it then that you are both on board?" Lombardi said slowly.

"No problems, Mr Lombardi. Sounds very inviting. An offer I, we, couldn't refuse. Eh, Leo?" Angelo said, putting his right hand around the back of Leo's neck and squeezing hard.

"Good then. I am about to tell you the prize. Have a seat boys," indicating that they should sit opposite him at the table.

"The job is this. You will be helping to take back some taxpayers' money. The fine taxpayers of Victoria will be making a withdrawal of sorts from Government premises."

A ram raid on some Government office. Bank job maybe? Angelo wondered.

"You read the newspapers," Lombardi asked.

Angelo nodded and then Leo opened his mouth to speak.

"Just the sports page Mr L. Got to see how Collingwood is tracking in the football. Don't read much else."

Lombardi looked over the head of Leo and continued speaking.

"Our State Government has decided that we need another three thousand police officers to save us from crime and criminals. Obviously then, there will have to be a lot of gear supplied to these fine recruits as they start to enter the Academy. That's where we come in."

Angelo's mind immediately went straight back to what they would be paid. This was going to be a big heist. Uniforms couldn't be worth that much of a reward. Only one thing could. Angelo closed his eyes in disbelief as Lombardi spoke again.

"Each one of these new little recruits will be supplied with a brand-new Smith and Wesson nine-millimetre shooter. We are going to relieve the Victoria Police Department of those shooters. To be precise we are going to take the three thousand firearms from them along with enough ammunition to start a war. Now what do you think about that, boys?"

Angelo's brain was seconds in front of the statement. Leo's mouth was opening and shutting like a goldfish.

Lombardi's eyes were as big as dinner plates. What came out of his mouth next convinced Angelo that he was trapped in the delusional world of this so-called crime boss.

"I am the King of Carlton, You two are now part of my army that is going to frighten this city into submission. When we have done the job people will realise that only one person could have masterminded this operation. They will never pin anything on me. These shooters will be out of the country within hours. No one will dare touch me. I will reign supreme wherever I decide to set up my empire."

Angelo realised that the only person Lombardi spoke about was himself. Everyone else was cannon fodder. All they could do now was to go along with the plan as long as he could speak to Leo soon and shut him up.

"Boys. You seem to be lost for words. There will be a lot of planning and work, but we have time. Ask all the questions you want to."

Angelo spoke very slowly. "Mr Lombardi. How are we going to take three thousand guns that actually belong to the Police, from the Police?"

"A good question", a laughing Lombardi replied. "What helps immensely is that I have an inside person who shall remain nameless except to say that I have drip fed his insatiable appetite for gambling over the last two years at the Crown Casino. He is now into me for over two hundred thousand dollars. He is a Police Support Officer at the Police Stores in Collingwood. I know you might think I am off my head to think this may work, but I can assure you this job can, and will come off."

"What are we going to do with three thousand shooters?" Leo asked.

"You are going to do nothing with them except steal them little Leo. I have already on-sold them. You don't need to know anything more than that," Lombardi said angrily. "These pistols are top of the range and are worth millions along with all the ammunition that will be with them. As I said, helping heist them is your job. You will be paid the money I promised, and I will arrange passports and the one-way flights to your new lifestyles and the overseas contacts for your future work."

The penny suddenly dropped with Leo. "Overseas contacts. What for?" He blurted.

"Listen up dummy," Angelo said, quickly intervening as he noticed Lombardi's face start to redden. "With a heist like this it will be best to live somewhere with no extradition crap with Australia. I can see this as a once in a lifetime chance to turn our lives around. Mr. Lombardi is giving us a great opportunity here. If we do this right, we will only have to work when we want to and then it will be with the best. Isn't that right, Mr. Lombardi?"

"You are catching on fast, Angelo. I am beginning to like you. You can see the future all mapped out, can't you? Work for me now and the world will be your oyster."

With that comment, Big Al Lombardi stood from the table and nodded to Joey and Feb, who immediately grabbed Leo, pinning his arms behind him on his chair. Angelo held his breath as Lombardi pulled a revolver from under the back of his coat, stepped up to the captive and force fed the barrel of the gun into the struggling mouth of Leo Carbone. He smiled and pulled the trigger.

Chapter Twelve

Angelo Morelli was choking.

He wasn't being held down and choked. He was not getting any air into his lungs because of the shock that his body had taken. He simply couldn't breathe.

The kitchen wall behind where Leo Carbone was seated had been transformed into a display so gruesome that even both his minders Joey Salessa and Feb Felagi had a hand over their mouths to stop from vomiting up their breakfast.

Angelo's eyes began to flicker from what remained of Leo's head that was still attached to his body to the splattered remains of bone, brains and whatever else his now shattered skull had contained. The kitchen wall looked like a brightly coloured mural of red and grey. Thin rivulets of blood were running down the wall and lumps of God knows what began falling to the floor with little plopping sounds as they peeled from the ceiling and dislodged themselves from the wall.

Eventually, Angelo forced himself to take a deep breath. When he did, he could see two people sitting at the table. Or to be more precise, one complete person in Al Lombardi who was wiping the barrel of his gun on the shirt of the other person. The other person being the half headless corpse of Leo Carbone. The noise of the firearm being discharged in the small room was still ringing in his ears as he watched Leo's body slowly fall to one side and onto the kitchen floor.

Turning towards Lombardi, Angelo opened his mouth to speak but no words came out. Instead, Lombardi spoke.

"Angelo. Your friend on the floor was dumb and getting dumber. Being dumb is one annoying thing in life I can't tolerate. If you are dumb, you are useless. You're not going to be dumb, are you?"

Angelo couldn't look Lombardi in the face but watched him as the cool and calm murderer of his friend quietly put the revolver back under his jacket.

Angelo didn't have to be told twice when it came to survival. With a quivering voice he replied quietly, "No, Mr Lombardi. Not me."

Big Al Lombardi stood from the table, looked at Joey and Feb, smiled and spoke.

"Boys. One less for you to baby sit. Clean this up. Hose the room down and while you're at it, open the windows. There's a bad smell in here and it isn't gunpowder. I think our friend Leo had time to have a little accident before I sent him on his way. Most unfortunate but understandable. Make sure Angelo helps too. It will reinforce his loyalty. Take Leo to Alfonse Moretti's funeral home in Preston. I will ring ahead. A family cousin. He'll double team our friend here with his next job to the Fawkner cemetery. There will be no questions and no trouble fitting young Leo into one of those big expensive Italian caskets with a new friend, now that he has been cut down to size a bit."

Joey and Feb nodded in unison. They didn't speak. They were still trying not to throw up.

Big Al Lombardi strode out of the back door.

Chapter Thirteen

"Kate, can you come in here for a minute please?" Tony called out as she passed his door.

Kate returned the other way and walked quickly into Tony's office.

"I've only been here for a few days," she said with a laugh. "Surely I haven't stuffed up already?"

"No, no. Not at all," Tony replied. "In fact, I have been keeping an eye on your management skills with the younger officers and I must say that I'm impressed. Part of the reason why I want you to take on a particular job. Have a seat."

Sitting down, Kate looked across the desk at her Senior Sergeant. "Shoot," she said.

Tony's eyes widened before speaking. "That's exactly what I'm going to talk to you about. Guns. Handguns to be more precise."

Tony proceeded to tell Kate the rumours that had been circulating about the possible theft of firearms on their patch and the concern it was causing at Divisional Headquarters.

"We have quite a few gun shops around Carlton and Brunswick, Kate. I know all of the owners and they are above reproach. They all run good businesses, and all have excellent C.C.T.V set ups. Some of the set ups were a bit old, but since I got the patrols to visit all the shops, they have all been updated. In addition, each shop has a direct line to the station just in case."

"What exactly do you want me to do, boss?"

"Senior Detective Max Tyler from Melbourne C.I.U. is doing all the follow up and legwork on any gun story that surfaces around the traps. He's an old Carlton boy and is sharp as a tack. I want you to liaise with him and be the Carlton end. Keep me up to speed at all times. Max is only doing temporary duties in town and I know he is loaded up with work just like all the other detectives. He is the one who brought me the story and I know he wouldn't worry me with it if there wasn't a solid basis to it."

"So, you definitely think there is something in it? None of the patrols have mentioned anything on their daily sheets and I haven't heard anything from the other Sergeants."

Tony replied in a serious tone, "Max came to me a while ago now and gives me updates when he can. So far, we haven't got anything else. What worries me Kate is where the story originated. It concerns two bikie gangs that might go to war if the rumours become fact. Max's source is solid. The two dumb bikie pieces of crap didn't realise they were being listened to. We need more. Headquarters needs more. The Critical Incident Response Teams have been given all we know so they are on heightened alert. Max gets out here when he can so see if you can get him to pop in and see you. I think you two could liaise well with each other. I don't want stolen shooters on my patch being used for some turf war. I know you have an interest in firearms because you belong to a pistol club. Any little bit of scuttlebutt you hear will be a help."

"I'll give him a ring today, boss. I'm going to the range after work. A couple of them down there work in the firearms business. See what I can track down," she said as she stood and headed for the door.

Tony slowly turned his chair around so that he could see out of his office window. The second story location gave him a panorama view of the Royal Exhibition Building.

Reckoned we'd cleaned the sewers of Carlton. Now some piece of shit wants to block them up again.

Chapter Fourteen

Big Al Lombardi knew it would only be a matter of time before he got a visit.

He had kept the planned heist of the firearms to an absolute minimum of people. He knew both Joey and Feb were loyal to him, but he also knew that they had connections with the Black Rats Outlaw Motorcycle Club. And that was where the problem lay.

Joey had come to him that morning and told him that some of his and Feb's bikie mates were asking questions about the pair's whereabouts. Since they had been guarding Leo and Angelo at the Brunswick house for over a month now, they hadn't been hanging out with their 'bros' from the Black Rats. Calls had been coming in asking why and they were running out of answers. Not a healthy plan when dealing with a bikies. Feb had said they were doing a job for Lombardi but couldn't say what. Word had got out to the President of the Black Rats, Tony Richards, that something wasn't smelling like linguini in Carlton town.

Lombardi thought back to a few weeks before he had come across the two inept car thieves, Carbone and Morelli.

It was a night upstairs at his Club Maximus in Lygon Street when Richards was full of 'ink' and starting to mouth off about a job he had in mind.

To save Richards from too many ears, he had taken him into his private office. It was more out of interest than business. Lombardi simply thought that if there was a job going down near his patch, then he had the right to know about it.

What Richards told him next about the incoming firearms was too good to be true. Richards had it on good authority regarding the future delivery of a significant number of handguns. Pistols to be precise. He didn't know exactly when but a fizz in Customs had alerted him to a shipment.

Lombardi knew it didn't take Einstein to figure out the possible destination for a legal and large delivery of pistols in Melbourne and it certainly wasn't going to be to a small gun shop in the suburbs. It had to be to the Police Department. More exactly to the Police Armoury in Collingwood. The very next suburb to Lombardi headquarters in Lygon Street, Carlton.

Richards wasn't the sharpest 'tool in the shed,' but he had given Lombardi an idea that his sharp, rat like mind would store away for good. It was only later when he read the morning newspaper article about the imminent recruitment of three thousand new recruits to the Police Academy that the light bulb in his brain switched on with full amps.

Since that time, he had slowly but surely worked his Victoria Police firearms contact with enough money to make sure his gambling debts at the Crown Casino reached breaking point.

Lombardi had gotten Joey and Feb to pluck the now broke punter from outside the casino one morning and make him realise that he owed the King of Carlton thousands of dollars. A quiet drive and a little gentle conversation back at Lygon Street with a promise to wipe the slate clean for information on delivery dates and access points to the armoury was the only way to avoid a one-way fishing trip out into Port Phillip Bay. Information was immediately forthcoming.

The concern now was setting up the heist without any of it getting back to the Black Rats. If anything leaked, Lombardi knew Richards would claim the deal as his own. Not only the deal but a sizeable amount of the profits.

Lombardi was thinking of the plan and raising his second short black to his lips when his office door crashed open courtesy of Tony Richards.

                                            The Calibre of Justice

Chapter Fifteen

"Hello mate. How the fuck are you today?" The tall leather clad bikie said in a threatening voice.

Wishing that Joey or Feb were here with him instead of being at the Brunswick house, Lombardi sat back in his big office chair, at the same time sliding his right hand under the expensive teak desktop to where a small Beretta pistol sat nestled in a holster strapped underneath.

Richards kicked the office door closed with his left boot as he also went on the offensive by pulling a .357 Smith and Wesson Magnum revolver from the back of his leather pants. He held it with a loose grip pointing towards the floor.

"Bad move, Al. You shift that hand another inch and I'll put a round through that lovely desk and blow your balls off."

Lombardi slowly placed both hands onto the blotter pad on the desk. Sweat started to soak into the thick white paper. He spoke with a very dry throat.

"Tony, what are you doing? It was only weeks ago that you were my guest here. You had my best girls and booze that night free of charge. What is upsetting you my friend?"

"You know what it is like, Al. You hear stories. At first you don't believe them. Or should I say, you don't want to believe them. When the stories keep resurfacing though, you start to wonder and then you start to worry."

"What stories, Tony? What are you hearing? Surly nothing is wrong between us?" Lombardi said nervously.

Richards stepped forward and placed the chrome plated cannon gently on the desk with the barrel pointing directly at Lombardi's midriff. He kept his finger on the trigger. Lombardi knew that if the trigger was pulled it would take out more than his midriff. It would blow apart his whole torso and the brick wall behind. Game over.

"Al, I'm not a person to be fucked over. Neither is my organisation. I want to know why you have my two Samoan bears tucked away somewhere. Word from some of my boys is that you have them doing a job for you. Now I don't really give a fuck what they are doing, but I want to know why they haven't been seen at the clubhouse. Why have you got them tucked away? What job have you got them working on? They're my boys, Al. My boys. Tell me now or I'll blow holes in this desk that I could drive your head through."

Lombardi knew he had to save himself quickly.

"Tony, Tony. Excuse the pun but you've jumped the gun on this. Cool it. Yes, I have them looking at a job but it's early stages. I was going to contact you next week."

"What job, Al? My trigger finger is getting very sweaty," Richards said as he looked down at the Magnum.

"Tony. You know. The one regarding the new shooters your mate in Customs told you about. We can take this on."

"What's this 'we' shit?" Richards said as he spat on the floor. "That was my idea, not yours. I want to know what my Black Rats are doing for you!"

Lombardi decided to take a chance.

"A good idea Tony, but that's all it was then. Have you taken it any further? Can you? Has your snitch in Customs come up with anymore on it? That's why I've been working the other end. You've come up with the idea, I'm coming up with the master plan and I'm going to need some of those bikie mates of yours to help carry it off."

Lombardi slowly rose from behind his desk, showing his hands all the time.

"Come on Tony. Put that piece away and let's have a drink and talk about how you and I can completely destroy the Police Department and probably the State Government at the same time."

Chapter Sixteen

Sitting at a table in the corner of his club with a still agitated Tony Richards, Big Al Lombardi laid out his plan to heist the firearms.

"Tony, it didn't register with me fully when you talked about a big government delivery of firearms. It was only when I saw the paper. Why else would there be a firearms delivery to this piss weak, nanny government. Who needs them? I'll tell you who. Three thousand new police recruits, that's who!"

Richards started to lean back in his chair whilst looking into his glass of Jim Beam and coke. The look of hate for Lombardi starting to turn into one of puzzlement.

"Go on," Richards said. This better be on the level or I will have my boys visit you twenty-four seven. It won't be Club Maximus anymore; it will be Club Ruin. It won't have any furniture left in it. They will turn this place upside down and recycle everything in it. Maximum will be minimum!"

With the mention of violence against his bar, Lombardi saw red. His voice went up and he barked back at the bikie opposite him.

"For fuck's sake you moron. Just shut up and listen. The Italian connection has been around this suburb longer than motor bikes were invented so don't threaten me with your bullshit. I have friends in all suburbs and states. You have heard of the word Calabria haven't you? It's in southern Italy but has connections right here. If you want in on this plan just sit there and drink free bourbon and open your fucking ears."

The air could be cut with a knife, the tension was that thick. Lombardi continued with a commanding voice.

"Do you want to act like some leather arsed bikie or show me how you can run your boys and between us we carry off the biggest snatch this state has ever seen. Yes, or fucking no?"

Richards slowly put both hands palms up on the table. Leaning in towards Lombardi, he spoke very quietly.

"Let's hear it all. If it's that good a plan with a shit load of shooters for the taking, then tell me how."

Inwardly, Lombardi felt a huge sigh of relief. He would tell Richards his plan with what would be the Black Rats involvement. He would tell him all right. He just wasn't going to tell him everything.

Chapter Seventeen

Saturday evening in Lygon Street and Dom's bistro was alive with noise, talk and families. Just the way the owner of the famous Carlton eatery, Dom Santino, liked it.

Dom had been a small child when, years before, his parents had decided that a new life was needed for themselves and their family. Thank God they chose Australia, Dom thought to himself.

His family had worked hard in post-war Australia. Settling in the northern Melbourne suburb of Carlton in a terrace house, his father had taken on all types of jobs from working in the fruit stalls of the Victoria Market to waiting on tables and washing dishes in the ever-expanding Italian influenced eating strip of Lygon street.

Dom's father, Rolando had always said the greatest gift he and his family had ever been given was a new life in this great free land.

Since the early eighteen hundreds, the Chinese, then Jewish and now Italian families had gravitated to the northern suburbs. They had all got along together because there was no time for any bickering or petty jealousies. Why? Because every member of every family worked long and hard hours to make life better for themselves and their neighbours. Birthdays and other celebrations were street affairs and it didn't matter where you came from. It was true diversity before the word had been politicised.

Dom's father eventually scraped together enough money to open the very establishment that Dom now called his own. There were many restaurants along the famous eating strip where you could be served delicious food from many countries; but there was only one Dom's. If you wanted a real family celebration in the true Italian style, then Dom and his wife Maria together with help from their three daughters Gina, Rosa and Silvana was where it started and finished. However, the finishing time was always open to interpretation. This was his restaurant and all who lived and ate in Carlton were his extended family.

Dom carried three drinks to a table situated in the back corner near the kitchen. It wasn't his best table in the restaurant by far. There was no view of Lygon street as such. You virtually sat with your back to the two right angled walls. Tonight though, it was occupied by three people, two of whom were old friends of Dom's. The third was a lady he didn't know but was sure he would very soon. Placing a glass of his best Chianti in front of her, he spoke as he waved his two arms around in the true Italian style.

"Dear lady. Forgive these two ignorant peasants for not introducing me. I am Dom Santino, the proprietor of this establishment. I can understand these two wanting to sit at this table, but not you. With such beauty you should be sitting centre stage." He then placed a Crown Lager in front of Max and gave a Lemon, Lime and Bitters to Tony, who then began to speak.

"My apologies, Dom. This is Kate McLaren, my new Sergeant at the station. Kate, this old Italian thinks he owns Lygon Street. His name is Dom Santino. He is an institution around this suburb and frankly sometimes I think he should be in an institution," he said with a smile.

Kate was thinking what to say in reply when suddenly, Tony stood, grabbed Dom in a big bear-like embrace and kissed him, first on one cheek and then on the other. To her surprise, Dom accepted the gesture with a hug that was just as bear-like.

Max Tyler, the remaining figure at the table leant across to Kate. "It's an Italian thing Kate. These two old legends have known each other for almost as long as this restaurant has been here, and believe me, that's a bloody long time."

Quicker than a flick knife could be produced, Dom and Tony lifted Max out of his chair and attempted to give him the same appropriate Italian kisses. Max fought back, pushing both of the laughing Italian faces away.

"Max, my young friend," Dom said. "My beautiful daughters are always waiting for a kiss from a young policeman like you. Do you now only come in here with this old dinosaur?" he said, throwing an arm towards Tony.

"Dom my friend," Max replied. "It's just that I can't decide where my heart lies. One minute it is Gina, the next Rosa and then I think about the lovely Silvana. They are all so beautiful."

Dom stood between the two police officers, who he had been through so much with, and squeezed them towards himself. Looking directly at Kate, he continued.

"Kate, you are now a Dom's resident. I have known these two, especially the very old one, for quite a while now and they are family to me. I am glad they have brought you in to dinner. You are like a rose between two thorns." He then looked at Tony and continued.

"This is Saturday night. You two are here for business, aren't you? That's why you reserved my special table down here near the kitchen. Otherwise I would have expected your beautiful wife Susie and gorgeous little Gracie to be here."

Tony sat back down and looked up at Dom.

"Yes, my friend. We'll all be here in a fortnight. It's Susie's birthday, so get some big tables ready, won't you? Tonight, is just about work. Now you are here though, I'd like to ask you a question."

Dom's face took on a serious look. Although some people might have thought he was just a big happy Italian restaurant owner, underneath that exterior was a very astute business person. White apron or no white apron, he had survived down through the years by being on top of any situation that may be about to happen in his establishment. He could spot upcoming trouble with a very sharp set of eyes and ears. Basic Italian cunning he called it. He knew from Tony's voice that he wasn't going to be asked the price of a plate of his best tagliatelle.

"What is it my friend? What do you need to know?"

Kate McLaren realised immediately that this man Dom was definitely more family than just friend to Tony. Looking at Max she got back a wink and a nod from the young detective.

"The Italian connection, Kate," Max said quietly.

"Dom, Max here has some rather disturbing information about an upcoming theft of guns that may take place somewhere around Carlton. Handguns to be precise. I know that you would tell me immediately if you heard anything around Lygon Street. Has there been any hint of something that has made you a bit suspicious?"

Dom immediately took a chair from the next table and sat down amongst the police officers.

"Nothing really, my friend," Dom whispered. "There has been no talk at all. When it comes to guns though there is always one person to keep an eye on. That piece of crap, Lombardi and his Club Maximus. Named it after a gladiator, so I am told. I put nothing past him."

A look passed immediately between Tony and Max. This was the second time Lombardi's name had come up. Once between the bikies at the Custody Centre when Lombardi was referred to as the King of Carlton and now with his old friend Dom.

"What makes you bring his name up, Dom?" Max interrupted

"I know that he has a lot of those, what you call Outlaw gangs at his place. You know the ones that are always on bikes or driving big cars. Bernardi next door, myself and several other restaurant owners are keeping an eye on his night club up the road. He is no good for Lygon Street. This is a family place. Has been for generations of migrant families."

"Yes Dom. Outlaw motorcycle gangs are what you are talking about. Is it mainly bikes or cars that these creeps are arriving in?" Max questioned.

"You always hear the bikes. Not our Italian ones but those big noisy Harley Davidson monsters. One car that is always there lately is a big black Chrysler. I have only seen one person in it and he looks like a nasty piece of work. I like to know what is going on around here. I took the number of it last week. The man doesn't do anything wrong, but he stays very late. There is always a parking space for it next to that Maserati that Lombardi owns. I'll get you the number," Dom said as he got up and hurried back into the kitchen.

"Let's check this out quickly, Max. If the driver is a bikie, then he is right up the chain otherwise he wouldn't be parking in a reserved spot next to the King, would he?" Tony said.

Dom came back and handed Tony a slip of paper with a registration number on it.

"Thank you, my friend. Good to have your eyes and ears helping us," Max said.

"Always. Always. This is a family area. We don't want this type around here. You know that I'll help whenever I can. I will come straight to both of you with anything," Dom said looking at Tony and Max.

"And Kate. She is helping Max on this and she is looking at the Carlton end while Max is looking further in at Collingwood, Fitzroy and Richmond," Tony said.

Dom stood. "Saturday night in two weeks eh? That will give Maria and the girls plenty of time. Upstairs will be all decorated and we will party the whole night."

Turning to Max, he continued. "Young Max, eh? Out of uniform and in a suit. I will tell the girls." Max reddened under the paternal stare.

"Kate. You will come, too. Tony will give you the night off. Bring your boyfriend as well," Dom said looking at her ringless left hand.

"No. I can't. Sorry, Dom. Think I am rostered on afternoon shift on that Saturday, aren't I boss?"

With a look of despair in Dom's direction, Tony replied.

"No, not now. The President of Italy has spoken, so you must attend."

Dom's face lit up. "Wonderful. You, Susie, little Gracie, Max, Kate and her boyfriend, Marie and the girls. Don't forget to invite Mr. Stone and his wife and Jill Norton and her husband.

Just a few for a quiet night. Family, wonderful family," Dom said, as he headed towards the outside tables on the footpath in bustling Lygon Street, with a huge grin on his face.

Turning towards Kate, Tony spoke. "Kate, by late that Saturday night you will have heard the history of Carlton from the early Chinese settlers through to the Jewish population, the Italian migration right up to the present moment, while you are presented with overflowing plates of pasta, bottles of his best Chianti amid happy, smiling Italian faces. I am used to it and so is Max. I apologise in advance, Sergeant."

Kate looked at her new work colleagues, the busy, noisy restaurant and the figure of Dom Santino waving his arms around while he entertained a family at one of his tables outside and couldn't help but think she had chosen a very interesting workplace.

Interrupting her train of thought, Max spoke as he looked down at his mobile phone. He hadn't dared answer the text while Dom was around because as far as the restaurateur was concerned, phones were banned at his establishment. He insisted people talked to each other face to face.

"Ah, boss. Now that Dom has gone, I've got some bad news to tell you. Phil Stone just texted me."

Tony gave Max a long stare. "You mean we not only have a possible shipment of illegal handguns which we can't find out any information on which may flood the suburbs and you have bad news? Tell me now before we eat."

"Phil Stone says that the bikie that spilled the information about the guns when he was on remand has been found dead at Barwon State Prison with a shiv in his back."

After a moment of silence, Tony motioned to the waiter to come over as he spoke to Max and Kate. "Well, that has just saved us a trip down the highway to interview him. Interesting though. Dom says the bikies are starting to infiltrate Lygon Street and the one that has screwed up by opening his mouth is silenced. Let's eat and then we will talk again on Monday when you, Max, will have some information on that car registration number."

Chapter Eighteen

Kate McLaren had been at her desk for two solid hours. The amount of paperwork she had checked, re-checked, authorised and not authorised because of mistakes, and then sent back to her team of Constables and Senior Constables was never ending. The early thoughts of getting out on the road with them had long since disappeared along with the vague idea of lunch. The electronic era of emails had certainly not diminished the amount of work she was churning through.

On her return from the mess room with an overdue coffee in her hand, she saw the screen of her mobile phone was showing a missed call. Picking it up, she gave a little smile to herself upon seeing Tom Cole's name above the phone number. She looked from the pile of paperwork in her in tray to the phone and back again. Decision made. Coffee and a phone call won hands down against checking another Brief of Evidence and report forms concerning everything from recreational leave applications to damage to one of the station cars where an overzealous young Constable backed it into the station wall on being called to a 'hot job'. Small incident but a lot of paperwork.

Sitting back with the coffee, Kate pressed her thumb on Tom's name and listened for the call to go through. He picked up on the second ring.

"Hey Sarge. How's the world of crime and corruption in downtown Carlton going?" Tom said with a relaxed tone.

"Just trying to get the outbox higher than the inbox at the moment, Tom. Where are you?" Kate said, quietly hoping that he was somewhere local and might be able to drop in.

"Miles away actually," Tom replied, turning off the ignition in his company security car as he parked outside the Carlton Police Station.

"Oh, okay," Kate said with a hint of disappointment in her voice. "That's a pity. I would have shouted you a cup of coffee. Maybe another time?"

"Only kidding," Tom said with a laugh. "I've just pulled up outside your station. Be with you in a minute."

Kate threw her phone onto some paperwork on her desk and found herself walking toward the front inquiry counter and looking forward to his visit. In fact, she realised it was brightening her day.

She had only seen Tom in cargo pants and a black T shirt at the pistol club recently, so when she saw the tall, well-built ex-soldier standing in the foyer in a smart grey business suit, white shirt, black tie and a pair of black wing-tipped shoes she was taken aback by his appearance. Standing about a metre from him, she couldn't help looking him up and down. To excuse herself from the obvious stare she said, "What's with the businessman appearance? Don't you wear a uniform at work with your security firm?"

"Where's the coffee you promised or does a member of the tax paying public have to invite himself in?" Tom shot back as he looked at Kate in her dark navy-blue uniform with the three Sergeant's stripes.

"This way to the mess room," Kate said, as she let Tom through from the counter. "Glad you dropped by. Have a big favour to ask you. Feel free to say no because it's on very short notice."

Taking a seat in the mess room, Tom realised he actually felt quite at home in the uniformed environment. Two Constables were just leaving as Kate handed him a cup of black coffee whilst pointing towards the fridge.

"Milk's in there and sugar is on the table," Kate said in a matter of fact tone. "Haven't made you a coffee before, so choose your own add-ons."

"Sorry to interrupt, Sarge."

Kate turned as Chloe Schaffer, one of the departing Constables looked at her.

"Yes, Chloe. What's up?" Kate replied.

"That Brief of Evidence I put in for authorisation. Did it look all right?"

Kate knew she was referring to an arrest that Schaffer had got on nightshift two weeks before. It had been a good bust for drugs and possession of a prohibited weapon. She had gone right through the brief and was very impressed with Schaeffer's legal facts and admissions from the offender. The brief had been authorised, but she wanted to go through it with the young Constable.

"Yes Chloe. It was good work, but I want us to get together and go through it and check the court date for both of us."

Schaffer looked at her Sergeant with a slightly bewildered expression.

"Why a mutual court date, Sarge?"

"Chloe. Have you ever had a brief like this before? A drugs and weapons one?"

"No, I haven't. Only small stuff so far, Sarge."

"That's why I coming to court with you. It's my job to see you through the paperwork and support you at court on the day. You are one of my Probationary Constables. We're in this together, mate. Come and see me tomorrow. All good. Don't stress. We'll take this wannabee drug dealing piece of shit down together. By the time you have finished with him in court, the Magistrate will want you promoted on the same day," Kate said with a laugh in her voice.

"Thanks, Sarge. That's fantastic. Good to have you there on the day." Schaeffer turned to leave and spoke quickly to her colleague with her in the doorway.

"So good to have her around. She is so supportive and good to work with."

Kate sat opposite Tom at the mess room table and was about to say something when he spoke.

"From the look on her face I think you may be a pretty popular Sergeant around here."

"It's not so much being popular. It's what I would expect from any supervisor. It's also what the boss here expects. These kids need support and that's my job. Anyway, nice of you to drop in even though you were nowhere near here," Kate said as she leaned across the table and smacked Tom lightly on the arm. "To what do I owe the pleasure?"

"Well, first off, you were about to ask me a favour. What is it?"

"Yeah, yeah. Almost forgot," Kate said, feeling a few butterflies in her stomach as she spoke. "Look, Tony Signorotto, the Senior Sergeant here, has a birthday bash on for his wife on Saturday week at Dom's restaurant in Lygon Street. I was with him and a detective at Dom's the other night talking about a situation we are trying to get a handle on in Carlton. Anyway, before I knew it, I had been invited to come along too. They've even invited your neighbour Jill Norton. She used to work here. I was just wondering if you wanted to tag along. With me, I meant."

She saw a look of doubt cross Tom's face. "It doesn't really matter if you can't."

Tom gave Kate a long, silent look before he spoke.

"Kate. I haven't really gone out much since Jo was killed. I'd really like to, but I've got little Summer to think of. If Jill Norton is going, then I've lost my babysitter."

A sudden silence engulfed the almost deserted messroom before the distinctive sound of Tony Signorotto suddenly made both Kate and Tom take their eyes away from each other and look in the direction of the door.

"Consider the invitation for you and your daughter. Dom's is all about family and she will have Jill there as well as Dom's daughters looking after her. Not a problem," Tony said as he approached the now standing Tom Cole. Both men reached towards each other for a handshake. Tom spoke.

"I take it you are the boss. Tony, is it? Tom Cole."

"Boss with a small 'b' actually. I have some good Sergeants here who can handle situations without any interference from me. Nice to meet you, Tom. Dropped in for a coffee with my Sergeant, have you?" Tony said with a slight grin on his face.

Before Tom could respond, Kate replied self-consciously.

"Tom's a friend of mine from the pistol club. Better shot than me."

"How'd that come about then? You being a better pistol shot?" Tony said.

"Army trained I suppose," Tom said slowly as his eyes met Tony's.

Tony continued with the same line of questioning.

"You weren't regular army then? To be a good shot with a pistol, I'd say you'd have been Special Forces. Correct?"

"Yeah, was actually. Afghanistan. Out now and back in civvy street."

"What do you do now?" Tony said as he poured himself a cup of coffee.

"Operations Manager for National Security Services."

Kate hadn't asked Tom who he worked for but cut into the conversation immediately.

"That's a big company. Good reputation, too."

"Yeah, it's well run. Got some good ex- police and ex-military running the show up top. Getting some worthwhile contracts. Just picked up one from Vic Pol, actually," Tom said.

Tony and Kate looked at each other with blank faces.

"Which contract's that? Haven't heard about any. Sure, I would have heard something from the Ivory Tower," Tony said referring irreverently to Police Headquarters. "Security for one of our new buildings? The Protective Security Officers usually handle that sort of thing," he said with a questioning look on his face.

"No, not a building. Escort job. Don't know exactly when but it concerns a new delivery of firearms for the induction of your supposed 3,000 new recruits. It'll be the pistols," Tom said.

Tony's eyes looked straight up from his coffee and bored holes right through Tom.

"Tell me more, if you're allowed. Any specifics?" Tony said quickly. The mention of anything to do with firearms was sending his radar off the scale these past days.

"Will be an escort job soon from the airport to your armoury in Collingwood. They all have to be de-greased and checked there I suppose before the newbies at the Academy get their hands on them."

"Tom. We have a lookout bulletin for a possible hit on firearms. Can't go into details with you, but can you keep Kate here up to speed on what's happening?" Tony said.

"Actually, because the delivery route will be going through a lot of Police Districts, I've been tasked with setting up meetings with the Senior Sergeants and Inspectors of the Divisions to give them the details of the escort and delivery route. I was sort of hoping that Kate here might be able to liaise between myself, N.S.S. and the police."

"Absolutely," Tony replied. "In fact, I'll ask Superintendent Phil Stone from Operations in town to set up a committee involving us all. Get the appropriate Highway Patrols on board, too."

"That would be great, Tony. I have only just been made Operations Manager, so I need as much help as possible," he said as he handed both Kate and Tony a business card with his detail on it.

"Leave it with me. I'll phone Phil today and tell him Kate is available to co-ordinate it. All right with you, Kate?"

"Fine with me. Would be good to get the Divisions together on this. Have you got any idea of when they will be coming in, Tom?"

"They're coming from the States. All nine-millimetre Smith and Wesson Police and Military specials. Same as what you are using now. Three thousand of them. It is down to the company in the U.S.A. and our Federal Police as to the arrival date. I would estimate about three weeks. The Feds will have been in contact with my company, so you'll probably hear from them very soon I'd say. It's probably already in your system at

Command level. If your Superintendent jumps on board now, we can get it going straight away with the Feds on the committee."

"Kate, I'm going to relieve you of all jobs now," Tony said. "If anyone asks, just tell them you are working on a big stats project that has come down from up high. I'll get Max Tyler on it also."

A few minutes later after some details had been ironed out, the conversation turned to a lighter subject.

"Tony, thanks for the invite to Dom's, but, as I said, with little Summer, I don't want to intrude," Tom said quietly.

"Tom, I have a hearing problem when it comes to knock backs for celebrations. You and Summer are coming. My wife Susie would kill me if she finds out I let you get out of this," Tony said as he stood, shook hands with him and turned to leave the mess room. "And don't forget to bring my Sergeant with you," he said with a quick wink in the direction of Kate who was turning a bright shade of red with embarrassment.

"Oh, Kate. Just one thing if I could see you out here for a second," Tony said as he walked into the corridor for some privacy. She quickly rose and walked out behind her Senior Sergeant.

"Kate. We've been searching high and low for some information on a possible arms grab. We have one dead big mouth from Barwon State Prison, and we have Lombardi's name being spruiked up and down Lygon Street. There has been no info from any of the gun shops and I trust those owners. I have been around long enough to smell a rat with this police pistol delivery. In fact, I smell a big fat King of Rats. As soon as you've finished, get onto Max and fill him in with this new angle. I'll get onto Phil Stone right now. This could be the dynamite we have been looking for. I just want to make sure we are holding all the fuses," Tony said as he headed with big strides towards his office.

Chapter Nineteen

Tony Signorotto was walking out of his office when the desk phone rang.

He had spent the last twenty minutes talking to Superintendent Phil Stone about the information Tom Cole had passed on about the shipment of firearms. By the end of that conversation he knew that the Superintendent would be emailing all the Divisional Inspectors between Melbourne Airport and Collingwood to set up a security meeting.

Picking up the phone, Tony spoke straight away.

"What have I forgotten, Superintendent?"

The reply that came back was filled with laughter.

"Thanks for the quick promotion, boss," Max Tyler replied.

"Thought it was Phil Stone again, Max," Tony said. "Just been on the phone to him about the shipment of new pistols for the recruits. He's only just been put in the loop about them. As the Superintendent in charge of Operations, I can tell you he isn't happy about the late notice. I won't unload on you now mate but you will be involved too. That new friend of Kate's, Tom Cole, who is the Ops Manager for Australian Security Services has been in here and told us about the transport security contract they have just got. I've got a hunch Max, that this could be the needle in the haystack we have been looking for. I think this is the missing piece. We have been looking locally at our gun shops but I reckon it is much bigger than that. Stand by to be briefed by an email from HQ, young Max. Anyway, what can I do for you seeing that you rang me?"

"Got some information on that car registration Dom gave us the other night. That black Chrysler. Remember?" Max said in an excited but controlled voice.

"Right. Almost forgotten about that. Who does it come up to?"

"Interesting boss. It comes up to a company by the name of A.R.D. Holdings. When I looked into it, it turns out that A.R.D. Holdings is actually Tony Richards Holdings. Based in a factory in Fairfield. A front for a luxury car business which sells mainly Jaguars."

"Good work, Max, but it doesn't get us any closer to who the head driving the car is?"

"Thought I'd practise playing detective. Put on some good jeans and had a wander through his factory pretending I was looking for a nice second-hand Jag. First thing I saw was the black Chrysler parked out the back. Took a few quick shots of some of the cars and made sure I had some head shots of the couple of dudes in the background that were coming and going from the office area. Guess what I turned up with when I showed the shots to a couple of mates in the O.M.C.G. Task Force. One of photos is Tony Richards. The Tony Richards who is the President of the Black Rats Outlaw Motorcycle Gang."

"Now we have a real connection, Max. Well spotted," Tony said eagerly.

"All seems a bit coincidental doesn't it, boss. One of the Black Rats has his wings clipped for good in prison and at the same time we have the President of the Black Rats making regular visits to the King of the Rats in Lygon Street," Max said.

"Max. This is all starting to come together—and it scares me! When you read your email, you'll know what I am getting at," Tony said.

"Boss, while I've been talking to you, I've been reading my emails. There's one here from Superintendent Stone and the invite list looks like a who's who of all the bosses from North West Metro Region. There's even the head of the S.O.G. and all the Highway Patrol Senior Sergeants. Even a couple of Feds have been told to come along. I'm the lowest rank on the whole ladder here. What's going on?"

"Max, your rank might not be as high as some on the list, but I can assure you that with the information you've got, you'll be the one who'll be answering all the questions. I think you, Kate and myself can expect some seriously long planning meetings and some even longer shifts coming up," Tony said.

Chapter Twenty

Big Al Lombardi now had information about the delivery of the police firearms. King Rat had it from two of his rodent sources! The first source was from his own 'fizz' in Police Support Services at the Police Armoury in Collingwood. His informant had been given a 'heads up' about the arrival of a shipment of handguns that Lombardi knew would coincide with the intake of the future boys and girls in blue.

You didn't have to be a Rhodes scholar to figure it out. All a person had to do was read the Sun-Herald newspaper and see the grinning State Premier pumping the hand of the Chief Commissioner outside the hallowed gates of the former monastery, now Police Academy, as they announced the upcoming first intake of rookies on April the First. The thought crossed the mind of Lombardi that the joke would be on them.

It was there for all to read in the newspaper. The State Government had agreed with the Police Department to start one hundred new recruits every month for the next two years. The promise from the top end of town was a solid gold handshake—according to who would be in the top end of town after the upcoming state election in three months' time. The Police Department knew that it could all collapse with a change of Government, but it wasn't about to look a gift horse in the mouth. Contracts had been signed for new uniforms and more equipment including the new firearms. It was full steam ahead on the political bullet train.

The First of April was only three weeks away. With each recruit taking five months to graduate, Lombardi guessed that they would start their pistol training after about four weeks. The arrival of the shooters at the Melbourne International Airport was probably inside the next couple of weeks.

His other source was the 'wanabee' Black Rats Outlaw Motor Cycle probationary rider who Tony Richards was working from his end. The young recruit was a Customs Officer at Melbourne International Airport. Unbeknown to all his mates at the airport, the young O.M.C.G. member was also tied in with several right-wing dark groups, of which all had a hatred of authority. Lombardi wondered how this kid could climb into his Customs uniform every day without wanting to tear it straight off. The fact that Richards was letting him ride one of his own possessions which he had paid for through dirty drug sales probably helped. You would have thought that a $30,000 Harley Davidson 'Fat Boy Smoker' would have raised a few eyebrows when he arrived at work astride the gleaming beast. If the registration had been checked it would have shown up as belonging to A.R.D. Holdings, the same shell company that Richards had his Chrysler registered to. Big brother helping out little brother in the harsh world of drugs and vice.

Lombardi was thinking about this as he handed a tumbler of twelve-year-old Macallan Scotch whisky to Tony Richards. They were in Lombardi's office above his Club Maximus in Lygon Street. There was no way he was going to the headquarters of the Black Rats in Fairfield. Even the chance that he might get a beer stain from that dump on his Versace suit made him queasy.

"Ice and water over on the bar," Lombardi said, indicating the expensive teak cabinet with the built-in fridge by the wall.

"Coke in mine," the laughing figure of Richards replied.

Lombardi stood and stared at Richards.

The sooner this job is over, the sooner I can eliminate this piece of garbage. Coke with Macallan. What fucking next? I only need him for so long. Just take a big deep breath, Al, he thought to himself.

Reaching out, Lombardi removed the crystal cut tumbler of expensive scotch from Richard's tattooed hand, walked over to the fridge and removed a cold can of Jim Beam bourbon and coke and tossed it to Richards.

"Yeah, more my style, Al," the biker said as he lounged with one leg over the armrest of the expensive Chesterfield wing back chair and at the same time ripped the ring top off the can, letting the sticky alcoholic drink spill onto the leather. He then proceeded to gulp down half the contents after which he wiped his mouth with the dirty sleeve of the cheap checked shirt he was wearing.

Lombardi stared coolly at the bikie before taking a deliberate sip of his scotch and ice, savouring the classic drop as he caressed the beautiful amber fluid around his mouth with his tongue and marvelled at the exquisite taste that piqued his senses. It was only then that he spoke.

"All right Tony. We are in this together for our mutual financial benefit, but I will be running this operation. Clear?"

The tall bikie removed his jean clad leg from the arm of the chair and leant further back in a relaxed pose and spoke.

"Don't know about that, Al. I have the club behind me remember. We are going to have to use a few of my boys to get this done."

Big Al Lombardi was done with holding his well-known violent temper. His words exploded over Richards.

"First things first, you dumb fucking bikie. If you put all the brain cells of your so-called boys together and changed the words 'brain cells' to the word 'dynamite', there wouldn't be enough collective force to blow your noses with. Understand? Secondly, I don't want any of your hyped up, beer swilling brainless mates involved until the last minute. They might have some muscle but that's all they are going to be used for. I will be doing the planning because I don't want any of this to leak out. They will not be told until the last minute what they will have to do in relation to stopping these guns going from A to B. Just think back to that one of yours at Barwon State Prison. He talked. He died. That was down to you. Get it? You are the arms and legs and I am the head and brains. If you don't like that you can take it up later on with some of my more down to earth mafia associates. By down to earth, I mean down in the earth. Quite clear my friend?"

Richards began to turn pale. People did not speak to him like that, but in his favour, he knew who and what he was dealing with.

"All right Al. All good. I just want a good share of the profits for myself. That's all," Richards stammered.

"Correct Tony. For yourself. So, we will keep this just between you and me. I'd hate for any of your brother Black Rats or, God forbid, the Carnivores to find out what you want for yourself," Lombardi said with an evil grin on his face as he held up his mobile phone and turned it towards Richards, switching off the microphone as he did. His insurance premium was now recorded.

Keep your friends close and your enemies closer, Lombardi thought.

Tony felt a bead of sweat run down his neck. Lombardi now had him by the balls. He had opened his mouth just wide enough to jam both his leather booted feet in.

Chapter Twenty-One

Big Al Lombardi didn't really mind Vietnamese food. It wasn't however real food like Italian food. In his mind it was just food for the hordes of immigrants from Asian countries that had populated Australia for years. He knew places like Vietnam, Cambodia and Laos were very popular places to visit. Just not for him. Europe was more to his liking. Italy especially. After all, wasn't it Italy that had given the world Da Vinci and Rome? It was chalk and cheese. Like beef and black bean sauce compared to home-made lasagne. Especially home-made lasagne that had been lovingly prepared by Big Al's mother. All right, but no comparison.

The problem was that Lombardi's contact from the Police Armoury wanted to speak to him and had booked a table for dinner at Ha Long Bay Vietnamese restaurant in Victoria Street, Richmond. The only reason that Lombardi was going along to the meeting place was because he needed more details of the who, what, where and when in regard to the firearms delivery. This had to be done privately.

He had arranged for Joey Salessa, his right-hand Samoan giant, to drop him off just north of the meet in Hoddle Street. He trusted Joey implicitly with driving his Maserati Gran Turismo simply because Joey knew that if he scratched, or God forbid, bent it then he would own it. Easy. He bought it with money or his life and both he and Joey knew he couldn't even afford the wheel nuts on the Italian chariot.

Lombardi made the decision to walk down Victoria Street to the restaurant because he didn't want any of the street crawling, drug addled patrons of the sewers of Richmond touching, or for that matter, *looking* at his four wheeled pride of Italy. Big Al had also changed out of his expensive suit into what he would have classified as very casual gear, notwithstanding the fact that most people inhabiting that area could hardly afford the price of the shoelaces of his twelve hundred-dollar Gucci Heart Dagger Ace sneakers. Just what the common garden variety lowlife would like to get his hands on in the United Nations melting pot of Richmond. It was a very rare moment indeed when you found Alessio Lombardi on foot, breathing the fetid air of postcode 3121. One of the reasons he always carried a box of air purifiers in his Maserati.

He was glad of the fact that the restaurant was only a short walk down Victoria Street. Stopping to cross the busy road, he suddenly felt a hand lightly brush across the rear pocket of his twelve hundred-dollar Escada jeans. Either this was a skinny little bird plying her sex trade or some ice ridden addict foolishly trying for his wallet. Either way there was definite pain coming for such an individual. Not that it would do the wandering hand any good, as Lombardi was carrying his usual five hundred 'folding' in the top pocket of his Burberry stretch cotton poplin shirt. If you added the cash to the price of his clothes you were looking well into the four-figure bracket.

Turning his head slowly, Lombardi looked at a scrawny, filthy, mid-twenties character who was standing to his right, but slightly behind the King of Carlton. Bad mistake on the part of Scrawny Filthy.

Scrawny Filthy spoke with a raspy guttural voice that was trying to sound full of menace but ended up sounding like a squeaky little child.

"I want your shoes and your money. I've got a fucking knife and I will use…"

Before Scrawny Filthy added any more to the one-sided conversation, Lombardi's right elbow crashed into his face with the force of a sledgehammer, driving broken and diseased teeth back into his throat. Scrawny Filthy dropped down to his home in the gutter, coughing blood and trying to utter more expletives to Lombardi's back as the King of Carlton slowly crossed towards the restaurant. If he had taken a look behind him, he would have seen Scrawny Filthy on his knees vomiting up his incisors, but Big Al Lombardi never looked backwards in life and definitely never in Richmond.

By the time he had entered the popular Vietnamese eatery, the incident with the local drug addict had completely left his mind. Not seeing his contact, he walked towards the rear tables out of habit. If his Victoria Police Support Staff informant had half a brain he would not have booked a table near the front windows. This was one thing Lombardi and most police had in common. Sit at the rear with your back to the wall so as to see the eyes and hands of your enemy if they approached uninvited.

John Moore, late forties, but appearing much older, looked up nervously as Lombardi eased his large frame into a chair at the small corner table. Moore knew he was into Lombardi for far too much money than he could ever repay. He was hoping that the information about the pistol delivery would see them square and he could get on with his life, but he knew that all he was doing was buying time. He was a worm on the hook. Lombardi would keep dipping him into situations for ever and a day. He would never be free. He had considered a cleaning 'accident' with one of the firearms at the armoury many times to end his misery.

"John, my friend. How are you tonight?" Lombardi said without a hint of friendliness or the pretence of a handshake.

"Good, good, Mr Lombardi. Would you like to eat first or?..." Moore's voice trailed off as he realised his mistake too late.

The dead eyes of Lombardi bored through Moore's skull.

"Don't ever use my name in public. Do you understand?" Lombardi hissed.

"Sorry Mr L. My mistake. Won't happen again."

"I know it won't, John. Otherwise our business will conclude very quickly," Lombardi said as his eyes flashed around the busy restaurant.

"Order now and then we will talk," Lombardi said with a calmer and more even voice. After all, this wasn't his patch, so he didn't want any trouble here.

Calling the young Vietnamese waitress to the table, Moore ordered a double serving of vegetarian spring rolls to be followed with duck rice paper rolls, curried beef with peas and jasmine rice. He offered to pour a cup of green tea from the thermos on the table, but Lombardi put his hand over the small porcelain cup and shook his head at the same time as snapping his fingers at the departing girl.

"What whiskies do you have?" He asked.

"Johnny Walker, sir," the young girl replied.

"Johnny Walker what? Red, Black, Blue. What label?" He fired back.

"Red and Black label," she replied slowly with a hint of steel in her voice as she turned her eyes to a very muscular and tall young Vietnamese man that was now hovering around the cash register.

"Double Black over ice. Two cubes," Lombardi said as he also followed the girl's eyes and saw the man stare back at him like a reptile. Lombardi was not out of his depth, just out of his territory. This was not Little Italy.

Cool your jets, Al!

"You have thirty minutes of my valuable time, John. What information do you have for me?" Lombardi said, as he settled his right hand around a tumbler of JW Black that had been delivered quickly and with the resounding sound of the glass being placed a little too firmly on the top of the Formica table. Big Al didn't respond. Not a drop was spilled by the girl. Looking again at the impassive face of the Vietnamese at the till, he realised that, he too probably had other businesses to run besides this restaurant. The girls were all too skinny for his customers in Carlton though, he mused.

Chapter Twenty-Two

Big Al Lombardi ate methodically as Moore detailed the facts that he had been given at a meeting the day before at Police Headquarters.

As senior ballistics adviser at the Police Armoury, he had been called in to give an estimate on how long it would take to strip down and check the new pistols before they were ready for delivery to the Police Academy.

Lombardi wanted the essential details.

"How many pistols are in the shipment?"

"I have checked the shipping invoice against the Department's order, and they are both the same."

Big Al leant across the food laden table and with a low threatening voice spoke slowly and directly at Moore's face.

"John. I am a businessman. I want to know how many and when they will arrive. I have plans to make."

"Exactly three thousand. They will be arriving two weeks from tomorrow."

"How are they being delivered?" Lombardi said as he looked cautiously around the restaurant. He did not need eavesdroppers.

"All I know from the meeting is what their Operations Manager said. Arrival time will be in the morning and we are to have the complete delivery dock clear for a large side loading truck and the escort vehicles. There will be three pallets to unload, each with one thousand pistols," Moore said at the same time as producing a business card and placing it on the table in front of Lombardi. It was for the National Security Service security company and had the name Tom Cole as the Operations Manager on it with his details.

Looking at the card, Lombardi spoke.

"Who was at this meeting beside you and this Tom Cole?"

"It was at Police Headquarters in Spencer Street in the main boardroom and there were a lot of senior police in attendance. Quite a few Senior Sergeants from the Highway Patrols between Melbourne Airport and Collingwood. It was chaired by a Superintendent Phil Stone and a Senior Sergeant Tony Signorotto from Carlton.

Lombardi's eyes widened at the name of Tony Signorotto. They had crossed paths before, and he knew he was not a person to be fucked with. The way it was when two Italians butted heads. Lombardi knew the history behind the demise of Benny Illarietti, the former mafia king pin and Signorotto's role in it.

Indicating to Moore to keep eating, Lombardi sat back with his JW Black in hand and took a slow sip after swirling the ice cubes slowly around the glass, He was not surprised at the details. After all, there was a lot at stake here for the Police Department and the State Government if something went wrong. Lombardi smiled to himself. That was exactly what he intended to happen. Something to go wrong.

Calling for a refill, Big Al knew he needed something else for this to succeed. Having John Moore at the receiving end and his other fizz at Customs was not going to help him stop the convoy which would have police cars and motor bikes buzzing around it from start to finish. The presence of the Highway Patrol at the meeting guaranteed that.

Lombardi's mind flashed to the moving convoy. He smiled coldly as he envisaged some of Tony Richard's boys going under the truck as they tried to intercept it. Who knew? Perhaps in stopping the convoy, Tony Richards himself might meet his end.

He needed someone else on his side of the fence and it didn't matter if it was by force or fear. His look switched to the face of John Moore stuffing himself with the aromatic rice and then slowly down to the business card from National Security Services that Moore had placed on the table.

"What's this Tom Cole like? This Operations Manager?" Lombardi said as he tapped a pudgy, gold ringed finger up and down on the card.

Chapter Twenty-Two

Moore stopped shovelling food, swallowed a mouthful and spoke.

"Mid-thirties. Ex-army from what one of the Police at the meeting said. Said he hadn't been with the company long."

Thoughts, possibilities and plans started to pop up in Lombardi's head like little explosions as he took out his mobile phone and snapped a picture of the card. He immediately stood, finished his JW Black, and announced, "I'm going."

"Okay. Will I see you again? Is my debt fully paid?" Moore said with pleading eyes.

"You won't see me in the near future. Consider your debt fully paid and stamped as such," Lombardi replied as he thought about the upcoming accidental death that he would have to get Joey and Feb to arrange for the future late John Moore.

Lombardi walked over to the large Vietnamese who was standing by the till, pulled out two one hundred dollar notes and placed them on the counter in front of the man.

Lombardi spoke. "Myself and my guest were never here. No receipt for the meal."

Picking up the money without taking his eyes off Lombardi, the Vietnamese giant gave the slightest nod of his head and continued to look around the restaurant as he slid the two large bills into his pocket.

Lombardi turned and walked to the door, ignoring the very relieved John Moore.

Chapter Twenty-Three

Phil Stone was sitting behind his office desk at Police Headquarters in Spencer Street. He had just finished a briefing session with the Deputy Commissioner for Crime on delivery of the new police firearms.

The briefing had included everything from the first overheard conversation in the courthouse to the bikie's subsequent death at Barwon State Prison. He also gave a complete rundown on the intelligence operation that Tony Signorotto had been operating through the local gun dealers with the assistance of Max Tyler and Kate McLaren.

Stone had convinced the Deputy Commissioner that beside the planning for the delivery of the shipment to the police armoury, which would be co-ordinated by the State Event Planning Unit in conjunction with the local Highway Patrols and the Special Operations Group, there also needed to be a local Task Force to track down who was behind the possible heist.

The Deputy Commissioner not only gave permission for the Task Force but put Stone in charge of it.

Stone looked over his desk at the hard-faced Tony Signorotto and spoke. "Top floor has given permission for me to form a mini Task Force to get this sorted. We have under two weeks till the shipment arrives and we have to find out who the snake head is behind it. Tony, you are going to be my second in command on this. Who else and what do we need?"

Signorotto thought long and hard before he eventually broke his silence.

"First off, I want Kate McLaren and Max Tyler. They are doing good work on this but they have their own workloads at their respective stations. That needs to change today, Phil."

"Done. It'll only be for a few weeks. I'll square it from this end about Max. Kate is your Sergeant, so you'll have to offload her work onto another Sergeant."

"I've got a good team at Carlton so that won't be a problem. We can't work between here and Carlton though. Too much wasted time. How about you shifting camp for the next few weeks? I have a few spare offices vacant after the budget cuts to some of our Support Staff. That way we won't be phoning each other all day long."

"Not a bad idea," Stone replied. "I can get out of here for a couple of weeks. Some of the committees I'm on won't miss me. I can delegate them down to the Inspectors. This way, anyone from the convoy side of things can slip into Carlton without having to come through all the red tape and accreditation crap that visitors need to get inside Fort Knox here. It's Monday now. I reckon we set up everything at your shop and be running by sparrow's fart on Wednesday morning. We can save so much time by doing it this way and I can tell you now the overtime is a blank time sheet. I'm like you Tony. Since that bikie bought it down at Barwon State, I've had a bad feeling about all of this."

"Phil, all the inquiries Kate and Max have made with the gun dealers around the traps have come up with zip. A lot of them have been ringing in with any sort of weird inquiries they may have gotten. This is definitely not a local network job. The firearms coming in are ours. Just about all of the local dealers have stopped any buying or importing of handguns till this is sorted. This has the smell of some sort of grand plan. A big one off. Mate, if this goes down, whoever is behind it will want to disappear really quick. And, if it does go off, we will be sitting back figuring out what to do in our forced retirement," Signorotto said, as he slapped his hand on Stone's desk. "Let's get these pricks."

Chapter Twenty-Four

Dom Santino gazed around his restaurant, a tired smile on his face. What a mess. What a beautiful mess.

It was early Monday, but his ears were still ringing from the noise of laughter and music that had gone on virtually all the previous night. A full and happy house celebrating a birthday of the ninety-year-old matriarch of a big Italian family from Brunswick. There had been at least eighty adults, teenagers and children who had taken over his restaurant the night before. Family and friends of all nationalities had come to celebrate. Copious amounts of food and wine had been consumed in what was a very joyous occasion.

Dom had sent his staff home around three in the morning knowing it would be a big clean up job upon their return. Now it was morning and along with his three daughters Gina, Rosa, Silvana and his wife Maria, he began the job of setting his restaurant back into order. He had told his kitchen staff not to return till later in the day in preparation for the evening influx of diners.

As he began to unravel the streamers that had been thrown into every high nook and cranny of the dining area, an old familiar voice emanated from the kitchen door.

"Dom. It's me. Binh. Binh Le," the voice said as the familiar figure walked into the restaurant proper.

Dom Santino walked towards the smiling Vietnamese giant who stopped half way across the room. Dom was pushed aside as his wife and daughters rushed to the visitor and enveloped him with hugs and kisses from all sides.

"Binh. It is so long since we have seen you," Maria Santino said as she held onto the smiling man whilst wiping tears from her eyes with her colourful apron.

"I know, I know. It is so busy at Ha Long that I don't know where time goes."

Dom stood back and looked at his one-time skinny dishwasher. Binh had been a young, thin refugee to Australia when he had walked into Dom's bistro years before and asked in broken English if he could have a job. Any job.

He had been to many restaurants along Lygon Street and had been refused work at them all. The reasons had varied from his skinny frame and his lack of English to the fact that many restaurant owners would not entertain a Vietnamese working in an Italian restaurant. It was European workers only. Dom had seen the look of despair in Binh's eyes that day and had given him a part-time job handling the big automatic dishwasher—a continuous job of filling and emptying the large machine which wore down men much larger than Binh.

After six weeks of watching the young, smiling Vietnamese boy at work, Dom called him aside one day to speak to him. Binh's face had crumpled as he obviously thought he was going to be sacked. Something he could not afford as he was helping to pay the rent and bills for himself, his mother, and his younger sister.

Dom, however, had no intention of letting him go. What he offered Binh was full time employment and the opportunity to work as a waiter. Binh had never looked back after that and had cooked many a Vietnamese dish in the kitchen after hours which Maria and the girls delighted in. Dom also, albeit reluctantly at first. The kitchen had become a truly multi-cultural feasting room before long.

Binh's ambition was to buy his own restaurant and serve the best Vietnamese food in Melbourne. The dream never left him and after ten years at Dom's bistro, the hugely popular Ha Long Café in Victoria Street, Richmond had come up for sale. The problem was that Binh could only raise enough capital to buy the business but not enough to update the décor and outdated kitchen. He had sat down one day after service and told Dom of his frustrations.

Binh had been left speechless when Dom and Maria had approached him that evening with their offer to finance the upgrade, interest free, with the only condition that he kept inviting them to dinner.

Dom was no fool when it came to the restaurant business. He kept a close eye on the fortunes of Ha Long and watched it become the premier Vietnamese restaurant in Melbourne. Binh had never missed a repayment and after the death of his mother came to consider them as his adoptive parents. He was the son they never had. The girls were delighted as well to welcome their new brother and sister to the family.

The mops and buckets were put to one side as everyone sat at a back table and talked as one. Italian, English and Vietnamese words gushed forward like a flood tide.

After coffee and snacks, Binh asked if he could have a private word with Dom. Maria could see that Binh had a serious look on his face so she ushered the girls back to the job of cleaning up. Dom then took up the conversation.

"Binh. It is always beautiful to see you, but I can tell that you have something on your mind. You didn't just come here for coffee. What is it?"

"Dom, a few nights ago I had two men sitting at back table. One I didn't know, but the other I sure I recognise from my time here in Lygon Street. I would have dismissed it as nothing but when the man was so rude to my sister when she was serving the table I began to look and listen without them noticing. I took photo of them on my phone," Binh said, as he held up a photo of the two men to show Dom.

Dom inhaled quickly as he instantly recognised Al Lombardi as one of the men. The other he didn't know. He spoke in a low voice.

"Binh. Remember that Italian gangster who would try and book in here quite often with all his friends. He gave up after I kept saying that I had prior bookings. Eventually he started going to some pizza place in Nicholson Street. That gangster's name is Al Lombardi. He is the one on the left in the photo. A no-good criminal. What did they say?"

The other man said something about 'three thousand and two weeks'. They spoke like ghosts to each other. Very secretive and very low whispers. This Lombardi look like he couldn't wait to leave. When he did, he said something like 'myself and my guest were never here'."

Dom reassured Binh that he would tell Tony Signorotto all about it. At the mention of Tony's name, Binh smiled and spoke.

"A policeman I like and trust. He and his friends always nice to me here."

"I will mention you to him, Binh. He will be glad you remembered him. Just send me that photo from your phone, please."

With the conversation over and the photo sent, Binh said his farewell to Dom and his family and quietly left.

Dom turned to Maria and spoke as he hurriedly took off his apron, grabbed his jacket from a peg on the back wall and headed quickly to his car parked in the back lane.

"Maria. I will be back as soon as I can. I have to see Tony right away."

As he unlocked his car door, Dom thought to himself that there were so many pieces in this puzzle. Police, crooks and now restaurants.

Chapter Twenty-Five

Tony Signorotto had just returned from Police Headquarters and was sitting down with Kate McLaren and Max Tyler when Constable Schaeffer's head appeared around his office door.

"Boss," she said. "Dom Santino is downstairs. Says he needs to speak to you urgently. Wouldn't tell me what about though. Shall I bring him up?"

"Yeah, bring him up, Constable," he said, looking directly at Kate McLaren.

The young Constable's blonde head disappeared back around the door.

Suddenly a red in the face and almost breathless Dom Santino rushed into the office just in front of the outpaced Chloe Schaeffer.

The Constable was about to apologise before Kate put up her hand to stop her.

"It's all right Chloe. The boss and Dom go a long way back," Kate said, as she politely waved the young Constable away. Schaeffer shrugged her shoulders and retreated for the second time.

Dom Santino began to speak with a gulping, short breath.

"Tony, Tony. I need to tell you something now. A friend of…"

"Whoa, whoa, Dom," Tony said indicating for him to sit and for Kate to shut the office door, before continuing. "Now. First things first, Dom. I presume this has something to do with keeping an eye on the comings and goings at Lombardi's club. Correct?"

"Yes, yes. Of course," Dom said as he slowly regained his breath.

"All right mate. You've done the right thing coming to see me. Don't ever talk to me over the phone about this. We have to keep any information just to us four. Now what is it you want to tell me?".

Dom Santino slowly and meticulously told the three of them about his visit from Binh. He emphasised the overheard conversation about the three thousand number and the delivery. By the time he had finished, Kate had filled almost half a dozen pages in her police notebook.

"So, you recognised Lombardi, but not the other man?" Max chipped in.

"No, I have never seen him," he said as he reached for his mobile phone. I got Binh to send me a photo of them. Here it is," he said with excitement in his voice.

The three officers looked closely at the photo on Dom's phone. Kate had never seen Lombardi in the flesh but recognised him from Police files she had been studying on the supposed King of Carlton.

"That's Lombardi, all right. Don't know the other one, though he does look vaguely familiar," Tony said. "I know every crook worth knowing in Carlton, Collingwood, Fitzroy and Richmond and have for years. Doesn't fit any lowlife I know," he said.

"I know that face," Max said suddenly.

"We all know it's Lombardi, Tony said."

"No. I'm talking about the other one. We know him, boss," Max said immediately. "The committee."

"Well, don't keep it to yourself, Max. Who the hell is he?" Kate said impatiently.

"He's Vic Pol. He's on the committee for the transport of the firearms. Name's Moore. John Moore. He's the ballistics man from the Police Armoury in Collingwood."

Chapter Twenty-Six

Angelo Morelli didn't know if it was just himself shaking, as what happened every night now that his nerves were so frayed, or if it was something else that was moving his head from side to side so violently. No matter what, it was just as terrifying.

The overhead bedroom light clicked on and sent a dazzling beam through his tired, aching head. Sitting bolt upright in the bed, he opened his eyes to see the close up faces of Joey and Feb hovering over him. An immediate sweat broke out over his face.

Joey leaned forward and slapped Angelo across the face with a stinging open-handed blow. Angelo's head burst into a kaleidoscope of bright coloured light. It took all of his resolve not to speak. He had seen firsthand, with Leo's violent execution, the result of speaking when you were not meant to. He was so far out of his depth that he feared for his life every waking minute—and these days there were more waking minutes than sleeping ones.

The big islander loomed large as he spoke.

"Get up. Mister Lombardi wants to see you."

"What time is it?" Angelo asked.

"Mister Lombardi said now, so the time is *now*. Get up and get dressed."

Angelo stumbled out of his bed and staggered around the tiny room trying to put first one leg and then the other into his jeans. His world had come down to being locked inside the house since Leo's murder .Everything had been taken away. No more booze, drugs or communication with the outside world.

"You want me in the kitchen to see Mister Lombardi?" Angelo asked the two hulking giants.

Feb replied. "No. He wants you at his club in Lygon Street. I think he's going to put you to work."

The Samoans didn't wait for Angelo to put his shoes on. He would have to do that in the van on the way to Carlton. Lombardi wanted Angelo standing before him as soon as possible.

Joey drove the black Mercedes van while Feb sat in the backseat next to Angelo. As it was early in the morning, the trip was a quick one and within minutes, the van bumped along the blue cobblestone alleyway, pulling up at the darkened back door of Club Maximus, the business home of Big Al Lombardi.

With a no-nonsense push to the centre of his tired back, Angelo was propelled through the back door towards the stairs leading to Lombardi's private office. One of the Samoans knocked softly on the door. Time stood still. Angelo's head was thumping, and he could feel his blood pressure rising.

"Enter!" Boomed Lombardi's voice from the other side of the steel framed door.

A large hand came over Angelo's right shoulder and pushed the heavy door open. He was unceremoniously pushed inside, and the door closed behind his shaking body. The giants did not enter. It was, Angelo could see, just himself and the self-proclaimed King of Carlton, Alessio Lombardi.

Lombardi sat with both feet crossed on his expensive teak desk. A pair of immaculately polished burgundy wing tip shoes shining in the soft low lighting. His right hand rested on the arm of his large antique leather and brass studded office chair. The fingers of his left hand were drumming rapidly on the leather inlay of the desk.

"Only one of you left now, Angelo. Sad about Leo. However, the bigger your mouth is, sometimes the smaller the relevance of your life becomes. Eh? What do you think? Eh, my friend? Am I correct? How big is your mouth?"

Angelo knew he had to give an answer and he quietly thought about how he was about to betray his friend Leo with his reply. Then again, he was only betraying the dead.

"Not nearly as big as Leo's, Mr. Lombardi."

Lombardi removed his feet from the desk and placed them quietly on the floor as he looked Angelo in the eye. He suddenly, and with alarming noise, lifted and then slammed his left hand down upon his desk. Angelo closed his eyes as he felt his blood pressure rise even higher. He could see white light behind his own eye lids. This was surely going to be the end.

The room was suddenly filled with loud laughter coming from the other side of the desk.

"That was a lifesaving answer my friend. You cut yourself loose from that loudmouth friend of yours and saved your own skin all in one sentence. I knew there was more to you than there was to that friend of yours, who, by the way, is now resting comfortably in the Fawkner cemetery. Don't know who he is with, but I can assure you they are very, very close friends for eternity," Lombardi said between bouts of laughter.

"Don't worry, young Angelo. I've said before that if you work for me your world will be your oyster. Do you like oysters?"

Angelo thought he would state it like it truly was.

"I like anything that keeps me alive and in one piece, Mr. Lombardi."

"A very wise statement my boy. I respect someone who knows they can work towards their future with confidence. Go over to the bar and get yourself a drink. I have plans for you."

"Mr. Lombardi. It's very early in the morning and the boys brought me in here without anything to eat. Could we possibly talk about your plans after some food?" Angelo said with trepidation in his voice.

Lombardi's eyes widened at the same time as his voice exploded.

"Feb. Joey," he screamed at the door.

The two Samoans fought each other to get in the door first.

"Yes, Mr. Lombardi," they said in unison.

Big Al rose from his desk and quickly stepped towards them.

"Did you not let Angelo have any breakfast before you drove him here?" Lombardi said as his voice rose an octave or two.

Chapter Twenty-Six

Joey and Feb looked furtively at each other.

Lombardi's right hand slapped one then the other.

"Bring us both hot food now, you idiots, or you'll both be the next Leo Carbone. Move," Lombardi exploded.

No sooner had the two thugs backed quickly out of the office than Lombardi walked the few steps towards Angelo, placed an arm around his shoulder and sat him down at his large office table.

"Breakfast for us both then we look at the plans."

Angelo looked at the dilated pupils set back in the dark recesses of Lombardi's skull then to the glass topped bar where he could see half a bottle of single malt scotch whisky, a near empty tumbler and a business card lying next to several lines of cocaine.

Be careful here Angelo. This man is very dangerous. Very dangerous and completely mad!

Chapter Twenty-Seven

Lombardi's pudgy, gold ring adorned left hand slid the photo across the table. Spinning it around so Angelo could see the image, he tapped on it heavily with his index finger.

"Memorise this face. This is the person I want you to follow wherever he goes," Lombardi said with a menacing voice.

Angelo looked up with a puzzled expression on his face. Too afraid to speak, he waited for Lombardi to continue.

"I will supply you with a car and you will sit within sight of the offices of the National Security Services in Fitzroy. You will not take your eyes off the place. When you see this person walk to his car and leave the yard, you will follow him wherever he goes. You will follow him for the rest of the day or until I tell you not to. You will be given a phone as well. It has no numbers in it and you will only receive calls from me. You will know it's me because I will let it ring five times and then hang up. Then I will ring again immediately. Do you understand this so far, Angelo? This is a very simple but important task you will perform for me."

"I know you will not make any outgoing calls because when I check, and be assured I will check, if there are any calls, the next call will be to your family in Broadmeadows. Speak to me Angelo. Don't sit there like you are dead. You don't want to be dead, do you Angelo? Not like Leo. Leo was a loud mouthed stupid young man who had bad manners and irritated me. I don't like to be irritated, Angelo," Lombardi said as his eyes bored into Angelo's.

Although terrified, Angelo Morelli began to see possibilities.

"Mr. Lombardi. I would never have questioned you like Leo did. Yes, he was stupid. He couldn't see the big picture. The future past his nose. He didn't realise the opportunities that would present themselves if he worked for you. Me, I can see a future for myself if you give me a chance to prove myself to you. To prove my loyalty," Angelo said with a very nervous sounding voice. He could see his speech was starting to have a small effect on this madman. Lombardi's eyes began to soften as his grovelling pitch washed over the King of Carlton.

"If you will give me a chance, you will not regret it. To become even a small part of your Empire would satisfy me completely, such is your reputation in the northern suburbs."

"Loyalty. That is the word I want to hear, Angelo. That is good. Feb and Joey are loyal. Loyal enforcers. What I think you can do for me is to bring me loyalty together with some rat cunning. After all, we Italians know more about Empire building than anyone else, eh?" Lombardi said, slapping both of his hands onto the table at the same time as throwing his head back, letting out a raucous laugh. Just as quickly as the frightening sound echoed around the room, it stopped. Silence reigned along with the sudden terror in Angelo's eyes. He really didn't know where he stood with this character. Seconds seemed like hours as the silence continued.

Suddenly, Lombardi's crazed stare at Angelo changed dramatically. The look softened as if someone had turned off an electric switch.

"Now, I will explain your mission," he said, sounding like an army general talking to one of his foot soldiers.

"The person in this photo is crucial to an upcoming business enterprise I am undertaking. His name has been supplied to me by a very good source as the overseeing person regarding a large shipment of firearms to a location in Collingwood. He has to be taken out of the equation."

The office door opened, and Feb came in carrying a tray of hot and cold food together with coffee and juice. Placing the tray carefully on the table, he quietly backed away.

"Come along my friend, you have a full day of work in front of you," Lombardi said, as he stabbed a large rasher of bacon with a fork and then stuffed it unceremoniously into his mouth.

Angelo, although initially hungry, had to force food into his mouth. He felt as though he was the condemned man eating his last meal.

While they ate, his head spun with the never-ending details Lombardi went into. The one thing that registered with him though was that this was the most audacious heist he had ever heard of. The theft of three thousand semi-automatic pistols from the police department was just plain suicidal. Angelo realised that Lombardi would never let him live after this, if it ever came off. The stakes were too high. He was a low-level car thief. What truly worried him was that he was being given way too much information for his liking. The more he knew, the more danger he was in. Just ask Leo, he thought, then shuddered. No one would get an answer from Leo again.

It was around seven in the morning when, after being given a mobile phone and the keys to an old Ford sedan that was parked in a nearby street, Lombardi sent him on his 'mission.'

Starting up the old car, Angelo placed his hands on top of the steering wheel then lowered his head onto them. It was now or never. Did he do what Lombardi wanted or did he flee with the possible, no, certain, repercussions that would be visited on his family and then on himself?

There was no alternative. He raised his head and with a quick U-turn he was headed to National Security Services in Fitzroy to begin his new 'career'.

Back in the office, with Feb and Joey looking on, Lombardi tracked Angelo via the app on his phone. With a smile on his face, he saw the 'ping' off Angelo's phone stop just short of the headquarters of National Security Services.

At the same time as he checked Angelo's location, he got Feb to ring Tony Richards. Satisfied that Angelo was obeying instructions, he took the phone off Feb and spoke to Richards.

"We have got all we need from that contact of yours at Customs House. I've got one of my boys sitting off Cole's workplace right now. I suggest you give your Harley riding snitch a ride by and offer him some free services at the Yellow

Blossom. Tell him what good work he has done but the pleasure gifts can only be given today. I've got the delivery date of the firearms and it's next Tuesday, so it's time you got your Fat Boy Smoker back my friend. We have to ramp things up a bit, understand?"

"Understood," Richards replied.

Chapter Twenty-Eight

"You aren't serious, Tony?" Phil Stone asked as he dumped some of his important carry over paperwork onto his temporary desk at the Carlton Police Station while looking into the face of his Task Force Senior Sergeant.

"Unfortunately, I am," Signorotto replied. "Only the Task Force and Dom Santino know who was in the restaurant with Lombardi. The owner of Ha Long is a friend of Dom's and he's not in the know at all."

"I can't believe it. That prick Moore is sitting on the Transport Committee for the firearms. What does Lombardi have on him to risk his job and a long gaol stretch?" Stone asked.

"Don't know, but it makes you think that either he is giving him plans of the Police Armoury for when the pistols arrive or just telling him how many firearms are involved. Either way we have to keep him under surveillance. Need to monitor his calls also."

"First things first, Tony. Needed to tell you myself. They've brought the firearms delivery date forward to next Tuesday morning would you believe. We have to get Lombardi's Lygon Street place, Club Maximus, under our eyes right away. I'll leave it to you to work up a round the clock roster for plain clothes surveillance. I want a log and photos of every person or thing that walks, crawls or slides into that sewer from now on," Stone said.

"First shift already on the way there, Phil. I'll sit down now and look at the next few days. Got a couple of good prospects from here who can help out. Like you, mate, I want this kept inhouse. If it gets out that we have rotten apples in the barrel, then it will blow our cover. Some money hungry copper will sell it to the newspapers for sure."

Sitting down, paperwork still in hand, Stone spoke. "This Task Force now has an official name. Operation Calibre. Pretty appropriate considering. I've just had a thought about how we can keep eyes and ears on that rat Moore. Give me thirty minutes and I'll get back to you Tony. Got to make a call to an old friend," he said, winking at the now departing Senior Sergeant.

I want to be the one to slam the cell door on this piece of shit, Phil Stone thought.

Reaching for his mobile, Stone flicked through his contacts until he found what he was looking for. He pressed the number and waited for it to connect.

"Superintendent Bob Archer, you old bastard. How are you?" Stone said in a way only an old friend could. After some friendly banter, he continued. "How would you like to get back on the horse, so to speak, my friend. Can you get into the Carlton Police Station within the next hour or so? I don't want to talk about it over the phone, but I am going to make you an offer that you can't refuse. You and I are going to team up again, mate." A minute later the call was over.

Forty-five minutes later, Tony Signorotto walked into Phil Stone's office with a draft surveillance roster in his hand. Max Tyler walked in at the same time.

"Max, I'm going to put young Chloe Schaeffer on this surveillance gig with you if that's all right? Tony said in front of Stone. "I've given her the heads up on this. You think she's up for it?"

"I was just coming in to say I'd do the handover with the crew that got thrown onto it tonight. Chloe and I can get there about ten tomorrow morning and pull a long shift if you like. She'll be a good fit for when we need to take a stretch. No one will pick her. I'm sure the crew from the Divisional Response Unit will have a lot of photos for us to look at by then, also. I'll brief her if that's all right with you both?"

"Fine with me," Signorotto said, turning towards Stone who returned the look with a nod of his head "I'll keep the Divisional

Response crew for the nights and give Kate the next day with another of the Sergeants that I'll pick and brief "

As they spoke an older man appeared at the doorway and smiled at Phil Stone.

Stone stood up from his desk and spoke. "Well, as I live and breathe. Tony, Max, this is Superintendent Bob Archer. O.I.C. of Police Forensics for the State."

Archer stepped forward and shook hands all around.

"What have you got me into here Stone?"

Stone continued. "Tony, Max. This man and I used to work surveillance operations back in the old days. Bob is one of the finest surveillance coppers I've ever known. He's going to help us out with our rat, John Moore."

"John Moore? He's my man at Collingwood. In charge of the Armoury. What's going on here, Phil?" Archer said with a quizzical expression on his face.

An hour later, Bob Archer had been fully briefed on the firearms arrival and the connection with John Moore.

"Yes, very interesting situation," Archer said slowly. "Moore is an expert in handguns. That's why he's in charge down at Collingwood. Even though I'm based over the other side of town, it doesn't stop me keeping my ear to the ground. I've actually had some phone calls over the last month or two from a couple of the support staff who work with him. Apparently, he's been leaving work early on a number of occasions and has turned up the next day looking like his world has caved in on him. I was going to let it slide for a while due to his expertise but then one of the staff contacted me because there had been a big argument at the mess room table just recently."

"What about?" Stone queried

"Money, it seems. He's been putting the hard work on some of his colleagues for loans from anything between ten and a hundred dollars. One of his mates even rang his house to have a chat with him but his wife said he had moved out weeks before. She said he had wiped out their bank accounts, so she threw him out."

Chapter Twenty-Eight

"Do you know the dates he left work early on?" Max asked.

"I've got them noted on my computer. Why?" Archer asked.

"I'll get onto the Casino Squad and get them to check the videos of the tables at Crown Casino for those dates. What's the bet he's hitting the Chinese punters late in the day when they may be down on their winnings and getting desperate. He wouldn't be able to play the VIP's at night. Leave it with me," Max said.

"I'll email them to you as soon as we finish up," Archer said. "Sounds like he might be up to his neck in debt. He must be desperate. In the meantime, though I'll think I'll do a quick office swap for a few weeks and re-locate to the Armoury. It's time I met a few of the new crew down there and maybe even do a bit of an inventory which the top brass have suddenly made me oversee. Sound good?" Heads nodded in silent agreement.

Chapter Twenty-Nine

Stepping quickly out of the change room at the Carlton Police Station in scruffy jeans and a hoodie, Max Tyler nearly bumped into Chloe Schaeffer as she too walked past in similar plain clothes. They were both in a hurry to relieve the night shift crew near Lombardi's lair.

Max knew the crew that they were to relieve would be exhausted as they would be coming up for twelve hours surveillance by the time he and Schaeffer arrived. He wanted to do a hot de-briefing and see if anything of significance had transpired during the night.

"Ready for a long day, Chloe?" Max said, as he grabbed the keys to an unmarked Toyota Camry that had been brought in overnight for them from the Transport Branch. "Now we know the delivery date is only days away, it's going to be full on from here on in."

"I'm up for it if you are," Chloe replied, winking at the jeans clad detective.

On the short trip to the sit off location, they stopped at a coffee shop to grab some coffees and toasties for their offsiders who, they knew, would be looking forward to the essential supplies. Max also filled Chloe in on the information about John Moore.

On arrival, both Max and Chloe quickly climbed into the back seat of the pale blue Kia Sorrento of the night shift crew. It smelled of stale tobacco and body odour. A typical smell of a good undercover operation. Chloe handed over two steaming cups of black coffee together with pods of milk, sugar sticks, stirrers and four rounds of toasted ham and tomato sandwiches.

"If you hope to get any information out of us, there had better be some Krispy Kreme doughnuts in this delivery," a tired voice said from the front passenger seat.

"Sorry fellas. Thought you would prefer the toasties," Max said as he introduced himself and Chloe.

The two front seat undercover police mumbled their thanks whilst giving their names as Leading Senior Constables Mick York and John Petran from the Melbourne Divisional Response Unit. After giving both the tired men a few minutes to throw some much-appreciated food and coffee down their throats, Max spoke.

"Okay. Feed bags off boys. Anything go down overnight?"

Petran handed over the Leica camera that they had used to take photos of the comings and goings at Lombardi's night club. Max started to slowly go through the images while Chloe Schaeffer checked the log against the times of the photos. A lot of punters had come and gone during the night.

"One interesting thing, though," York said. "That club has a closing time of three in the morning—I checked with the Licensing Inspector before we started the shift. After that time, it sorts the so-called patrons from his closer contacts. Two islanders arrived with another dude about four-fifteen and then they all left about six, but the white guy drove off in an old Ford. The other two drove off in the van they had all arrived in. The numbers of both are in the log," he said, indicating the entry to Schaeffer.

"Looks to me like some sort of pond life business meeting," Petran said in-between gulps of coffee and large bites of the nearly demolished toasted sandwich. "We'll leave it to you to check the registrations."

"Anything else of interest?" Schaeffer asked.

"Not really," York said, brushing crumbs from his scruffy beard. "Just the usual hookers and their pimps operating out of Argyle Square. God if I was in vice or traffic, I could have swapped around all night arresting hookers and those punks flashing around here on their café racers. Are we back on tonight?"

"Yeah. Sorry about that. Back here about ten. Thanks, fellas," Max said as he and Chloe got out to go back to their own vehicle to start the next observation shift.

"No problems. Just make up for it tomorrow morning with the Krispy Kremes, eh?" Petran said turning the ignition before heading off back to their office and then hopefully to bed.

Settling into their own car, Max turned to Chloe.

"Get on the blower to the registration people and find out who owns those two cars. I'll get back onto the Casino boys. They should have had time to look through their video tapes by now. After that, settle back and keep your eyes on Lombardi's. I think though, that like all gutter crawlers there will be more out tonight than during the day."

Chapter Thirty

Angelo parked a short way back from the National Security Services in Harold Street, Fitzroy. From this position he had a clear view of the front of the premises and the driveway that led into the car park. Anyone who wanted to go into the premises had to walk out of the car park, along the footpath a short distance and then up the front steps to the front door.

From his vantage point, he could see the top of the building and its many communication towers. He thought to himself, that if they had employed Cole then he must have had some serious entries on his C.V. He settled himself in to await the arrival of the man in the picture, whilst wishing desperately that he could report to Lombardi that his target never arrived for work.

Angelo Morelli had never been a very lucky person. This morning proved no different. About two hours after arriving and parking the old Ford, he saw a late model Toyota Camry swing into the car park from the opposite direction. As he watched the driver's door open, he immediately matched the photo of Cole to the person now standing by the car.

Not just a man, Angelo thought worriedly to himself. This was a big individual. Lombardi had mentioned that Cole was ex-military. Morelli didn't know anyone in the military, but even he could tell that this individual looked like more than your average soldier in build and even in the way he held himself. He appeared as though he could drill holes through a person by just looking at them. This was not a person to cross paths with. There was something quite scary about him.

He watched Tom Cole make his way slowly out of the car park, along the footpath and take the front steps of the National Security Services two at a time, shoving open the heavy wooden and glass doors with a simple push of one hand. Angelo's mind began to race in circles. He had never been a person who liked any sort of physical confrontation.

Do I stay? Do I do a runner and just dump the car? Would Lombardi find me?

The third question had a frightening answer. *Yes, he will find me, and I'll end up with Leo for eternity.*

Angelo was frozen to his car seat. He didn't know if he was just scared of Lombardi or what a person like Tom Cole would do to him if he crossed paths with him in a bad way.

He put his head in his hands and began to sob quietly. The real answer was that he knew he was just a coward, and this was his worst nightmare.

A shrill sound filled the interior of the old car. The mobile phone that Lombardi had given him was ringing. Grabbing it, he immediately punched the green button. "Yes?" He tried to say, but his voice came out as a hoarse whisper.

"I fucking told you I'd ring five times. Do you not understand, or do I simply cancel you and get a replacement?" Lombardi's voice screamed through the phone.

"Sorry Mr. Lombardi, sorry," a distraught Angelo whined back.

"Has Cole made any attempt to leave the building yet?" Lombardi said with a now completely calm voice as though he had just begun speaking to Angelo.

He's mad. He's absolutely fucking mad! Angelo thought.

"No, Mr. Lombardi. He hasn't come out at all," Angelo said quickly.

"Next time wait for the five rings. I don't want you answering anyone but me. Understand?" Lombardi said.

"Yes, yes," Angelo began to say into the phone which had already been disconnected by Lombardi.

The day passed slowly. Angelo was now hungry again even after the early morning feast with the King of Carlton. The only time he had gotten out of the car was to take a piss up against a nearby tree. He had been abused by two young office workers who had threatened to call the police but ended up laughing at him because he was so nervous, he had pissed more on his jeans than on the tree.

The car clock was showing just shy of three o'clock in the afternoon when Cole appeared from the office with a large file under his arm. Striding with purpose, he quickly got into his car and exited the car park after a few minutes flicking through the file. Angelo fired up the old Ford, took a big gulp of air and began to follow the Toyota from a safe distance. Cole did not seem to be in a hurry, which made the tailing easier. Angelo realised he was quite at home doing this as he had done it many times with Leo when they were following future car theft opportunities. *Good days now no more,* he thought.

Passing the Edinburgh Gardens in Fitzroy, Angelo kept his distance as the Camry headed south along St. George's Road then continued into Nicholson Street towards the city.

The right-hand indicator of the Toyota started to flash as the car turned right into Kay Street and then right again into Charles street. Changing indicators, the Camry pulled left to the kerb and stopped. Angelo pulled slowly to the side in Kay Street. It wasn't hard to see Cole, as the house he entered was only three or four along the street. He noticed that Cole was not only carrying the same file he had previously seen but other items as well.

Before he had turned off the ignition, the mobile phone rang again. This time he let it ring five times and stop. It soon rang again. Angelo hit the green button. He didn't speak.

"That's better," Lombardi said. "Do you have an update for me?"

Before he could reply, he saw Cole re appear from the house, walking a small child with him to the house next door and enter the gate. At the same time, an elderly woman waved to them from the first house. The little blond-haired girl, who looked about six years of age, waved back.

Angelo's heart went cold. *No, not kids! Not kids!* He thought.

Lombardi's voice boomed again. "I said. Any fucking news?"

"No, Mr. Lombardi," Angelo said over the clacking sound emanating from the idling old motor of the Ford. "He's just about to drive off. I've got to go."

"I'll get back to you, soon, you hear me?" Lombardi growled into Angelo's ear.

"Yes, yes. I hear you," Angelo said as he stared at the little girl.

As he turned off the ignition, he wondered why he had lied to Lombardi. He certainly feared him but at the same time he knew that Lombardi was totally deranged-and deranged people would involve anyone in their bizarre dreams, including children.

Chapter Thirty-One

Max and Chloe kept eyes on Lombardi's club while they both went about their own investigative work. The advantage was that Club Maximus, although open for business, wasn't going to attract the dark side of the punting fraternity until much later in the day. The strippers and pole dancers weren't of the 'evening quality' at this time. The girls working in the club now would be lucky to get any tips at all from the lunch time crowd except on how to show more of what the punters had come to see.

After a quick phone call to Vic Roads regarding the registration of the two vehicles in question, Chloe studied the results she had scribbled down. No real surprises in the answers. Both the van and the Ford were registered to Lombardi Enterprises with the van having the Lygon Street address but with the twenty-year-old Ford coming up to an address in Brunswick.

"What do you make of the two addresses?" Chloe said to Max, who had only just got off his phone to a contact in the Casino Squad.

"He probably uses the van for transporting his clients back and forth between whatever sleazy place they're staying at and here. He'd be offering them a Booze and Broads package. Getting a skinful of booze into them and as much money out of them as he could."

"I'm new to all this Max. As a famous politician said once, please explain."

"He'll be using the van to ship his cashed upped punters around various bars, strip joints, brothels and back room casinos that he controls. This is just the meet and greet starting place. This is where he starts them all off on top shelf booze and a few lines of coke before they get into the van for a night of wine and women. By the time his clients have finished at some seedy cockroach infested brothel down in St. Kilda or Footscray, the booze and girls will have gone from Dom Perignon and classy ladies to finishing with watered down whisky and pin cushion pros," Max said as he looked at Chloe.

"Pin cushion pros?"

"They will be that pissed or drugged on cheap crap by the end of their tour Chloe, that they won't realise they started the night on eighteen-year-old Glenfiddich and laying Lombardi's top of the range girls on silk sheets and finished in the morning with a screaming headache from downing backyard hooch and screwing sixteen-year-old illegals with arms so full of holes that they look like pin cushions. Without doubt though, most of the bus load will end up at the V.D. clinic in Richmond after a few weeks, wondering if they should tell their wives or girlfriends about the so-called party bus night. Lombardi will also have taken about a grand off each one of them for their unforgettable night out. He usually sends about six on the bus with a couple of his heavies so there are no problems. It's always cash up front before they head off."

"I've only been in the job about a year and at Carlton less. Didn't realise Lygon Street was like that," Chloe said with a startled look on her face.

"That's the thing, Chloe. It's not. It's a fantastic eating strip for families. Take Dom Santino's place. Families all the time. He and blokes like his mate Bernado with his family restaurant are keeping tabs on Lombardi and trying to gain enough evidence so they can take Lombardi up before the Liquor Control Board. They have to be careful with their spying though because if Lombardi finds out, he would firebomb their restaurants. He's had his goons do over a few places along here. The Malaysian Penang Inn and the Indian Curry House takeaway have been threatened repeatedly."

"Geez. What an absolute slime bag this Lombardi is. Love to see him get taken down," Chloe stated icily. "By the way, any luck with the Casino Squad?"

"Yeah. Turns out that our boy John Moore has been playing the tables very heavily and not been lucky at all. Has lost big time but keeps coming back for more. Plays late afternoon like we thought. That's why he has been leaving work early. I'd better let the bosses know. Superintendent Archer will want to be briefed so he can cover all bases with Moore back at the armoury. If you want to go for a bit of a walk around the block and check out his club, I'll phone in. I've downloaded some of the photos the boys took last night onto my laptop here and I'll email them into the Task Force."

Chloe walked slowly along Lygon Street. She couldn't get over what a laid back atmosphere the street had, even at this time of the morning. Cafes were just starting to open up and the various waiters and owners were sharing a joke whilst having a coffee themselves on the footpath. The one place there was no congregating was outside Lombardi's joint. Stopping nearby, she tried to look in through the darkened window. Suddenly a voice spoke from behind her.

"You don't want to know anything about that joint, lady," the voice said.

Turning around she saw a mid-thirties man behind her.

Playing along, she decided to ask him a few questions and was surprised at the fear in his voice.

"What's wrong with the place? I was thinking of getting a coffee in there."

"Come into my place here," the man said, indicating the café next door called *Sergio's Pasta Paradise*. "I will give you a coffee for nothing before I let a girl go in there," he said with a low voice, all the while looking as though someone would burst out of Club Maximus and hit him. "It's not a nice place. It's a strip joint and a lot of other things."

"Who owns it?" Chloe pushed.

"I don't want to say names, lady," the man said. "None of the restaurants here have anything to do with them in there. They give us a bad name."

"Thanks for the offer of the coffee, but I think I'll keep going," Chloe said. "Thanks for the warning too," she watched the man move quickly back to a table outside his restaurant where three other men who looked like café workers, sat in a huddle looking at her with concern.

Upon Chloe's return to the car, Max gave her a quick progress report.

"First things first. Tony is going to get the boys at Brunswick to do a drive-by of that address where the Ford is registered. Turns out the photos were quite interesting. A lot of wannabee dudes in them, but the ones of the black van arriving with the three heads and then leaving in two cars raised eyebrows. Kate turned out to be correct when she said the two Samoans looked like bikies. She called in one of our undercovers who rides with another O.M.C. gang. He pinned them as two of the Black Rats. Apparently, a lot of questions have been floating around about their whereabouts. They haven't been seen around their headquarters in Darebin Road at all."

"You think they work for Lombardi?

"Most of the Black Rats have some sort of part time jobs in the transport and car industry," Max continued. "From what our undercover contact said, he has heard on the grapevine that these two have been doing a bit of work for Lombardi. I'd say they are probably some of the drivers for his punters when he needs them. They'd keep a tight control over a bus load of Lombardi's shit clientele. No one would make any complaints while those two are around. He gave us names, too. Joey Salessa and Feb Felagi. The connection between them and Tony Richards can't be overlooked. Richards must know who they are working for and is just riding with it."

"What about the third guy who ended up leaving in the Ford. Any ideas?"

"Photofit has him coming up as a small-time car thief by the name of Angelo Morelli. Hasn't done time yet but is on the way to Barwon State if he keeps boosting high end rides. Don't know the connection but he certainly doesn't look like a happy camper in those photos. The first one when he arrives has him looking pretty dishevelled when he gets escorted in by the Samoan army. Looks even less happy when he leaves."

"Bosses say anything about John Moore?"

"Superintendent Archer is going to tap his work phone and trace any calls he makes by his mobile. See what happens. Obviously in way over his head money wise at Crown Casino. If he's dealing with Lombardi, then he's in real debt," Max said, suddenly sitting upright in his seat and looking intently through the windscreen.

"Well, well. Look what just crawled up. The black Chrysler that Dom gave us the number of. Grab the camera Chloe and get some head shots of the driver."

Chloe aimed the long lens of the Leica SL camera through the front windscreen and started the auto shot. As soon as the driver got out, she hit the button and the camera took ten shots every five seconds until he walked in the front door of Lombardi's establishment.

"Got about twenty action shots of our boy there."

"Well done. I'd know that head anywhere. That's Tony Richards himself. Why would he be going into Lombardi's early in the morning? It won't be for coffee, and the lap dancers would still have their pants on at this time. What's this gutter crawler up to, Chloe?"

Chapter Thirty-Two

"Bob Archer here, Phil."

"Yes mate. What have you got for me? Has he panicked yet?" Phil Stone said.

"He must be desperate. Either that or just very stupid. I'm glad I set up my office here so soon. The techs I got in from the Shadowers Unit had only just finished tapping his phones a couple of hours before when that email came through about the bringing forward of the firearms delivery. I reckon it only took him ten minutes before he started making calls."

"Did the techs get any recordings?" Stone asked anxiously.

"Every little word of a lovely incriminating conversation with Lombardi. Almost called him Mr. Lombardi. Stopped just short after King Rat told him to shut up. Moore thought he must be clever by telling him that his Australia Post-delivery would be at 'T' by seven o'clock on Tuesday morning."

"Quite the code! T for Tullamarine. Moore's desperate all right. Anything else he talked about, Bob?"

"Yes. Moore asked him if that delivery by Australia Post finished their contract."

"What did Lombardi say?"

"Moore seemed happy with his answer. Poor fool. You and I would look at it another way, Phil. Lombardi told Moore that his contract would now be terminated."

"Christ, I think we both know what terminated means when a dog like Lombardi uses it," Stone said with a hard edge to his voice.

"Let me know when I can arrest this prick will you Phil? I want to give him his own Australia Post delivery. Right to the door of the County Court."

"Will be my pleasure. About time you did something to earn your wage, you desk jockey," Phil Stone said with laughter in his voice.

Chapter Thirty-Three

Max's brain was working harder than a one-armed paper hanger. What Richards was up to was definitely business. Something did not sit right with him in this visit. He grabbed his mobile phone and called Tony Signorotto.

"Boss. Richards has just gone into Lombardi's place. I've got a feeling that we may see some action soon," Max said hurriedly.

"I've got you on loudspeaker here, Max. Superintendent Stone and Sergeant McLaren are listening in," Tony said.

"Lombardi has obviously been busy. What with his goons bringing in that guy Morelli this morning and now Richards? I don't think he's in there for a lunch date so if he comes out, I think we need to tag him. That all right with you?" Max asked.

"Four-way conversation here," Signorotto said as Max waited. He didn't hear anything and couldn't see the Carlton based Task Force nodding their heads in agreement.

"It seems like Lombardi has been burning the midnight oil with his meetings. We reckon that if Richards comes out, it would be the right decision to tail him, Max," Phil Stone said.

"Thanks, boss. If he just cruises back to his factory in Darebin Road, we will come straight back. I don't want us to be sprung hanging around down there."

Ten minutes after finishing the phone call to the Task Force, Richards reappeared through the door of Lombardi's dive and walked quickly to the black V8 Chrysler SRT. The beast roared into life and took off quickly north along Lygon Street. Max had been sitting in the passenger seat and hadn't had time to swap over to the driver's side of the unmarked police car.

"Stay with him Chloe but hang back about four car lengths. Let's go," Max said hurriedly as she eased the Toyota out into the two north bound lanes.

Before long, it became obvious that the Darebin Road factory was the destination. Chloe Schaeffer didn't have a problem tagging the black monster.

"These bikies want to fly under the radar when they aren't on a patched ride, but they drive these things that stick out like dogs' balls. That thing's just an extension of his dick albeit a different colour. Can't believe how many white cars there are on the road. We blend in pretty well," Chloe said as she deftly manoeuvred the unmarked police car so as to maintain sight and distance.

"World's most common car colour, I read somewhere. Second in line is black," Max quietly chuckled as they headed along Queens Parade in Clifton Hill, then onto Heidelberg Road before turning into Grange Road.

"He's going to his business all right," Chloe said, as she saw Richards turn right into Darebin Road and pull into the driveway of 351A. A green and gold sign over the entrance said. *Tony Richards Classic Cars.* Two late model Jaguars were parked haphazardly on the dirt apron area out front. Richards stepped out of the Chrysler and tossed the keys to a black T shirted dude. Both the dude and the black Chrysler looked completely out of place next to the sleek Jaguars. Richards proceeded to walk over to where a late model Harley Davidson motor bike sat, partially hidden from view behind the Jaguars. Stepping astride the Harley, he put on a matte black helmet he had taken off the handlebar and kicked the American roadster into life with an ear shattering twist of the throttle.

From their parked position behind a tray truck, Max and Chloe had a clear view of the proceedings. "What's he up to now?" Chloe said, shaking her head.

"Don't know, but he's about to take off, so stand by," Max said quickly.

Richards pulled the monster motor bike back onto Darebin Road and roared obliviously back past their car without even a look. He powered left back onto Grange Road, heading back the way he had come.

Chloe made a quick U-turn and just managed to turn back into Grange Road through a yellow traffic light. By this time, they were some distance behind their target.

"Just need to keep my ears open for this. Don't think it will matter too much if we lose sight of him for a second or two. Every time he gives it some throttle, I can hear him a mile away," Chloe said with a sarcastic laugh.

The Toyota dodged slowly from lane to lane as Richards headed back towards the city and then down into the Docklands area.

The two police officers hardly said a word to each other on the tail back. Max knew he would have to say something if he didn't think Chloe was up to the task. He stayed silent the whole time.

"I've given up guessing where he's going," Max said. "If he ends up turning onto the Tullamarine freeway and then maybe the Calder to the Western Ring Road then we are going to have to call for a swap over because he'll spot us for sure." Max cut off his own words as he watched the big motor bike glide to a noisy halt outside Customs House, the headquarters of the Australian Border Force in La Trobe Street. Chloe pulled the police car into the kerb behind a large delivery truck so as to give themselves some cover. Both of them stared in disbelief as Richards dismounted, removed his helmet and went in through the main door.

"Border Force? What's going on here for Christ's sake?" Max commented.

Chloe didn't reply, but the answer was soon forthcoming. Richards came back out the door and went and stood by his bike, took a cigarette out of his top shirt pocket and proceeded to light it as he lent against the Harley. All Max and Chloe could do was look on in confusion. Suddenly Chloe spoke.

"He's got to be waiting for someone. He wasn't in there long enough to make a genuine inquiry."

Five minutes passed before they both suddenly turned towards the now familiar sound of a revving Harley Davidson motorcycle which was coming out of the Customs House garage behind them. They immediately slunk down in their seats as the bike cruised up behind Richard's steed. They watched as Richards strolled back to the rider of the second bike and gave him a brotherly hug.

"A mate in Border Force! Cat in the cream factory, eh?" Max said.

Max and Chloe looked on as Richards mounted his bike and performed a U-turn in La Trobe street, followed by the second rider. He didn't have to say a word to Chloe. She already had the camera focussed on the second bike, shooting frame after frame while he looked intently through his high powered Olympic mini binoculars at the figure on the second bike.

"I know you got shots of the bike, Chloe. Well done. That second rider looked like he had a pair of blue uniform pants on with a dark blue shirt under his leather jacket. I reckon it's a Border Force uniform. Let's see where they're going. If he's Border Force and working from Customs House, he's probably on a lunch break or taking time off."

Chloe got the car into a position where they could follow discreetly behind the two big Harleys back along La Trobe Street. Just short of King Street they both peeled off into the open driveway of the Yellow Blossom massage parlour.

As they drove slowly past, they saw Richards get off his bike and pull down the steel roller door behind him.

"Time to park and email those pictures back to the Task Force and check on who owns that second bike. That rider looked relatively young. If he's a Border Force guy just doing a nine to five job back there, I'd like to know where he gets the money to ride that hog," Max said.

"Looks expensive," Chloe replied.

"No change out of thirty thousand. That's a late model Fat Boy Smoker," Max said, as he quickly punched the registration number of the bike into his computer.

"Well, well," he said thirty seconds later with a grin on his face.

Chapter Thirty-Three

"Surprise me," Chloe said.

"A.R.D. Holdings. Richards' shell company. Whoever the Border Force guy is I'll bet a month's salary that he's part of the Black Rats set up. If he's working for Border Force, he wouldn't dare have a part timer anywhere else. I'm going to get onto the boss. He can contact Customs House and find out who he is. There won't be two of them riding Fat Boys at Customs," Max said sarcastically.

An hour went by during which Max had several conversations with Tony Signorotto and Phil Stone. The connection between the President of an Outlaw Motorcycle Gang and a Border Force officer conjured up some very dangerous scenarios.

"At one end of this chain we have a fizz in our department who dines with Lombardi," Tony said to Max and Chloe over the open phone. "We know that Moore has obvious money problems and it doesn't take Einstein to figure that Lombardi is blackmailing him to get information on the firearms shipment. Either Moore tells him what he knows about the guns or I'd reckon Lombardi would punch his ticket very quickly. Then you have the nexus between Lombardi and Richards which has been proven by his visits to the Club Maximus in Lygon Street. Lastly, but not least, we now have a link between Richards and Customs. Basically, we have a chain between King Rat, the head of an O.M.C.G and two others, one where the shipment comes in and one where the shipment should end up."

"It's starting to fall into place," Phil Stone said over Tony's open phone. "A connection between the start and the finish points. Why though, beside needing Richards' contact at Customs would Lombardi risk bringing in an O.M.C.G? Any ideas, people?"

"What about this angle?" Kate McLaren said to the five persons hook up. "Lombardi needs the Customs contact which belongs to the Black Rats and he is looking at two ways of getting the firearms. One is at the destination, being the Armoury or the second is hijacking the shipment on route. He'd need real back up for that, and that's where the Black Rats come in."

"Yeah. I get the idea," Max said. "But would you risk taking on the Special Operations Group and the Highway Patrol on the road from Tullamarine airport to Collingwood? Even Lombardi knows that this shipment will be covered seeing that there has been so much press about the new intakes to the Academy. There'd be no guarantee that the S.O.G. wouldn't massacre the lot of them in a firefight. It'll be a no brainer. Lombardi will have an ace up his sleeve. He's a rat, but rats are cunning."

Ideas kept being tossed around amongst the Task Force. Notes were being furiously scribbled on white boards. Eventually, Tony Signorotto called a halt to it.

"All good theories, everyone," Tony Signorotto said. "Thing is though, that's all they are. Theories. No doubt one will turn out to be the jackpot, but in the meantime, we need to keep any eye on the movements in and out of Lombardi's place. He is central to the whole operation. Anyway, while we've been theorising, Kate's been on the phone to Customs House."

"Turn up anything, Sarge?" Chloe chipped in with, so as not to feel overshadowed by all this information in what was her first Task Force operation.

"G'day, Chloe. Glad you are keeping up to speed," Kate McLaren said. "Yes, I spoke to one of the Border Force Inspectors by the name of Mount. I didn't think he was too surprised when I asked him about his man with the Harley. He wanted to check out who I was, so I got him to ring back on the Task Force number and clear it with Superintendent Stone. Turns out that our rider is a lad by the name of Billy Stevens. He's Border Force, Level One and been at La Trobe Street for about a year. Has hit a few hurdles in his time there for associating with some pretty shady characters who are O.M.C.G. prospects. He only gets about sixty thousand a year, so there's no way he could afford that thumper he's riding. By the way, good work getting the details so quick. Anyway, I asked Mount where Stevens was today and it turns out he came to work but reported sick a few hours back. You obviously sussed him riding off with Richards."

"Well, he's been in the Yellow Blossom for a while now with Richards," Chloe replied.

Tony Signorotto chipped in. "Yes, Chloe, that's a massage parlour that Lombardi has a share in along with a few other characters of note who are connected with O.M.C. gangs. Probably a money laundering front for the Black Rats. I'll have to check with Organised Crime about that. Anyway, good work you two. Now hightail it back to Lygon Street."

After Tony finished the call, Chloe hit the ignition button on the dashboard, but as she did, she noticed a small motor bike low loader recovery vehicle pull up outside the Yellow Blossom and then slowly back through the now opening metal gates. On the driver's door on the all black truck, written in gold lettering, was the name *"Hog Ties"* with the same address as A.R.D. Holdings in Darebin Road. The gate closed in front of it.

"Looks like another connection, Chloe. Let's just wait a while and see what's going on," Max said.

Through the steel grilled gate, Max could make out a large, well-muscled goon manoeuvring a motorcycle at the back of the small truck. Suddenly with the familiar, thudding sound, the bike was ridden up onto the flat-top and stopped.

"Someone's not riding away from there," Chloe said with a cold edge to her voice.

There was no reply from Max as he concentrated on seeing what he could through the binoculars. Minutes passed without any movement. The steel gates then began to open, and the low loader was driven out into the street and turned left giving both Max and Chloe a direct look at the motor bike on board. Chloe snapped away with the camera as Max spoke.

"That's the Harley Fat Boy Smoker that Customs Boy arrived on."

Both officers stared at each other as their police brains came up with many possibilities of Billy's fate.

"We aren't about to bust in there, Chloe. There could be a good explanation. I seriously doubt it, but we can't blow our undercover op on what ifs. Let's get back to Lombardi's."

Chapter Thirty-Four

"Mate. Today was the only time I could give you the full treatment here at Yellow Blossom. You deserve everything you are going to get. I have to go out of town for a few days on business, so I thought I'd show my appreciation for all that information you have gotten me," Tony Richards said, as he guided the young Black Rats prospective member past an array of gaudily decorated bedrooms inside the massage parlour. In the doorway of several of them were half naked girls of various nationalities displaying their wares for potential customers.

"No problems at all, Tony," a gobsmacked Billy Stevens replied, salivating over each hooker he passed. "I told them I was crook after you turned up at work. Wasn't going to pass up this chance. Think I'll be able to recover pretty quick after a session here."

"I've got someone very special for you today, Billy. You just get yourself into this room," Richards said as he gently nudged Billy through an open doorway into a room with a king size canopy covered bed. Next to it sat a table laid out with sex toys, bottles of massage oil and tubes of lubricant. Two small plastic pouches of cocaine were also within easy reach. Billy's heart rate began to soar. He sat on the edge of the massive bed and let his imagination run riot.

Richards returned some minutes later with a young Asian girl who was wearing nothing but high heels and a red leather G string.

"Billy, this is Hanh. She is here to take you on the stairway to heaven, with a few stops on the way to enjoy the ride." The grin on his face matched the one on Billy's. "I'll leave you alone to explore every possibility you can think of my friend."

Richards walked over to his now quickly undressing guest and gave him a brotherly hug. "You're off to paradise and beyond, mate," he said, as he then walked back to the door, closing it quietly behind him.

"We start with a slow massage, Billy," Hanh said with a sultry voice as she stood in front of the mesmerised lad, rubbing her small breasts in his face. Billy's breathing was getting shorter and shorter. "You take clothes off and lay face down on bed."

Billy stood up and stumbled around the room trying to get his jeans off, fumbling with his large motorcycle boots in his attempt. Eventually he lay face down on the black silk sheeted bed and looked sideways at Hanh, who was kneeling next to him displaying a chrome set of handcuffs in her left hand. Billy's eyes widened. With her right hand, she poured some warm, scented oil between his shoulder blades. Billy could feel himself getting hard as he anticipated what was going to happen.

"We have big fun now Billy. Eh?" Hanh whispered into his left ear.

"You do anything you like, Hanh. I don't care what or for how long. I just want that happy ending all the boys that come here talk about," Billy said after Hahn handcuffed both his wrists to the bedposts as the warm liquid trickled slowly down his back., She then slid across his back, making sure her nipples caressed the back of his head.

"Now I need you put strong legs apart. I do same again," Hanh said as she showed Billy another two sets of larger cuffs. As he parted his legs, she placed a hand between them and massaged his erect cock. Billy just moaned as she then clicked the third and fourth set in place. He was now face down, buck naked and unable to move. "You are now my prisoner."

"Please. Please," young Billy whispered eagerly with a voice that was becoming increasingly hoarse.

Billy thought Hahn was getting some other erotic pleasure article ready for him as he felt a breeze cross his bare back. Moving his head to see where the air was coming from, he suddenly heard a muffled sound, and at the same time there appeared to be white feathers everywhere around his head.

Billy screamed, as suddenly, Hahn's bloodied head appeared at bed level, inches from his face. Her head slowly rotated on her slack shoulders showing a gaping hole in the side of her skull. A grey, glutinous mass started to ooze from the jagged cavity. Her head then slid out of sight as the rest of her now dead body pulled it below, and out of his sight to the floor. Billy Stevens started to struggle violently against the four sets of restraints that Hahn had put on him. He couldn't raise himself up at all and he could feel the wet, warm feeling of urine on the mattress he was lying on. He had pissed himself.

Turning to the other side, all he could see was the business end of a large handgun pointed between his eyes.

"What the fuck? What is this?" Billy screamed at the figure behind the .357 Magnum that Tony Richards held in his right hand.

"Sorry pal. I didn't have to go out of town on business. I lied," Richards said, with a quiet laugh. "My business was all here. Little Hahn was the first part of the agenda. Silly girl had been skimming the packets of coke that were set out for the clients. She fucked up badly when I set her up with one of my boys who doesn't touch the stuff. No drugs, no piss, just sex. When he had finished banging her, she took the two customer packs. Told my manager that he had used both. Silly girl. Now she really has had her brains blown out."

"What have I done to you, mate?" Stevens pleaded from his trapped position, as Richards ran the chrome barrel of the revolver across his face.

"I just don't need you anymore, Billy. You've had your fun on my hog, and I've got the information I need about the shooters. You don't honestly think that I would let an employee from fucking Border Force ride with my outfit, do you?"

Billy started to cry loudly as Richards pulled the hammer back on the Magnum and placed a pillow between it and the back of Billy's head.

The smell of urine and excrement permeated the air as the muffled boom from one of the world's most powerful handguns discharged a round through the head of the young Border Force operative. Brains and blood spattered over the bed as one of Billy's eyeballs exited from the front of his skull and stuck itself to the wall in front of the bedhead. It then slowly slid down to the floor.

Richards pulled the gun backwards and wiped the barrel on the black satin sheets. Turning to two of his patched, leather clad bikies, he indicated for them to remove both the bodies of the young Vietnamese girl and Billy Stevens.

"Make sure you destroy every shred of that Border Force uniform he was wearing," Richards said coldly.

The two, silent, Outlaw members walked over to a cupboard and removed several large rolls of thick black plastic and began the gruesome task.

Richards walked out into the corridor. There was no-one in sight. Little did Billy know that after he had passed every one of the girls in the corridor before entering his Nirvana, they had been ushered into their rooms, told to get dressed and take the rest of the day off. When Billy 'eyeballed' the bedroom wall, the only people to see him on his way up the stairway to heaven were three bikies.

At least they were wearing leather, albeit black and a little larger than Hahn's outfit.

Chapter Thirty-Five

"Sarge. Phone call for you. Somebody from Border Force. Says he got some information for you," the inquiry counter Senior Constable's voice said into the upstairs Task Force phone.

"Put him through," said Kate. "Sergeant McLaren speaking. You're on speaker. I have with me Superintendent Phil Stone from headquarters and Senior Sergeant Tony Signorotto who is in charge here at Carlton." She spoke into the speaker which was now on an open connection on the table in the centre of the cramped Task Force office.

"Gary Mount here, Sergeant. You were making some inquiries about Billy Stevens yesterday. Just thought you should know that he didn't front up for his shift this morning."

"Hadn't requested a day off or anything?"

Gary Mount replied with a chuckle.

"Our Inspectors here at Border Force have to do a bit more paperwork than most of your officers, I think Sergeant. I do the roster and, no, he didn't request a day off. He went sick yesterday after a few hours. I've rung him on his mobile and even sent a crew to visit his flat in Northcote. No sign of him at all. They didn't get in but they said they made enough noise to raise the dead," Mount said.

Phil Stone spoke with a nod and a wink towards his fellow Task Force crew in the office.

"An underworked Victoria Police Superintendent here, Gary. Phil Stone's the name. Did they check any of the neighbours? If he had gone somewhere on that hog of his, I'm sure they would remember the noise of that thing waking them up every morning on a regular basis."

"Yes, Superintendent. One of my crew did make inquiries and none of the residents could remember it starting this morning. They checked the car park and there was no sign of his bike."

"Tony Signorotto here, Gary. A question. Has Stevens ever not turned up for work and not called in?"

"Never, Tony. Taken a couple of sick days from time to time but has always called in, or if it was more than one day, he always produced a sick certificate."

"So quite out of character then?" Tony continued.

"Yes, and to be honest, I probably wouldn't have checked up on him except for the phone call from Sergeant McLaren yesterday. Just pinged my radar a bit."

"Thanks for that. Put our radar on alert now, also. Let you get back to your paperwork while we all go up to Lygon Street for a latte or two," Phil Stone said, laughing.

"Sorry about the paperwork crack. I know your guys in town are always treading water when it comes to work levels. Forgive me?"

"Phil can't answer that, Gary. Too busy dunking another doughnut in his coffee. Been great talking to you. Anytime we can help your boys out, get in touch. Good to know someone down that end of town," Signorotto said.

"No problems, Tony. Thanks Kate. You too, Superintendent," Mount said before hanging up.

They all looked at each other before Phil Stone spoke.

"Pretty obvious that something has happened to Billy Stevens. I say that with that Border Force information combined with Stevens and Richards both riding into the Yellow Blossom yesterday and Billy's bike being towed away. I think we'll have to contact Vice and get them to do a warrant on that place. See what they can find. I wouldn't put anything past Richards and Lombardi where three thousand pistols are concerned. That shipment disappears and it's big, big money for those two."

Chapter Thirty-Six

Big Al Lombardi could not get the nagging thought out of his head.

Ever since his contact at the Police Armoury had told him that he had been at a conference regarding the firearms delivery, it had given him some sleepless nights.

"Fucking Signorotto," Lombardi said over and over to himself. He had heard that name too many times over the years. His Italian 'brothers' were always saying that Signorotto should be avoided at all costs. Even when he had asked the 'retired' head of the local brotherhood, Benny Illarietti, he had been warned off. Lombardi thought the warning was most likely because Signorotto was Illarietti's nephew. Family was sacrosanct, but when Illarietti had said that Tony Signorotto would be too much for Big Al, the self-appointed new King of Carlton saw red. Something had to be done to keep that copper in place, and that place was to be far enough away from interfering in any of the King's plans. Benny Illarietti did not want to know any of Lombardi's projects. He had just smiled and waved an admonishing finger in Al's face. "

Lombardi knew there had been a big fallout a couple of years before between Benny Illarietti and Mickey Midolini, his former lieutenant. Midolini had subsequently disappeared and had never surfaced again. Soon after this, Benny had been stood down by his brotherhood. Scared old men, Lombardi thought. He hadn't been around then, but as sure as hell, he was now, and that was all that mattered. Time to let the world know who ran Carlton!

Lombardi knew that it would have to be something of significance to get Signorotto away from concentrating on the firearms shipment, but not something that would point back towards him. Thoughts skittered through the rat-run passages of his mind as he drove his Maserati through the backstreets of Carlton. There was always a favour to be called in for an overdue gambling debt, and in this case, he knew exactly where to go.

Parking the big Italian showpiece in Leicester Street near the corner of Pelham Street, he looked at the now empty building site where the Corkman Irish pub had stood. Before the Corkman it had been called the Carlton Inn, an establishment where many a famous Carlton footballer from the thirties and forties had knocked back a pot of beer or two. The only thing that Lombardi knew about the site was that there was now a fight going on between the so-called developers who had knocked the Corkman hotel down whilst it had a heritage overlay protecting it and the Melbourne City Council. Lombardi smiled to himself when he remembered that it had been bulldozed early on a Sunday morning before any of the local residents could do anything about it. He appreciated the audacious cunning of the developers as much as he despised the Melbourne City Council.

The old Corkman hotel was only used for one thing by Lombardi in days gone by. To get young first year university students hooked on drugs. The hotel was the watering hole for many kids from the colleges, dorms and houses from the surrounding Carlton streets. He had his lackeys ply their trade around the area every day. Enough drugs of their choice to keep them coming back and working for him. A vicious merry go round where he always looked on from the outside as he collected his cash.

The King of Carlton stared at the rubble strewn site and thought of his rise in the crime world since those days. His trade was so much bigger now. Brothels, strip joints and more. He knew he could keep his lavish lifestyle going by just doing more of the same for years, but he wanted something bigger. A jewel in the crown. A nine-calibre jewel. In fact, three thousand nine calibre jewels. This would make every two-bit crim look up to him. It would be all in the planning. He had no misgivings about getting rid of Richards or his henchmen when it was over. The blame would all lead back to the ongoing feud between the rival bike gangs, the Black Rats and the Carnivores. He would be over one million dollars richer and in the clear. His dream then would be to take over some of those so-called family restaurants in Lygon Street and grease enough palms at the Melbourne City Council to maybe even rename the strip Lombardi Boulevarde. In the meantime, though, there was something he had to do.

Picking up a burner phone from the console of his Maserati, he dialled the number of one of his dependents who he knew lived in Pelham street. A giant of a Russian by the name of Ivan Volkov. Lombardi had him pegged for thirty thousand dollars that the big man had racked up in debt at one of his back-street gambling dens where cheap vodka flowed freely. He also knew that Volkov had beaten a murder rap in his home country where he had apparently snapped the neck of someone he just didn't like. At this moment, according to one of his 'fizzes' in the Department of Immigration, the Minister was going through his file with a possible intention of sending the Russian back to his homeland. Lombardi didn't care if he got deported. There was nothing he could do about it, except try and get thirty thousand dollars' worth of quick work out of him.

Volkov was the perfect loner. He had managed to get to his new homeland of Australia before word had leaked to Canberra about his past, and the more the Australian government found out about some of his habits back home, the more they were trying to get him on the next plane back. In Melbourne, he had refused any help from members of the Russian community. His one downfall, was gambling. Especially any form of Russian card games. He was addicted. He would have some good nights, but then he would have bad nights, playing his favourite, Durack. Lombardi had seen the look in his eyes when a fellow Russian had suggested the card game be played at one of Big Al's casinos. Lombardi knew how to get people hooked on anything from drugs to sex and gambling. He didn't mind Volkov racking up the thirty thousand-dollar tab, but he didn't let him go any further after a few weeks. He was then just another customer who owed him a favour, and now was the time to reel him in—like a Russian sturgeon.

The call was answered after a few rings.

"Yes?" Volkov answered in guttural English.

"Ivan the terrible. Your banker here. Al Lombardi."

Volkov did not answer immediately, indicating to Lombardi that he was very aware of why he was ringing.

"Yes," the Russian said again.

"Ivan, we need to meet and discuss some repayment plans for the thirty thousand dollars you owe my company," Lombardi said with what he hoped sounded like an attempt at authority. In actual fact he was scared shitless of the hulking Russian.

"I am not working Lombardi. I cannot repay," Volkov replied gruffly.

Lombardi was prepared to take a chance.

"Ivan. You are not the only person who has outstanding debts with me. I also have a person who works for the Federal Government in the immigration area. If you want, I can make some inquiries in relation to your application for permanent residency. However, before I make that call, I will be repaid the thirty thousand dollars either in cash or kind. Do you understand me, Ivan?" Lombardi said with a steely edge to his voice.

"What do you mean?" Ivan asked.

"What I mean, Ivan, is that you can repay me by doing a job for me and that cancels the thirty-thousand-dollar debt," Lombardi said, at the same time thinking that the word cancel would definitely be in the Russian's vocabulary. He would have cancelled more than one person back in his homeland.

Silence ensued for several seconds before Volkov replied.

"We meet and talk. Where, when?"

"A comfortable place for you, big man. *Borsch Vodka and Tears* restaurant in Prahran. One hour. I will pay," Lombardi said.

"I be there," Volkov replied, hanging up.

Lombardi sat back in the leather driver's seat of his Maserati and thought to himself about involving Volkov in this side plan. Ivan would never be told about the heist. There was no need to tell him anything. He just had to be wound up and pointed in the right direction like a G.I. Joe action figure. Big Al did have a slight concern though. People like Ivan Volkov were notoriously stupid in his estimation. Time would tell if he could follow simple instructions and the timeline. It was a job that had to be done immediately.

Lombardi knew that what he had in mind for Volkov would only count for a few small lines in the morning paper, but he believed he had an answer to that.

He sat back in his Maserati, picked up a copy of the paper and scanned it for the name of the city crime desk reporter. After ringing the paper on a burner phone and being put through to the crime desk, Lombardi spoke to the bemused reporter.

"Listen to me carefully. Tonight after dark there will be an incident take place outside the Carlton Police Station which you should have a reporter and a photographer in place for. I can guarantee you a headline story."

"Can you give more details. I am not sending a crew on a wild goose chase just because of a phone call," the crime desk reporter replied.

"Terrorism grips the world. Russia knows all about terrorism."

"Why do you say Russia?"

"You will have the jump on all the other papers. I am only telling you, no one else. It will be a story you will have to follow up," Lombardi then ended the call.

At the other end of the call, the crime reporter sat and looked at his phone before making up his mind and walking in to the chief reporter's office.

"Chief. Got a job on tonight which I need a photographer for. Could be nothing but I have a feeling we may have a headline for the morning edition. The man who rang didn't sound like a crackpot."

Chapter Thirty-Seven

Lombardi knew exactly what Volkov was. A stone-cold killer. He had heard about the man through various sources and had even thought about putting him on his payroll. The thought was a short one because he didn't like hiring people he couldn't control. He always considered Russians useful, but dangerous. He knew though that he would take up his offer of wiping his slate clean of debt.

Borsch, Vodka and Tears was definitely not Big Al's restaurant of choice for two reasons. Firstly, being in Chapel Street Prahran, it was out of his comfort zone of the northern suburbs. Secondly, he couldn't comprehend why people would eat such peasant food as borsch. He realised that to get this hijack over the line he was seriously putting his culinary reputation at risk. First, Vietnamese and now Russian / Polish food. His mouth watered when he thought about some of his Italian favourites like Cozze in Padella and Fiore Di Zucchine. For this meeting though, he was willing to sacrifice his taste buds, and at least he could park his Maserati Gran Turismo in Chapel Street near the restaurant. It was far better than having to be dropped off in the sleaze bag suburb of Richmond. At least here his car would be surrounded by a Porsche or two and maybe even a Ferrari, and would look all the better for it.

He had made an early lunch booking for himself and Ivan the Terrible because he wanted the job to be done that night. Not the next day, but that same night. Signorotto had to be given something to derail his mind away from the firearms delivery. If this plan worked, the Carlton Police Station would be in the news and that prick Signorotto would be the centre of attention of all the reporters.

Lombardi walked into *Borsch, Vodka and Tears* and could see the big Russian bear already seated and talking to a waiter. The last thing he himself wanted was to stuff himself full of borsch like he knew Volkov would do. He also didn't want his guest having a gutful of vodka before the job. He couldn't outright refuse him a drink because with Russians, it was an insult not to drink vodka, especially with a meal. Going straight to the table, he took a seat opposite the Russian killer. Volkov didn't look up but kept talking to the waiter who was attempting to translate the guttural English and scribble down his order at the same time.

"For me, white borsch, some slivovitz, cured salmon with sour cream and red kraut. What you eat, Lombardi? You pay, you order. What you like?" The Russian said with a deep voice, as he looked across the table with slate grey eyes that reminded Lombardi of the colour of the gravestones at the Melbourne General Cemetery. He had seen many of those after attending funerals of his countrymen following turf wars around Melbourne.

"Not really that hungry, Ivan," Lombardi said, casting his eyes over a menu that nearly made him vomit. He wanted the 'contract' wrapped up quickly and did not envisage an afternoon of casual chit chat and exchange of cultural pleasantries with this man. Without giving much thought to the menu, he pointed to a couple of selections without speaking, while he forced himself to remember that this was being done for Volkov's benefit as much as his own. The waiter started to walk off when Lombardi called him back and spoke.

"Scotch. Double with two cubes. Single malt. No rubbish. I'll be able to tell the difference," he added with a sneer as he looked around the restaurant. Turning to Volkov, he continued. "Vodka for you, Ivan, I presume?"

"Yes," the Russian said without even a thank you.

"What's the best vodka you have in this place?" Lombardi asked.

"That would be Legends of Kremlin. One hundred and forty dollars a bottle," the waiter said, raising an eyebrow at the heavyset Russian.

Lombardi noticed the look and saw the opportunity to impress his guest.

"One more look like we are peasants, and I will buy this dump and ship you back to your homeland in a crate. Get my friend here his large vodka and my Scotch right now. Understand?" Lombardi said viciously with both of his hands pressed flat on the table.

The waiter turned quickly and weaved back through the restaurant quicker than a bullet in the back from a Kalashnikov.

Looking at a smiling Volkov, Lombardi gave his briefing.

"Ivan, I would like to see you remain in Australia, and I can, with my contacts, make that happen. Simple fact. One job for me means two things for you."

"What two jobs? You say one," the Russian growled angrily.

"Listen and don't talk, Ivan. I said two things, not two jobs. One thing is that you won't have to pay me back the money you owe me. Firstly, the job must be done tonight and secondly because of that you can't have more than one vodka. You all right with both these things? Job tonight. No more vodka today. When it is done, you will find a crate of Legends of the Kremlin on your doorstep."

Volkov looked disappointed with the possibility that a long, free liquid lunch had just been tossed out the window.

Lombardi knew the mention of firearms would not even cause Volkov to blink.

"Tonight, after dark, all I want you to do is stand across the road from the Carlton Police Station and, with the pistol that will be supplied to you, put six shots through the upstairs windows. I just want to scare someone, so you do not, repeat not, shoot through any window that has a light in it. If you do it at about ten o'clock there will be no one in those offices upstairs. The police bosses will all be finished for the day. There will be police downstairs in the station, but you will not direct shots at anything else but the dark windows upstairs. Do you completely understand me, Ivan?" Lombardi said as he looked into the Russian's cold eyes.

Chapter Thirty-Seven

"This all I do to not pay you money I owe?" Volkov said slowly.

"That and then walk into the Exhibition Gardens and throw the pistol into the front yard of the empty gardener's cottage. You then walk away and when you get back to your house there will be a crate of Legends of Kremlin waiting on your doorstep. A very simple operation. This is a lesson to someone who works there not to interfere with me," Lombardi said.

"Easy job. Shoot upstairs windows. Walk to park. Throw gun in front yard and go home," Volkov repeated.

"There will be one of my people watching you, and they will want to see you throw that pistol into the empty front yard," Lombardi said with a knowing smile which was slowly returned by the Russian. "Just so you fully understand, absolutely no one is to be injured."

Volkov slowly nodded his large head and reached for his vodka, which had just been delivered to the table along with Lombardi's scotch.

"Nostrovia," Volkov said, raising his glass in a salute. Lombardi did not return the gesture, but just took a large mouthful of his golden liquid, feeling it burn into his gut like liquid fire.

"Only one drink for you, Ivan. You have work to do," Lombardi said in a serious tone.

After Volkov had demolished his meal and Lombardi had pushed most of his around his plate, a well-dressed man walked quickly through the restaurant door, ignoring the waiter walking towards him. He was carrying a Samsonite bonded leather attaché case. Arriving at Lombardi's table, he placed the case on the chair between the two diners, turned around and left without saying a word.

Volkov looked at the case, leant across the table and spoke quietly to Lombardi.

"What type of weapon?"

"Your type, Ivan," he said, trying to avoid the Russian's foul breath. "Makarov semi-auto with a six-round mag. You may keep the case as a token of my appreciation, but you must dispose of the firearm as I said," Lombardi gave Volkov a smile that left no doubt in the big Russian's mind that if he even thought about keeping the pistol it would be a seriously bad move.

"As you say in this country, Lombardi. A walk in the park," Volkov said slowly.

Fifteen minutes later, Lombardi excused himself from Volkov's company. On the way out he took hold of the frightened waiter he had earlier threatened and spoke quietly in his ear.

"Under no circumstances is my friend to be served any more alcohol. Do you understand ?" Lombardi said with a tight grip on the waiter's arm. He then left the restaurant gulping fresh air as he did. The only good food to smell was Italian food.

The diminutive waiter could do no more than stand still and nod his bobble head up and down.

Chapter Thirty-Eight

Ivan Volkov could not understand Australians. He was standing on the centre median strip of Rathdowne Street, outside the imposing facade of the Carlton Police Station, holding on to a very expensive attaché case which contained what he knew was a very expensive semi-automatic pistol, realising that when he had completed his job there would be a very expensive case of beautiful vodka waiting for him on his return home later that night. All this and he didn't even have to kill anyone, because there was no target except for a couple of windows. No one to be hurt, Lombardi had said. In Russia for such gifts as the case and vodka you would be expected to dispose of at least half a dozen people. No questions asked. Strange country, Australia.

Volkov had been slowly walking up and down the street from about nine thirty that night, making sure that the top floor windows were dark. He was convinced there were no people working upstairs in the station.

Upstairs and inside the darkened office, albeit at the other side, Senior Sergeant Tony Signorotto and Superintendent Phil Stone were quietly talking about the leads that the Task Force had so far unearthed. They were the only ones in the office. An hour before, the Inspectors from the Highway Patrol and Special Operations Group from the subcommittee of the Task Force had left after giving Stone and Signorotto their ideas of how they could transport the firearms from the Melbourne Airport to the Police Armoury at Collingwood.

It had been a long day for both men, so Signorotto had quietly closed the door and turned out the lights. Only a few dimly lit computer screens were glowing softly. Stone was leaning back in his chair sipping on a large Scottish Ledaig single malt whisky of which he had brought a bottle back from the Isle of Mull off the west coast of Scotland on a trip there some months before.

The smooth peated alcohol was being swirled around inside the cut glass crystal tumbler along with two cubes of ice. Tony Signorotto, who had now been off alcohol for over two years, was quietly content with his can of sugarless Coca Cola. Both men were dog tired, and after their drinks had been finished, about to head home.

The sudden cacophony of sound caused Stone to drop his expensive tumbler of scotch to the floor.

"Get down, Phil. Get down," Signorotto yelled, as glass shards from two of the now demolished windows flew in their direction. Six shots came in rapid succession, causing mayhem as they hit the overhead hanging neon light fittings and the metallic air conditioning vents in the ceiling. The air was filled with smoke and debris as the two veteran police officers lay face down, their hair and uniforms covered in glass, dust and plaster.

Tony Signorotto realised immediately that all the shots, which had now stopped, were aimed at the ceiling. They had to be. There was only the Exhibition Gardens opposite. The angle of fire had to have come from below.

As Phil Stone crawled through broken glass towards the doorway leading downstairs, Signorotto duck-walked to the only unbroken window and carefully stood to one side, slowly and carefully peering down at the street below, catching a quick glimpse of a large body, attaché case in hand, walking with determined steps towards the Gardener's cottage just inside the boundary of the Exhibition Gardens. Turning quickly with the intention of heading downstairs, the now enraged Signorotto flicked another look very quickly out the window and saw something else in the street. Running across the office, he bounded down the stairs passing Stone in his hurry.

Swiftly side stepping a Senior Constable who was crouched behind the counter with his service pistol in a double handed grip pointed towards the front door, Signorotto shouted loudly, "Give me your gun and get on the radio for back up."

The Senior Constable slid his semi-automatic Smith and Wesson pistol across the floor to his boss who shouldered open the front door at the same time as picking up the sliding firearm.

The old habits of cover and concealment had not left him. Hitting the footpath running, he took cover behind one of the station cars parked directly outside. He knew he was breathing heavily, but what he had seen upstairs gave him some hope. He smiled to himself as he heard the young voice boom at the top of her voice.

"Police. Get down now or I will shoot. Get the fuck down. Hands out to your sides." The command was followed by a loud grunt coming from a prostrate figure. Signorotto came out from behind the police car to see a large male, pistol kicked to one side spreadeagled on the ground with Chloe Schaffer holding her service pistol at the back of his neck while Max Tyler ratcheted on a set of handcuffs. It was only then that Schaeffer holstered her firearm and snapped the safety down.

A smile of pride and satisfaction spread across the sweating face of their Senior Sergeant as he walked up beside them. Before he could say a word, two men approached quickly from the footpath with one calling out loudly.

"Crime desk Sun Herald, Senior Sergeant. What's the story. Terrorism related? Shots fired at the Police station and a man arrested. What's the situation here? Why do you think he did it?" The reporter said to a confused Tony Signorotto as the other one took photo after photo of the prone and handcuffed prisoner and the three surprised looking police.

"What the fuck is this about?" An enraged Signorotto said to the reporter before realising that a mobile phone was being held towards him, most likely recording everything that was being said.

"Is this a terrorist situation we have here in Carlton? Shots have been fired. Could this be an attack on authority here in the centre of Melbourne by a terrorist cell, Senior Sergeant?"

"I don't know what the situation is yet and we won't know more until we get the offender inside. Now will you get out of the way please," Signorotto said. "Is there a possible bomb scenario?" the now excited reporter demanded.

Tyler and Schaeffer dragged the handcuffed Volkov up from the ground as the reporter and photographer abandoned Signorotto and ran to the prisoner. The reporter shoved his microphone past the extended arms of the two police officers and spoke directly to Volkov.

"What is this for? Why are you shooting at the Police? What have they done to you to make you do this?"

"I shoot windows," the big prisoner said in a confused Russian accented voice before being dragged away to the station.

The reporter and his offsider stepped back and went to their car where the reporter calmly talked into his phone recorder.

"Possible Russian terrorist organisation involved in shooting at Carlton Police Station." He then switched off the microphone and turned to his workmate. "I think we have our headline wrap and pictures for the morning paper, my friend."

Chapter Thirty-Nine

"I saw you two out of the top window, just after those shots busted up our office. What were you doing there?" Signorotto said, as they shoved a handcuffed Ivan Volkov through the front door of the police station and into one of the interview rooms.

"We'd been sitting off Lombardi's place. The changeover crew said he'd been out during the day but had come back by the time Chloe and I had swapped over with them. His Maserati was in the back lane and there were a few cars behind it. Appeared as though he was in for the day. There was virtually no foot traffic going into his club so we thought we might as well come back here," Max Tyler said.

"Lucky you did," Phil Stone chipped in with, as he tried to brush plaster and debris off his epaulettes. "Who is this guy, Tony?"

"I'm about to find out, sir. Give me fifteen minutes with him before you ring the Armed Offenders squad, eh?" Signorotto said with a note of steel in his voice.

"He's got a shitload of charges facing him. Gave the name of Ivan Volkov," Tyler said.

"You're probably right, Max, but I want to know why he did it in the first place," Signorotto said, before slowly opening the interview room door and then quickly closing it before anyone else could enter.

"Put in a call to the Armed offenders Squad, Max, but not before you and Constable Schaeffer have a well-earned coffee," Stone said.

"I'll make the call right now, sir," Max said in reply.

Stone turned immediately to face the pair.

"I just think we need Italy to meet Russia for ten minutes, thanks troops. I'm sure that Senior Sergeant Signorotto has lots to talk about with his newfound friend. I absolutely insist that you two wind down in the mess room. In fact, I am making that an order," Stone said staring directly at Max Tyler.

After a 'light bulb' moment, Tyler turned to Schaeffer.

"Come on Chloe. Coffee. Now," he said as he pushed the young Constable to the back of the station. "Where the hell did those news guys come from?"

Stone walked immediately to the internal phone and rang the extension of the interview room where Signorotto was with Volkov. It was answered immediately.

"Tony, Phil here. Tyler has already got the offenders name as you know. What we need is a reason he shot out the windows. He seemed too calm coming into the station. He'll have a history somewhere and people like him don't go around shooting up police stations just for the heck of it. What's your take on him?"

Signorotto replied very quietly so Volkov couldn't hear the conversation.

"Working on it now. This guy is either nuts or has been set up. Get someone onto the computer right away. I need some information on his shooter. It's a Russian pistol and that narrows down where it came from. If we can link the gun to something or somewhere, we may buy us some time before the heavies from the Armed Offenders Squad or the Anti Terrorist boys descend on us like a ton of cement. We'll have to hand him over eventually."

Signorotto hung up the phone and turned to look at Volkov. The offender was showing no facial expression at all. A quick hand motion from the Senior Sergeant removed the Senior Constable that was standing guard in the room. Volkov did not even blink, but stared coldly at the opposite wall. Signorotto picked up the phone again but kept his finger down on the button so that the call was never connected.

"Turn off the video recorder in this room. That's right. Turn it off now," he yelled into the receiver. Volkov sat upright in his chair. Signorotto walked the few steps towards Volkov and stood directly behind him. The Russian braced himself.

Suddenly he was forcibly lifted out of his seat by his handcuffed arms.

Volkov's eyes began to dart around. His wrists were grabbed roughly and then suddenly freed. The handcuffs were thrown onto the steel table in front of the big Russian at the same time that the equally big uniformed frame of Tony Signorotto stepped around from behind and stared into Volkov's eyes from inches away. Volkov braced himself for a punch to the midriff. None came. Signorotto spoke directly at him with a calm but clear voice.

"Why did you try and kill me and another police officer?"

"I did not try kill anyone. I put shots through windows. I not know who you are," Volkov said slowly but firmly in reply whilst returning the stare from Signorotto. He knew this cop was not about to be intimidated. He was the same height as himself with an attitude to match.

"There was no one in the room I shot. I know. Lights were not on. I check for hour before."

Signorotto put a hand on the shoulder of Volkov and slammed him downwards into the bolted down interview room chair and grabbed him by the throat.

"There were two of us in that office," Signorotto said through clenched teeth. Volkov's eyes were now wide open. He said nothing. Signorotto could see the blood draining from the face of the Russian. He eased the pressure on his throat slightly.

"We have the fingerprints from the gun you used tonight. There are two witnesses, both police officers. Save us both a lot of time and yourself a lot of pain. Why, is what I want to know," Signorotto said.

Volkov looked up at the enraged police officer, just as there was a sudden knock at the door.

"Come in," Signorotto yelled.

A uniformed Senior Constable stepped into the interview room and handed a computer printout to the Senior Sergeant who, after reading it, realised he now had the bargaining chip he needed.

"Thanks, Senior. Just made my day," Signorotto said to the smiling member leaving the room.

"I have some details here about you, Ivan. You are on a temporary visa here in Australia. Very temporary, I would say after tonight. I want you to confirm your name and date of birth for me."

"Ivan Volkov. Born September '83."

"Great start, Ivan. Now why did you shoot at us?" Signorotto asked.

Volkov knew that he couldn't be charged with anything that would get him more than a couple of years in prison. At least for the next year or so he would be top dog in any soft Australian gaol they threw him in.

"Charge me! I do not worry about your holiday gaol. I do it on my ear," Volkov said with a sneer.

"Ivan. You should have thought through your plan a bit more. That Russian piece you used on our station. I have the history of it right here," Signorotto said as he shook the paper in the face of the Russian thug.

"Good Russian pistol. You can trust things from my homeland," Volkov said with arrogance in his voice.

"I wouldn't trust you as far as I could kick you. That pistol you used was a Makarov semi auto. In fact, it was one of the firearms that our Australian government let your Embassy keep in Canberra. The big problem is the fact that this particular one was reported stolen from your bloody Embassy about eighteen months ago," Signorotto said staring intently at the now silent Russian. Seconds passed as Volkov's mouth opened and closed silently.

"You charge me with shots and stolen gun. I not worried about you," Volkov spat back.

A beaming Signorotto pulled his ace from the pack.

"Ivan, listen to me carefully. The fact that you had the gun forces me to hand you over to our Federal Police. It was stolen from Canberra and from an Embassy. This is no ordinary theft you dumb fool. As far as I'm concerned you are Russian, and you stole from your own Embassy. We'll let the Embassy deal with their own problems. Your little house in Canberra will be informed that we have found their property and also have one of their citizens for the theft. They then take over. It won't go through an Australian court. We'll hand you over and they will pack you into the next diplomatic pouch, maybe in pieces, and ship you back to the Motherland. If you land in one piece you will be taken to Butyrka gaol. Bye bye, Ivan the Terrible," Signorotto said, as he gave the wide-eyed bear a mock wave to his face.

He just hoped that Volkov bought the pack of lies he had just invented.

"Your Australian visa will be torn up and thrown to the four winds. What do you think about that little bucket of Russian caviar, comrade?" he said with a knife-like edge to his voice.

"It not my gun. It given to me. Not steal, just use."

"Work with me, Ivan. I need more than that before I can help you. Where do you live?

Volkov replied with a North Carlton address.

"Who got you to do this, Ivan?"

Volkov did not reply, as he thought about the consequences of punishment between an Australian prison, a Russian gulag or a bullet from Lombardi.

"All right. We will play it your way, Russki. You have two hours before I hand you over to the Feds, who will drag you to your Embassy in Canberra and dump you in their front yard. That's it," the confident Senior Sergeant said, looking at the now very worried Russian in front of him, as he opened the interview room door and called for the Senior Constable from the counter.

"Cells for him," indicating Volkov. Ivan's going to have a little rest and a big think."

Volkov was forcibly pulled from the room by two officers. A loud clang of the steel cell door reverberated around the station.

Chapter Forty

Tony Signorotto walked into the mess room with Super-intendent Stone, where Max Tyler and Chloe Schaeffer were seated. Stone spoke.

"I know you've been on the go all day, but what we need now is for you to get over to Volkov's address. There has to be more to this shooting. A pay off or something. I want to find it so when we hand him over in the next few hours to one of the Squads, we have got all we need from him. He thinks he's sitting in the cells making us sweat, but if we find out the reason, I will hand him over without a word and watch him scream the place down. I don't want him thinking he can decide the outcome. Your Senior Sergeant has let him think that he has options, where in fact what he was told can't happen. He can't be handed over to his Embassy, much as we might like to, but we will have him charged with a heap of firearms offences and while he does his time down at Barwon State Prison, each day will get him closer to a flight back to Moscow. You never know, when you get to his house, it might have an open window that, excuse the pun, needs looking into. I think I can hear a call for police assistance from his house already. Understand?"

Max Tyler looked at Signorotto, who was standing, with raised eyebrows, next to his Superintendent. It was definitely a look of 'ask no questions and be told no lies' coming from him. Before Max could say anything, Stone spoke again.

"Come on, move. Let me know what you find. Be quick and discreet." Tyler and Schaeffer walked quickly between their bosses and headed out to their car.

"Let's just see what we find, eh Chloe?" Max said, looking directly at the very junior officer.

"Max. I don't mind a little breaking and entering between friends when we are trying to find out why he shot up the place.

If some bloody import wants to put bullets in us, then stuff his rights. I'll wear the consequences."

Fifteen minutes later, they got out of their unmarked vehicle and walked slowly up to the front door of a rundown little miner's cottage at the address they were given. An overgrown, weed-strewn front yard led to a dilapidated front door. Two overflowing, stinking wheelie bins full of rubbish stood to one side.

"God, Max. If the inside of this dump smells as bad as the outside, we will need a couple of forensic plastic suits before going in," Schaeffer said with a screwed-up face.

Both front windows either side of the door, had vertical wrought iron bars on them, which was pretty normal for houses in the area. There was no access to the side yard. A steel gate was topped with half a metre of razor wire.

"I don't think we are going to get in anywhere but the front door," Max said, as they both returned to the front of the falling down shack.

"Hang on a minute. What's this?" Chloe said, spying a cardboard box wedged between one of the bins and the rotten weatherboard front wall. Putting on her regulation blue plastic gloves, she dragged the heavy container out from behind the bin. As she did, the loud sound of glass knocking against glass could be heard from inside the container. Flipping back the lid, they could see half a dozen labelled bottles inside.

Schaeffer removed the pistol from her holster and flicked on the powerful mini torch that was attached to the underneath of the barrel of her Smith and Wesson nine-millimetre Police and Military Special pistol.

"What have we got here? Unlike everything else around here, Chloe, this looks brand new," Max said as he removed one of the bottles which was filled with clear liquid. The label read *Legends of Kremlin. Finest Russian vodka.* The six bottles appeared to be identical. A red, white and blue card was attached to the neck of one of the bottles. Schaeffer opened the card and read it to Max.

"We hope you enjoyed your lunch with us today. Please accept this as a gift for your patronage." The card was dated with the current date and bore the moniker of the Prahran restaurant, *Borsch, Vodka and Tears*.

Holding a bottle towards the young Constable, Max noticed her eyes widen.

"Something wrong?" Max said.

"A few of the girls at Carlton like a vodka or two, including me, but that stuff is way above our pay level. It's over a hundred bucks a bottle. If some punter buys you a shot of that, they are either pissed or want to get into your pants. The second usually follows the first," Schaeffer said with a grin.

Tyler looked down at the bottles and spoke.

"This is strange, Chloe. It's got to be a payment. No restaurant would do this unless someone has ordered it. It would probably be worth more than the lunch. I'm going to ring the boss. What do you think?" the detective said to the young Constable.

"I was just thinking about the gift and not the motive behind it. Suppose that's why you're the detective," Schaeffer said in reply.

"Maybe. But you found it, I didn't." Hitting Tony's number on his phone's speed dial, he was relaying the find to his boss within seconds. Stone listened intently as Signorotto put the call through the phone's speaker. The two looked at each other with the same thought pattern bouncing between them. Signorotto spoke at the end of Max's description.

"I'll ring ahead, but I want you to get over to that restaurant quick and check it out. Also, see if they have C.C.T.V. of the inside of the place around lunchtime today. Someone has sent our friend Ivan on a mission. What they didn't plan on was him getting sprung by us. The Superintendent and I will wait here till we hear from you. Good work troops. It's a pity old Ivan will never get to wrap his lips around an open bottle of that stuff."

Chapter Forty-One

By the time Schaeffer and Tyler arrived at *Borsch, Vodka and Tears*, the last of the evening patrons were just leaving the up market eating establishment. The head waiter approached, a nervous smile on his face.

"You are the two police officers someone rang about?" The diminutive man said.

"Yes. I'm Detective Senior Constable Tyler and my partner here is Constable Schaeffer."

"What can I do to help you? It won't be a licensing problem. We enforce the rules stringently here and it can't be a food problem either, because you are police, not council."

"No one is any trouble. We just need to know if this person was in your restaurant around lunchtime today?" Max said, showing the man a mug shot of Volkov taken back at the station.

The waiter did not waste time replying.

"Yes. Lunchtime. He was at table number four over there," indicating a table with four chairs near the rear of the room.

"Was he with anyone?" Schaeffer said quickly.

"Just one very rude, frightening man," the nervous waiter said as his eyes flicked from Max to Chloe.

"Can you describe him?" she continued, at the same time as removing her police notebook from the back pocket of her jeans, ready to take down the description.

"No need for notes, officer," he said. "After the threats I received at lunch from this man, I told the owner and he took some freeze frame photos from the C.C.T.V. and printed them off. The owner is a good man and he will never allow this individual back into the restaurant."

Minutes later he returned with a large colour photo of the lunch table. On one side of table four was Ivan Volkov and on the other side was none other than Big Al Lombardi. On the chair between them was the Samsonite case that Volkov had on him when he had been arrested earlier that night.

"Do you know anything in regard to a shipment of *Legends of Kremlin* vodka that was possibly sent to this man?" Tyler said, indicating Volkov.

"We were contacted later in the afternoon and told to deliver half a dozen bottles to a house in Carlton somewhere. When our owner asked how they would be paid for, the caller said if they weren't delivered, there would be more tears than vodka and borsch at this restaurant. It cost us over six hundred dollars, but it was better than being firebombed.

They thanked the waiter and left. Sitting in their car, Max Tyler phoned Phil Stone.

"Sir, you're going to love this. I can see pieces of this falling into place. This was Lombardi's work.

Upon returning to the station, the group had a round table conference.

"What's your theory, Max?" Stone said after being shown the photo from the restaurant.

"We know that Volkov is on a temporary visa. We also know that Lombardi has his fingers in a lot of government pies. It wouldn't surprise me if Volkov had been promised a bit of government help to stay in the country. We've checked his status with Canberra, and I don't like his chances of remaining here without a golden handshake. For some reason, Lombardi has conned him into this, but what I can't figure out is why he would just get him to shoot the station up. He's thinks he's the King of Carlton, so why bring attention to himself? He didn't have to."

Chloe Schaeffer gave a small cough.

"Speak up, Constable. We are all in this together. You are the front line of the Task Force. Any idea is worth listening to," Stone said encouragingly.

"We know that Lombardi is connected to the possible heist. He doesn't know what we have found out so far. So why not, from his point of view, set up a big diversion that will keep this station on its toes and away from anything he is planning. The press coverage for some fake news about terrorist attacks or bombs will keep you, Superintendent, tied up for a few days until it is all proven otherwise. That reporter will get his front page in the morning and people will be swarming all over here. Everyone here will be thinking about the bullet holes in this place rather than a heist of firearms that only a few of us here know about. When he finds out that Volkov has been pinched, he will have to get his plan underway quick smart. Getting some big press coverage was one thing, but Volkov actually being nabbed wasn't in the plan, I bet. If it was, Lombardi wouldn't have had that vodka dropped off. Leads straight back to him. Big ego mistake. That's my take on it for what it's worth."

"Smart thinking, Chloe," Stone replied. "While everyone is thinking terrorist plots and other bad shit, we will have to keep our focus. I can see myself being tied up with headquarters and the press for the next day or so thanks to the papers. No prizes for guessing who set this up. Lombardi has with the newspaper bit. It wouldn't have taken long for the pictures of Volkov to be recognised by someone. If it wasn't for you and Max nabbing him I think he would have had probably been at home safe and sound for a few days drinking Vodka. The station would have been drowning in Anti-Terrorist coppers from here and Canberra looking for a scalp. At least with him being caught in the act we can by-pass the diversion and concentrate on the shipment."

Chapter Forty-Two

Joey Salessa was going to make sure he stayed out of reach of his boss, Big Al Lombardi, when he knocked on his office door at Club Maximus late that Thursday night. He knew from experience that the reaction would be a violent one. He had witnessed Lombardi blow Leo Carbone's head clean off his shoulders, Anything could set him off: And the news he was about to give him definitely would.

"Come in," Lombardi said in a voice that Joey knew would descend into rage when he dropped the bombshell on him.

"Ah, boss. That guy you wanted me to check on. The one you wanted to shoot up the cop shop?" Joey said in a timid voice.

"Yeah, Joey. That will give that prick Signorotto something to think about. The press will be all over a story about a shooter on the run. It'll be days before he can think about anything else. His bosses will be all over his arse," Lombardi said with a loud laugh. "It'll be all over the morning paper. I can just see the headlines now. Glad I dropped that phone call to the paper."

Salessa didn't say a word. His mind was too busy trying to think of the best way to give Lombardi the news. *Why the fuck didn't Feb get the tagging job?* he thought.

Lombardi held out his right hand as he walked towards Joey.

"Give me his gun so I can get rid of it," he said, walking across the deep pile office carpet to a now visibly shaken Samoan. Joey just blurted out the words.

"The cops have it, boss."

Lombardi came to a sudden halt, whisky glass in his hand and a look of disbelief on his face.

"What! What the fuck are you saying? Didn't he drop the gun in the gardens?" he said as his voice rose like an erupting volcano.

"He let the shots off all right boss, and he hit the windows, but then two plain clothes cops came out of nowhere and jumped him. One of them was policewoman, and seriously boss, I thought she was going to blow him away right there. He didn't make it across the road. They flattened him. Press were there like you said but they got more than the shooting. They got the arrest," Joey said sheepishly.

Lombardi started to scream at the top of his voice.

"He was supposed to make sure there were no cops around. He said he'd make sure for fucks sake."

"Boss. He was there casing the copshop for an hour before he pulled the shooter out. I sat off him like you said and watched him sus the place out. There were no uniforms or cars out the front. I couldn't even see the reporters until it all went down. These two cops came out of nowhere and saw him unload. He started off across the road and then that crazy young bitch went nuts," Salessa said.

Lombardi screamed at the top of his voice as he hurled his Norlan whisky glass, half full of an expensive single malt scotch, across the room and into the heavy wooden door. Glass fragments flew everywhere, as did the contents which splashed across the back of Joey's head, the throw being so close.

"Fuck! Fuck! What happened then?" The enraged King of Carlton shouted.

"They cuffed him and by the time they went to drag him up, an older cop had come out of the copshop. He just ran out straight to them. He picked up the pistol and then they just dragged your guy into the station, but not before the reporter had started yelling about a terrorist attack and Rusia or something. I didn't hang around after that. Came straight back here."

Lombardi, by this stage, was stomping back and forth across his office, swearing at the top of his voice while holding his head in his hands.

"Get out! Get the fuck out! Lombardi bellowed at Joey, who couldn't believe he had heard sweeter words said to him in his whole worthless life. He shot through the door quicker than a buttered bullet.

Outside he could hear Lombardi storming around the office smashing things and swearing. Joey was relieved that he wasn't the object of the smashing and beatings taking place on the other side of the office door. He knew ages ago that he shouldn't have taken up a casual job with this crazy son of a bitch. Being a full blood brother in the Black Rats O.M.C.G. was like being in a kindergarten compared to being around this prick.

Inside the office, Big Al's mind was in turmoil. It didn't take a Rhodes Scholar to figure out that the older guy would have been Signorotto. He had come across him on a couple of occasions in and around Lygon Street in uniform checking up on some of the licensed premises. Any time he had come into his establishment, he had made sure his paperwork was up to scratch and he wasn't around. It was always the bar manager that handled any questions. It wasn't that he was scared of the big cop: Or was he? In hindsight it hadn't been a good idea to get Volkov to shoot at the copshop, but in his mind it was just another way of keeping this cop away from him. Too many stories from the Brotherhood traced back to no-win situations for them. The fact that Benny Illarietti had been forced to 'retire' and nothing had happened to Signorotto sent a shudder down Lombardi's spine. If the Brotherhood didn't want revenge, then why wouldn't he try and keep his distance. Benny's lieutenant, Mickey Midolini had also disappeared without trace. Big Al didn't mind disappearing but it had to be somewhere of his choice, not a six by four cell at Barwon State Prison with a twenty-three-hour lockdown. If Volkov fessed up, the law would drop on him like a sledgehammer.

There was no alternative now. He would have to go to another plan he had been toying with. A 'just in case' plan. Just shut the business in the morning for a few days and get his accountant to oversee not only the finances of the Lygon Street nightclub, after putting in a new manager, but also take over the money side of his two massage parlours. His financial guru would be told after a few months that his holiday to Italy would become permanent and that a new owner would have to be found for Club Maximus. The massage parlours were no problem as they were run by one Asian madam who was paid very well. The safe house in Brunswick would fetch a very nice price now that the suburb was appealing more and more to the new generation of latte sippers. All the money would be laundered here and magically appear in his oversees accounts in due time. It was worth paying his accountant the exorbitant amount he charged.

Time to head to Brunswick. He had rented a large factory residence that would become headquarters and home for the next few days. After that, Sydney for the money and Italy for retirement. He had it all mapped out. He was Maximus. He was a gladiator.

It was now Thursday evening. He had to get the main players in for a war council. The timeline had to be brought forward and he had to get himself and his entourage to the new premises quickly.

Half an hour later after a phone call summoning Tony Richards to his Lygon Street club, Lombardi walked downstairs to his bar and looked around. The business had been good to him, but his money in an offshore account, together with the cash from the upcoming firearms deal with his Sydney counterparts would buy him a completely new life in the Dolomite mountains region of North East Italy. A shiny new Maserati from the showroom in Modena would handle those mountain roads with ease.

He could forget being the King of Carlton. He would now become the King of Cortina d'Ampezzo and rule the Dolomite region of northern Italy.

Chapter Forty-Three

Five o'clock the next morning saw the arrival of the key figures that were needed to carry out what Lombardi considered the heist to beat all heists.

Tony Richards, bleary eyed but eager to share the bounty, slouched in one corner of Lombardi's office. With him were his Sergeant-at-Arms and another enforcer from the Black Rats Outlaw Motorcycle Gang. The three bikies looked as though they could start a war all by themselves. None of them wore their leather 'patched' colours. This was no club ride. This was big business. The other individuals skulking around in the shadows of the darkened room were a very reluctant Angelo Morelli, constantly flanked by Joey Salessa and Feb Felagi.

Lombardi stood, hands on hips, and spoke to the gathering like Caesar to a phalanx of centurions.

"All of you get downstairs and raid the kitchen for anything you can eat. Joey, make sure all the remaining food is packed up and put into the van. No booze though. The time has come gentlemen for us to relocate our operation for a few days. I will outline my plan and give you my orders when we get to our new headquarters. Tony, I need you and me to have a private briefing while the others are downstairs."

Richards uncurled his sinewy, snake like form from one of the leather seats and indicted to his cohorts to go downstairs. The two bikies nodded their consent, never taking their eyes off Lombardi. They would take orders from their President, but never from Lombardi.

Dragging an office chair to the opposite side of the desk where Lombardi had seated himself, Richards began to speak before his so-called partner could.

"Don't start acting like some pissant army general, Al. None of my boys will wear that. They are loyal to me only. You want them to do something, you come through me. Got it? That yank George Patton might have waged war with the Nazis mate, but just remember this. We are the new Nazis and I lead the Melbourne chapter of the ugliest Nazis in the southern hemisphere. So, I guess then that I'm Hitler and you are Mussolini: And you know what happened to Mussolini, pal? Strung upside down by the locals."

Lombardi's eyes slowly glazed over, and his face reddened as he reached into his waistband and removed a semi-automatic Beretta pistol, before placing it on top of the desk with the barrel facing Richards. If it was meant to intimidate his partner in crime, it didn't work. Richards just smiled and pulled back one side of the black leather vest he wore and with his right hand removed a Ruger Super Blackhawk forty-four Magnum revolver. He placed it next to the Beretta, a battleship moored next to a dinghy.

"If you want to compare dick sizes, Al, forget it. My two boy's downstairs carry 357 Magnums. Why don't we just cut to the chase and talk plans. Actually, before we do that, how about we talk dollars after this comes off. What's my cut of the action?"

Lombardi knew he was dealing with a violent thug who couldn't plan his way out of a one door room, so he didn't mind Richards show of firearm power because that's all he could do—show! Richards wouldn't even have come into his calculations except for the muscle he would need.

"All right, Tony. Here's the bottom line. When my Sydney connections get these firearms, they will be paying eight hundred and fifty dollars apiece for them. That includes the ammunition. That's more than what they cost through a gun shop obviously, but there is no way anybody, except me, can get their hands on three thousand of them. They can sell them in batches on the black market for whatever they can get, which will probably be up around the twelve-hundred-dollar mark. I don't give a fuck as long as I take two and a half million for them and the ammunition. My connections already have the money waiting. I will take one and a half mill and you will get one mill.

How you divide that up with your crew is up to you. I'll look after mine, you look after yours. When we go our separate ways next week, you can have your two Samoan bears back also. I won't need them," Lombardi said, while internally laughing to himself about what good two dead Samoans would be to Richards.

Richards stared back at the reptilian eyes that swivelled around in Lombardi's pudgy face. He himself was thinking that the survival rate at the end of this job would be virtually nil for Joey, Feb and the other one they constantly flanked and knew full well that if he was thinking that about them, then Lombardi would be thinking the same thing about him and his boys. This did not faze him one iota. As Ned Kelly said, *"Such is Life!"*

"I have a little side plan also," Lombardi said quietly. It will happen this afternoon. That Tom Cole, the head of the security company who is escorting the guns is going to come home from work today, and along with his little daughter, disappear. He will be more than willing to help us when we have his kid."

Richards' head snapped upwards at the mention of the child.

"No way am I or my boys helping kidnap a kid. Forget it," Richards fumed.

""You won't be involved in the grab. My boys will do that. I've already had Morelli track Cole to his house. We won't be hurting him or his kid when the heist takes place. The boys will have balaclavas on the whole time. They will be bringing them to our new location in Brunswick. While you have been taking care of your loose ends like Billy Stevens, I have been busy planning ahead," Lombardi said.

"Lay it all out for me now, Al. Every little detail."

Lombardi smiled, rose and walked to the table in the middle of the office and sat again, beckoning Richards over. Sitting on either side of the expensive teak table, with the firearms left on the desk, Big Al Lombardi proceeded to outline his audacious venture to an incredulous Richards.

Chapter Forty-Four

"You don't have to go along with any of this. Let's just get out now while we can," a highly agitated Angelo Morelli said to Joey Salessa and Feb Felagi.

They were parked in Charles Street, Carlton, six doors down from Tom Cole's house. Angelo kept up his pleading from the back seat of the old Ford sedan.

"Guys. Think about it. We're sitting here looking at a house where Lombardi wants us to kidnap two people—and one of them is a little kid! We'll all do twenty years inside for this. Come on, think about it. This will be the end of our lives," Angelo said loudly as he leant forward between the bucket seats and talked directly to the two sweating Samoans seated in front of him.

Feb Felagi twisted in his seat and faced Morelli, grabbing him by the front of his shirt, screaming into his face as he threw him backwards into the seat.

"What fucking choice do we have?"

Angelo's mind raced back to the last minutes before Lombardi had killed his friend Leo Carbone. The three of them in the car now were the only witnesses to the shooting and if it still terrified him, he knew it still terrified the others.

"You know what he wants. You both heard him at the house before he shot Leo. He wants these pistols at any cost. I'm telling you; he will kill all of us. You saw what he did then. He's totally fucking mad. You know it and I know it. He doesn't care about us, just himself," a desperate Morelli pleaded.

Joey Salessa turned to the visibly shaking Morelli and spoke.

"The Black Rats will take care of us. We take our orders from Tony, not from Lombardi. Tony and Lombardi have spoken, and Tony wants us to grab them both when they come up to the house. We won't be hurting anyone unless we have to. Tony is the President and wouldn't send us in here unless he thought it was all going to work. The Black Rats are brothers. We are blood."

"Yeah? Well fuck you two. I'm not one of your fucking Black Rats. I've been kidnapped myself for the last few weeks and I know how it's going to end up. There's only a few of us going to this place in Brunswick where we have to meet Lombardi. He's already killed Leo, so, what's not to say we're not next? Just fucking collateral damage at the end of this. Lombardi wants big money for these guns. Do you think he's going to share any of the takings with you and me? Not fucking likely."

"Any plan he has will only work with Tony. He needs us. Now just fucking shut up," Feb said as he tossed a black balaclava at Morelli. "Put this on when we get to the house, all right? All we have to do is pick up and run back to the car. The plates have been changed on this shitheap, so no one will know where it's from," Joey said.

One stupid fucking try at stealing a good car and this is what happens. Leo is dead and I'm either going to the can for life or I'm going to die for it!

Angelo looked around desperately. He could feel his world coming to an ugly end. Clutching the balaclava with one hand, he reached with the other and tried to wrench open the back door in an attempt to run and escape the impending situation. Lombardi's plan was one thing, but kidnapping was another.

He looked down at the handle as he yanked it up and down. Locked! He just caught sight of the butt of the sawn-off shotgun that Joey was bringing down on him when Feb grabbed Joey by the arm.

"Check the car," Feb called, causing Joey to spin back around just in time to see a Toyota sedan pull up outside a house on the opposite side of Charles Street.

The three kidnappers saw a big man step out of the car and stretch.

"That him?" Feb asked Angelo, who didn't answer, but looked with terrified eyes back at the two Samoans.

"I said, is that him?" Feb said angrily at the same time as he delivered an open-handed blow to the left side of Angelo's head, causing the scared back seat passenger to put both hands up to ward off further blows.

"Yeah, yeah. All right. That's him," Angelo answered meekly. "He'll go next door to get his kid. There's some old woman and her husband who look after her when school's out."

The large frame of Tom Cole walked to the house next to his own, opened the gate and strode up the path. Joey and Feb grabbed their balaclavas along with a short aluminium baseball bat. Both slid out of the driver's door quickly. Feb opened the rear door and dragged Angelo out.

"We're in this together," Joey said, as he pushed a now compliant Angelo across the road and out of sight of Cole's next-door neighbour's house. The three of them walked quickly up to the side of Cole's house and hid just around the corner from the front door.

As they all knelt down, Joey turned to the other two.

"When they come up to the door, I will king hit him from behind. Morelli, you just grab the kid and cover her mouth with this piece of gaffer tape," Joey said, ripping a piece of the sticky black tape from a roll he pulled out of his pocket. "Pick her up and get to the car. Drag her if you have to but get her into the front seat. Me and Feb will do the same to him. Have the boot undone. He won't know what hit him. When he's in the boot Feb, make sure he is cuffed," Joey said as he stopped to take in a large gulp of air before continuing.

"When he comes up to the front door, he has to open the screen door left to right. He won't be expecting anybody to come up behind him. Morelli, all you have to do is grab and tape the girl then get to the car. Understand?"

Feb nodded quickly while Angelo Morelli's body just shook all over.

Chapter Forty-Five

Tom Cole stretched both arms out from his body as he stood next to his company car. Yawning, he looked over its roof at his house, and realised what a long day it had been. The planning for the delivery of the police firearms the next Tuesday had just about been finished and put to bed. He would have to pop back into work for an hour the next morning, but after that he wanted to spend the rest of the day with Summer. He was also quietly looking forward to Tony Signorotto's wife's birthday party on Saturday night. The fact that Kate McLaren was going too was an added bonus.

Walking up the path to Jill Norton's house, Cole could hear the friendly laughter emanating from behind the screen door. He counted his lucky stars to have Jill Norton and her husband as neighbours.

"Jill. Tom here. Come to pick up that blonde-haired ball of trouble you've been minding," he called out down the passageway of the Victorian terraced house. The screen door flew open as the little six-year-old leapt onto her father and wrapped her arms around his neck. Tom looked over the mass of blonde curls at the smiling face of the ex-police officer standing in the open doorway.

"Thanks so much, Jill. Don't know what I'd do without you," a grateful Tom Cole said.

"Anytime, Tom. She's a pleasure to look after. You two are coming to Susie's birthday bash tomorrow night at Dom's, aren't you?" Jill asked.

"Absolutely. Got to pick Kate up on the way though. She hasn't met Summer yet, so I thought I'd do the driving and they can chat. You know. Girls stuff and all that," Tom said with a laugh.

"You're a quick worker. She does seem like a nice type," Jill replied with a smile. "Don't know if I'd get involved with a female copper though. They're pretty hard cases. Look at me."

"Yeah. You're a real hard type, Jill. By the way, how many home-made biscuits have you fed Summer since you got her home from school?" Tom said brushing crumbs from his daughter's face.

"That's girls" business only. Isn't it pet?" Jill replied with a wink to the little girl, who nodded back with a smile as Cole carried his daughter back down the path before dropping her onto her feet just outside Jill's front gate. Turning around towards Jill, he called out.

"Got to go into work for an hour tomorrow morning to tie up a couple of loose ends about a big job on Tuesday morning. Any chance…?

"Not a problem. Just don't give her breakfast. I'll do some strawberry pancakes for us. That little poppet needs feeding up," Jill said, as she received a squeal of delight and a wave from Summer.

"Thanks, you hard old thing," Tom said heading to his own house.

Chapter Forty-Six

After reaching into his coat pocket and retrieving his keys, Tom unlocked the wire security door, but was then suddenly distracted by a sharp tugging on his left arm.

"Hang on a minute," he said to his daughter, who was impatient to get into their house.

Suddenly, a balaclava clad stranger appeared at his left and grabbed his daughter, lifting her off her feet at the same time as clamping a hand over her mouth and spinning her around to face away from her father.

Cole's army training, combined with the immediate reaction to protect his daughter, kicked in, as he lunged towards the back of the stranger with the intent of putting him in a headlock. He never saw the short aluminium baseball bat coming down on his head, as he felt himself sag to his knees, unbelievable pain shooting through his skull, causing him to see stars as his vision disappeared.

"No one is going to hurt you, kid," Angelo Morelli said in a raspy voice while slapping the sticky black tape across the young child's mouth. He had made sure she didn't see her father being hit or falling to the ground, and he didn't even look back to see what Joey and Feb were doing to Cole. He just picked the little girl up and bolted to the car.

Once inside the sedan, Angelo leant over and hit the boot release before speaking to Summer in a voice filled with emotion.

"It's all right, kid. You're not going to get hurt. I won't let anyone touch you. Your dad will be okay too. Promise."

His immediate reaction to the look of terror in the little girl's eyes was to rip the black tape from her mouth so she could breathe properly. She looked up at him, but just shook with fright at the balaclava covered form, without saying a word.

Morelli put her head down towards the floor so she couldn't see any of them when they took off the balaclavas for the drive to the rendezvous. A slamming noise erupted after the other two dumped Cole's inert body into the boot. Joey had jumped into the front seat after throwing the Toyota keys to Feb.

Joey fired up the old car and sped off along Charles Street, followed shortly after by Feb driving the Toyota. The whole kidnap had lasted about two minutes.

All Angelo could do was hug the child a bit closer as he saw the tears begin to run down her cheeks. Heavy sobbing and crying were all you could hear.

Morelli stared at Joey, who was sweating profusely as his hands clenched the steering wheel. His knuckles were white. Angelo spoke with a venomous edge in his voice.

"No matter what happens from now on in, this little kid stays with me. Understand? No one comes near us. You can do what you like with this job, but this kid will stay safe. We've just given ourselves life sentences by snatching her, but no one, and I mean no fucking one, harms a hair on her head."

"No arguments from me, mate," Joey said, as he wiped perspiration from his forehead with his left hand onto his T shirt. The smell of sweat and fear permeated the interior of the car. "You'll just have to convince Lombardi of that."

Chapter Forty-Seven

Big Al Lombardi didn't get out of his matte grey Maserati Gran Turismo until the big garage roller door was down and locked.

Sliding his hands around the leather steering wheel, he knew he would miss the luxury feel that enveloped him every time he slipped into the driver's seat His only consolation was the thought of picking up a new model from the factory in Italy.

Looking through the windscreen, he saw the figures of Tony Richards and his two men The van and the old Ford that Joey Salessa had brought Lombardi's bargaining chips in were also there. In a corner was a pale blue small Isuzu truck along with the company car belonging to National Security Services. Cole and his daughter had already been taken to one of the office rooms of the old factory and accommodation set up.

Lombardi had rented the large premises for several reasons. It was the old Sam's Tyres factory in Brunswick Road, near the partly renovated Sarah Sands hotel, which would make for a quick left turn into Sydney Road after they had transferred the guns into their truck. The long holiday weekend with the rostered day off for construction workers being added to the following Tuesday had been a bonus. No one would return to the area until at least the next Wednesday. The rent deal had been done via an email address that could not be traced back to him. If the police ever figured their way through the electronic maze, they would find it all led back to a shell company providing more questions than answers. If the name Alessio Lombardi ever popped up he would be well ensconced in the mountains of Northern Italy. Even the Italian government would not enter that region for extradition purposes for fear of extreme retribution.

The premises itself combined ample parking with a lounge and meeting area and several rooms that had been converted into sleeping accommodation for what Lombardi presumed were for long haul truck drivers prior to heading up the Hume Highway to Sydney. Cole and his daughter would be well looked after—as long as they co-operated.

Lombardi and Richards had warned everybody connected to the job that gloves must be worn at all times. Even Big Al had on his Italian leather, skin-tight driving gloves. There was to be no trace of fingerprints left anywhere when they vacated the factory after the heist.

Turning to Joey Salessa, he motioned him to the meeting room.

"Any problems with Cole and his kid?"

"No boss. Cole will have a sore head but is coming around. Feb has him cuffed to a rail in the living area and we've got his mobile phone. He's a big bastard though. Might be an idea to let him see that his kid is okay and won't be hurt in this. Morelli is paranoid that we are all going down over this job and doesn't want to leave the kid alone," Joey said.

"I've got a part for him to play in this. You just leave him to me. None of you have shown your faces to Cole, have you?" Lombardi said urgently.

"No boss. Balaclavas on for the grab. The kid couldn't see anything during the drive here and Cole was in the boot. Morelli kept her face down on the floor the whole time. We put them back on when we got here. If we have to go into their rooms, we will make sure they are back on again," Joey said.

"The rooms they are in have everything. There aren't any windows and the place has C.C.T.V. set up to keep an eye on them and the outside. I'll be talking to Cole on the internal phone soon and tell him what he has to do to keep his precious kid safe. No one can make external calls from that phone, so he's just going to have to wait for me to speak to him. I'm going to let him sweat for an hour," Lombardi said.

Minutes later, Feb had been rung by Joey with the instruction for him to release the cuffs off Cole and for him and Angelo to come out of the room and lock it. When Morelli appeared, he screamed at Lombardi.

"Leave her out of this. She's just a kid."

Lombardi reached into his coat pocket, produced his Beretta pistol and stepped up to Angelo. He brought the butt down hard on Morelli's shoulder, causing him to fall to the ground, crying out in pain. Lombardi bent over him while the rest of the crew looked on.

"Angelo, you are fast becoming more of a liability than an asset in this operation. You will either follow instructions or I will fucking kill you in a heartbeat. Just remember back to your friend, Leo. Understand me?" Lombardi bellowed, pressing the business end of the Beretta into his forehead.

Morelli slowly nodded his head in agreement. Lombardi continued to speak after indicating for the crew to go into one of the rooms.

"Angelo, if you want to stay with this operation and make some big money, just sit outside his room after we have finished here. Do not have any contact with Cole or his brat. Now, so we are all on the same page, I will fill you in on what Tony and I have planned. Some of you already know of the prize, but Tony's comrades don't," Lombardi said.

"Tuesday morning at seven-thirty there will be a shipment coming into Tullamarine airport. It contains three thousand pistols for the new police recruits that our State Government has promised to fill the Police Academy with. Our job is to change the delivery of these pistols from the State Government to us." He let this sink in before continuing.

"They will be off loaded from the plane at a private hangar away from the main terminal. We know this because Tony and I have inside information."

"We know that the truck, a white five-ton Hino will be parked in the loading bay from tomorrow morning. How do we know it is a white five-ton Hino? Information from another source. This person has control over this government vehicle from his job overseeing police firearms in Collingwood," Lombardi said.

"Just prior to the firearms crates being put into this vehicle, the Australian Security Services driver will be relieved by his boss, whom we have in the next room as our guest. He will tell the guard to take up the position as passenger in the rear National Security Services car that will follow the truck. Of course, they will be flanked by police motor bikes, and at the front will be Police vehicles set up for this operation including the Special Operations Group. Don't worry, we will not be engaging them on their turf," Lombardi said as he saw some raised eyebrows amongst his crew.

"Once on the Tullamarine Freeway, there will be a little diversion set up for those pricks and the rest. Let's just say that the Black Rats and the Carnivores will have a bit of an argument amongst themselves. Tony is setting this up himself. The cops will have to deal with that. After all, they have to protect the public, don't they? The finer details will be gone into over the next couple of days but for now I want everyone's mobile phones handed over to Tony. I don't care who wants to contact you or who you want to phone. No one, including myself, will have any contact with the outside world until Tuesday morning. Now, I know all of you except for Angelo have shooters on them. I want them locked in the Maserati for now. Tony and I have figured out the money side of this heist and let me tell you, it is worth a lot. At the end, I will look after my boys and Tony will look after his. You will all be paid out very well: Have no fears about that, "Lombardi said.

"So, let's set up house. Tony, get your boys to unload the van and get some food into the kitchen. Feb, you and Joey start checking the C.C.T.V. this place has. I want around the clock watch of the outside of this place. Anyone that comes around for no reason, I want to know about. Also..."

One of Tony Richard's boys stepped up to his President and spoke quietly, letting Lombardi see, but not hear.

"You got a problem, pal?" Lombardi questioned.

Before he could answer, Tony Richards spoke.

"My boys and I ain't handing over our firepower, Al. No fucking way. End of discussion," Tony said as he and his two boys stared back at Lombardi. "Should have asked me about that before you said it, Al. Let's just keep this nice and tidy. I know you don't trust me and my boys sure as hell don't trust you and will never go along with you giving them orders. All your requests will come through me. As for setting up the kitchen, just remember that Joey and Feb are my boys, too. They're just on loan to you at the moment, Al. They can all figure out who does what. Okay?" Richards said with steel in his voice.

"Whatever, Tony. Let's just get the job done," Lombardi replied with a dead pan look on his face. He walked away thinking at the same time.

Don't make the mistake of thinking this is an equal partnership, you idiot. You'll see what I mean on Tuesday. Equality comes out of the barrel of a fucking gun.

Chapter Forty-Eight

Tom Cole had a splitting headache. That didn't concern him though. There were plenty of problems that came before that. The immediate one was his daughter, Summer.

The two men had just backed out of the room after one of them released him from the handcuffs which had been fastened to a steel railing on the wall. He knew that he could have got himself released by gradually working at the wall holdings, but his priority was Summer's safety and getting a plan of what was going on before he blindly started an escape plan. He had no idea of what was outside the windowless room. His S.A.S. trained mind did however, notice the strange behaviour of one of his captives when Summer had received a pat on the shoulder as he backed out the door.

Cole immediately got to his feet when the door slammed shut on their prison. He picked up his daughter and gave her a hug as he whispered in her ear.

"You okay, sweetheart?"

Summer did not answer immediately, but kept hold of her father as he spoke again.

"Did they hurt you at all?"

Summer pulled back from the hug but kept her arms around her father's neck as she replied.

"The tape over my mouth was sticky, but the man took it off slowly. Where are we, daddy?"

"I don't know sweetheart, but I intend finding out. These men will have to answer to me as to why they took us from our house."

Cole placed Summer on her feet. She gripped his hand tightly as he walked her slowly around the large room which contained two fully made up beds. Inspecting the kitchen, he found the cupboards had ample food and even packets of lollies. Cole's mind automatically realised that this was most likely planned with a child in mind. The one thing he was looking for, he found in every room except the toilet. Ceiling cameras. They covered all aspects of the rooms. Everywhere they walked, they were being watched. To his mind, this was a positive. The fact that whoever was on the other side of these walls was not about to do anything to himself or his daughter quickly. That would have already happened in a rushed or botched kidnap. This had been thought through—to this point.

The only memory he had of the event so far was regaining partial consciousness as he was lifted out of the boot of a car before having a metallic object shoved under his chin as hands walked and dragged him to the room they were now in. There was one other memory though and it was something that he had remembered for years and would never forget. The lingering smell of gun oil.

During his time in the armed forces and especially through his tours of Afghanistan, it was an essential and daily routine to thoroughly clean any weapon you carried. The last thing you wanted was your firepower to jam up when you got into a firefight with the Taliban. The smell of gun oil would forever stay with him as a reminder of his service to his country.

Cole sat at the table in the eating area, picked up Summer and put her on his knee. He knew they were being watched through the cameras but decided to test if they also had microphones in them. He spoke out aloud.

"I don't know who you are or why you've taken us, but you'd better leave my little girl out of any plans you've got. Understand that from the start."

He deliberately said no more as he waited for some reaction from their kidnappers. Within a minute, the wall phone next to him rang. He picked it up slowly, put it to his ear but didn't speak. He wanted some sort of control over whoever was on the other end. He wanted the caller to go first. When the voice came over the line, he knew he'd had won on the microphone guess. His caller had heard him.

Lombardi spoke into the phone from an office next to the rooms where Cole and his daughter were held. He was sitting at a desk, looking directly at the computer screen that was displaying both his captives.

"Do as you're instructed, and you will both be released without harm when this is over," Lombardi said quietly into the speaker.

"What is it and when is it over?"

"It will be over on Tuesday. Relax. Make yourself a coffee and I will explain the what," Lombardi replied.

Win number two. Microphones and the job is on Tuesday. Got to be the Vic Pol job! Cole thought.

Tom Cole knew no matter what happened going forward, Summer's safety was paramount. The only way for this to happen was to play along with whatever game plan the person on the other end of the phone wanted him to. It was now Friday night and he had time to plan: And forward planning was what had kept him alive in the deserts of Afghanistan.

"Okay. Give me ten minutes to settle the child and I'll listen," Cole said, thus taking some initiative over the situation. He had set the small time frame to gauge the caller's reaction.

"Ten minutes and I'll call back. Remember Cole. I am in charge of this," Lombardi said with determination in his voice.

Microphones, Tuesday job and now my name. Definitely the police job! Win number three.

Chapter Forty-Nine

Coffee in hand and Summer settled on one of the beds watching the television that had been set up in the room, Cole waited calmly for the phone to ring. When it did, he picked up the receiver and again listened rather than talk. *Control the situation, Tom. Control.* He thought to himself.

"Cole? Or do I call you Tom?" Lombardi asked coolly.

Cole was not going to jump on the caller, but at the same time, being a trained negotiator himself, was not going to let the opposition have everything their own way. In a calm voice he replied.

"Whatever," he said, nothing else.

"Okay Tom. This is what it's all about and what you are going to do," Lombardi said, before being quickly cut off by Cole.

"Nothing is going to be done until I am guaranteed that my daughter is left completely out of whatever it is you have planned."

"She will be with you right through to early Tuesday morning. Nothing will happen to her" Lombardi said evenly.

"What happens after whatever it is you want me to do?" Cole said, deliberately leading the speaker to the end of the job rather than go straight to the start of it.

"You'll both be locked in here until you manage to get out. I'm sure you aren't the head of a security firm because you know how to rattle doors on night shift to see if they are locked or not. By the time you get out, my crew will be long gone. You are just an outsider in this, but an important one. Now, enough of the questions. Let's get to your part in the job itself," Lombardi said impatiently.

Win number four. 'My crew.' I'm talking to the planner then. Cole smiled inwardly.

"Go on," Cole said flatly.

"There is a shipment of firearms coming into the airport here on Tuesday morning. You are the Operations Manager for National Security Services, who have been given the contract to get them to the Police Armoury in Collingwood. I am now going to give you your instructions as to what you are going to do to execute my plan. I want you to listen up now and I'll come back to you in an hour for any questions you have. I may answer them or I may not, but it will make you feel as though you have contributed to my exit plan. This will be the heist of the century. Ready to listen, Tom?"

His plan. Not his team's plan. Doesn't trust the team. Paranoid? Exit plan. Not hanging around. Exit Australia? How does he know about Collingwood? Rat in the ranks, I bet.

"I'm listening," Tom said, settling back with his coffee.

Chapter Fifty

Big Al Lombardi sat in one of the partitioned office spaces thinking all the time of how he was going to bring off his masterplan. He only had one concern. That concern was in relation to his captive, Tom Cole.

He had only given him his part in the execution of the heist the next Tuesday morning, emphasising all the time the need for co-operation because of his daughter. Telling Cole this part of the plan did not worry him in the slightest because he would be long gone before he could get out and tell his story to the police.

What ate at him was the obvious lack of fear or respect in Cole's voice. Nothing seemed to faze him, when it was explained that he would be the truck driver in the heist. He showed a disinterested attitude towards the job. Cole had asked few questions and had that look and sound about him that he thought the job could never work. He acted almost bored with the whole plan. Although Lombardi studied him closely over the monitor, he noticed that Cole's demeanour never changed. Cole was either very dumb or very calculating. And it was safer to assume the latter.

The door opened, and the forms of Tony Richards and his two wingmen appeared. Richards spoke immediately after he had placed himself in a chair opposite Lombardi and his two associates had draped themselves over a nearby lounge.

"All right, Al. Time to get this little decoy sorted out. Let's explain to my boys here what they have to do to earn their money. I want it going off without a hitch because it's my pay day, too. Okay?"

Certainly is going to be your pay day, pal. In a way you'll never know about, Lombardi thought, snapping out of his mental block about Cole.

"Gents. The plan for you is probably one you will enjoy, especially as you say you are the new Nazis in Australia. This should suit you down to the ground. It's a chance to dominate your nearest rivals," Lombardi said, with a crooked grin on his mouth, before continuing.

"It's simple. When the convoy swings off the Tullamarine Freeway at Brunswick Road to cut through West Brunswick and Carlton on its way to the Police Armoury at Collingwood, the Special Operations Group vehicle, a black Toyota Landcruiser, with probably four of those arseholes on board, will be the first vehicle car in the convoy. Second will be one of those new Highway Patrol BMW M 5's. Behind that will be the truck carrying the shooters and behind that will be one National Security Services sedan with two on board. Also, there will be two Police solos somewhere from front to back. Knowing how the S.O.G. work though, the solos won't be around them just in case something goes down quickly. Those bastards would run over their own grandmothers to get into some action. We will be supplying them with just that. Action. What Tony will explain to you now is how the Black Rats are going to create another Milperra bikie war without getting themselves shot—hopefully.

The mention of the infamous Father's Day bikie massacre in nineteen eighty-four between the Comancheros, Bandidos and Gypsy Jokers outlaw motorcycle gangs in the carpark of the Viking tavern at Milperra, south west of Sydney, where seven people lost their lives, brought the associates of Tony Richards to full attention. He took over the briefing.

"Where we are now is only down the road from where it will take place. It will happen in the car park of the Brunswick Italian Social Club which is right next to the freeway at Brunswick Road. When the convoy goes under Moreland Road, Al will see it and ring me. I'll then make an anonymous call on a burner phone to Police Communications telling them there is a bikie shooting war about to start at the Brunswick Italian Social club car park between the Black Rats and the Carnivores. By the time they jump on that they will have no choice but to divert the nearest S.O.G. unit to it, convoy or no convoy. They will come up the Brunswick Road exit, turn left and then immediate right and down into the car park of the club. Those pricks will be that amped up, they will go down there just itching to run over a heap of Harleys and blow the bikie world into little pieces."

Richards stopped talking so that his two offsiders could take in what had just been said. His Sergeant-at-Arms spoke up.

"How exactly are you going to set up this car park shit?"

"We have a parcel which is on ice at the moment in a freezer van. It will be dumped outside the headquarters of the Carnivores very late on Monday night. It used to ride that Harley that is down the back of our headquarters. Our former probationary member from Border Force decided to hand it back. The body will have a toe tag saying that the Carnivores had him killed and the Black Rats want retribution. It will also contain a challenge to come to the Italian Cub car park the next morning, tooled up, to settle the matter. An eye for an eye deal. I know the President of that shit pot club will ride in, all guns blazing. They will think it is a set up when they see the black van from here, with the Black Rats patch on its side and blacked out windows parked in the middle of the car park. You two will have left it there earlier on. You will be long gone by the time those dickheads arrive. Their idiot President will pull out a sawn-off twelve gauge from his paniers and start using the van as target practice. He won't give a fuck if there are Black Rats in it or not. His dumb mates will fall in line, also. They should be in full shotgun mode when the cavalry rides over the hill. It will be the shootout at the O.K. Corral all over again. I'd love to see it, but I'll be up the road setting up the next bit of the plan. You two will need to make your way back on foot to the factory via the side streets. That's when we will need you for the transfer of the shooters to the other truck."

"That takes care of the S.O.G.," Lombardi said. "What will happen then is the lead cop car with their fearless leader, Tony Signo fucking rotto, on board will be taken out by Tony here with the old Ford at the intersection of Fleming Street. We've had a bull bar fitted to it at Tony's factory. He will hit that Beemer right across the front so that it will be fucked for driving any further. Hopefully, whoever is in it gets whacked, too.

Without doubt, the two motor bike cops will stop to comfort their fucking brothers. Tony will have stopped just up the road so it will look like it is just an accident. As soon as the bike cops get off their bikes, Tony will take off along Fleming Street. Next, our Mr. Cole who will be driving the shooters truck that has stopped by this stage will slam it into reverse and go right into the front of the Security vehicle so hard that it will be out of action. He is under no illusions about this and his next move which is to then go forward and knock over the two motorbikes. His daughter's life depends on both these hits. He then accelerates up Brunswick Road and by the time he swings into the factory, we will all be back here." A victorious smile appeared on his demented face. Richards then spoke again.

"We've checked the train timetables for the rail crossing up near here at Brunswick Road. It's going to be early on Tuesday morning and it's a public holiday, so that won't be a problem. I've also checked the factories around here for C.C.T.V. and the Sydney Road and Brunswick Road intersection for traffic cameras. There is one camera over near the Seven-Eleven on the opposite corner, but that will be fixed with a can of spray paint the night before. The Techs that fix those things won't even bother to look at it for days. Mr. Lombardi and I have put a lot of work into it. We will not only take the shooters but hopefully the fucking cops will play ball by taking out the other shooters. The fucking Carnivores!"

Lombardi watched the smiles spread on the faces of the bikies as they imagined the demise of the Carnivores.

Yes. Take out the Carnivores and shoot down the Black Rats. These three won't be flying anywhere.

Chapter Fifty-One

Jill Norton looked up at her kitchen clock sitting above the fridge. It was nine-fifteen Saturday morning. She had read and re-read the Sun-Herald Saturday morning paper thoroughly and had put it to one side. It sat next to the pancake mixture that she had made earlier. The breakfast that she had promised Summer. She knew the little girl loved pancakes with strawberry jam.

She wondered if she had misheard Tom. No! She was sure he said he had to go to work this morning and would she look after little Summer.

When the clock showed nine-thirty, she got up from the table and went to the open back door where she could see her husband working away in his vegetable garden. Calling out to him, she said.

"Going next door to Tom's to see what's going on with Summer. Don't forget we have Susie's party at Dom's tonight."

Jill got back a wave from her husband's left hand as he bent over a carrot patch he was tending to.

Walking out of her house to the street, the first thing she noticed was that Tom's Toyota wasn't there.

Strange. Gone to work? Where's Summer? Take her to work? Never did before.

Up at the front door, her police training kicked in. The fly wire door was ajar but the wooden front door was locked.

Not like Tom. In or out of the house, he always made sure the security door was locked. Just the way he was. Not like him at all.

She rapped on the door. At first lightly, and then quite loudly. There was no response.

An early call to work? He knows he can leave Summer with us anytime day or night. Better give him a call.

Standing in the front yard of Tom's house, she flicked through the numbers on her phone and rang him. The call rang out and went through to his message bank.

"Tom. Jill Norton here. Can you give me a ring, please? It's about nine forty-five on Saturday morning."

After putting her phone away, she walked back next door to her house and decided to wait a while longer. Tom's absence didn't worry her too much, but she did think it was a bit strange.

After lunch, and with her husband glued to the television, showing the replay of the football from the night before at the Melbourne Cricket Ground with a dominant Carlton win over Richmond, she went back to Tom's house only to find nothing had changed from her previous visit earlier in the morning. No Tom. No Summer.

Surely, he wouldn't have taken Summer to work for this long.

This time, she hit the speed dial on her phone for the Carlton Police Station.

"Senior Constable Sheahan, Carlton police. How can I help?"

"Mr. Sheahan," Jill said dryly to the officer she had trained at front counter duties a couple of years before. "Nice to see you are answering the phone with such a sweet, kind and helpful tone."

Sheahan cut straight back, recognising his mentor's voice in a heartbeat.

"My dear, what can I do for an esteemed elder member of the beautiful suburb of Carlton?"

Jill smiled to herself. "Listen son. How'd you like me to come down there, pick up the roster clipboard and give you a whack over the head? I'll show you what an esteemed elder citizen is capable of."

"Geez, Jill. Hope you've been doing your weights since you've retired. The roster isn't on a clipboard any more for your information. It's on Microsoft Excel on the computer. You'll have to pick up the desktop and throw it at me," Sheahan said laughing at the same time before continuing. "Jokes aside, Jill. Could do with you back here. Some of these kids from the

Academy are so far up themselves they walk around on tiptoes. Think they have the answers to everything as long as it's on a bloody computer."

"That's exactly what I said to you the day you arrived at the old station. Actually, I think it was my go-to speech for all of you wet behind the ears saviours of the free world when you were all freshly pressed uniforms, shiny shoes and wide open starry eyes. You in particular along with young Max Tyler. He thought he was Superman and you thought you were the Lone Ranger," Jill Norton said, with a hint of the old mother in her voice.

"Hey, don't compare me with some cowboy from your black and white television days. Anyhow, citizen. I am a busy little copper here at the moment. Enough chit chat. What's up, Jill? What can I do for you?"

"Just wanted to know if your lovely Sergeant McLaren is in, Mick?"

"Yep. I'll put you through. I think she's upstairs. Before I do though, I hope you're coming to Susie's party tonight at Dom's. Wouldn't be the same without our Valour winner," Sheahan said in reference to the prestigious award that had been presented to Jill Norton after the famous night shift shootout with Mickey Midolini in the watch-house of the old Carlton Police station a couple of years back. The photo from her Valour Award investiture at Government House hung proudly in the foyer of the new police station.

"Be there with bells on, Mick. Expect your wife Colleen to be there so she can keep an eye on you and Dom's wine cellar," Jill signed off with as the call was transferred.

"Jill. Lovely to hear from you. What's up?" Kate McLaren said.

"Hi Kate. Sorry to sound a bit presumptuous. Tom said to me yesterday that he was going to pick you up on the way to Susie's party tonight. Just wondering if you know where he is at the moment. He was going to drop Summer over for breakfast this morning before going to work for a bit. He never brought her over and his car's gone. Did he say anything to you at all?" Jill said, with a note of concern now creeping into her voice.

"No Jill. Nothing at all," a surprised Kate McLaren replied. "He and Summer are meant to be picking me up about seven. That's why I'm doing an early shift toady. Got heaps on with a special job at the moment for Mr. Stone. Some planning that will keep me going all day. Have to rush home after that and get ready. To be honest, I wasn't expecting to hear from him until he picked me up."

"Okay, Kate," Jill said with a flatness to her voice. "I'll have to put the strawberry pancake mix away for another day. Was looking forward to discussing girl stuff with little Summer over breakfast. Better than listening to those bloody television commentators going on about Carlton being the red-hot premiership favourites just because they beat lowly Richmond."

"Tell me about it," the exasperated Melbourne supporter said. "I had to throw the morning shift van and car crew out of the mess room and back on the road. It must be a prerequisite that if you work at Carlton you also have to barrack for the damn team."

Jill laughed as she replied. "Don't complain to that bloody Bluebagger Signorotto or he'll have your name down with the Special Events office in town to work the Carlton Cheer Squad bays for every Carlton home match at the 'G' for the next two years. Anyway, Kate, thanks for listening and I'll see you tonight."

Hanging up, Jill walked slowly back to her house.

The two experienced police officers, one retired and one working, both went about their days, however, neither could help thinking as Saturday afternoon dragged on, that something, just something, was strange about Tom and Summer's no show.

Chapter Fifty-Two

Tom Cole and his daughter had been left alone through Friday night into Saturday. He was not about to do anything but look after Summer. Now was not the time to do anything drastic: That time would come.

The first thing was to get her some breakfast in their 'prison cell' and try to explain to her what was happening to her child's world. Summer had tossed and turned all night in the strange bed away from her toys and normal surroundings. Cole himself had done what he had always done in his S.A.S. days out on the field of battle. He had trained himself to sleep with his eyes partially closed, so that he could be fully awake in a millisecond. He also sat upright with his back against the only entrance door. He could easily go three nights in this fashion and still function perfectly, both physically and mentally. Knowing that whoever was looking at them through the cameras would think it very strange brought a wry smile to his face. It was obvious to him that the kidnappers had never checked his background.

Cole deliberately ignored the internal phone when it rang. He was having breakfast with Summer and at the same time explaining to her that she would be going home soon and for her not to fret.

"These people here want me to help them steal something that doesn't belong to them. I don't want to help them, so I think we are going to let them think we are for a while. Let's treat it all like a game and pretend we are having a holiday in a caravan without windows," he said with an animated voice as the phone began to ring again.

Stepping away from their breakfast, he picked up the phone and looked directly up at the camera above him so the caller could see his face. He didn't give the person a chance to speak.

"I am talking to my child. You can call back in half an hour," he said, quickly replacing the receiver into its cradle.

On the other end, a furious Lombardi threw the phone onto the desk and screamed at Tony Richards, who was standing beside him.

"This prick thinks he's in charge of this show. Put a balaclava on and get in there and show him otherwise."

"Al, this guy is no fool. He's been around and run things his own way before. He's winding you up to see how you react. Can't you see that? On the day of the job he will cooperate because if he doesn't, he is putting his kid at risk and we know he won't do that. You should have snatched him without the kid. Kids just fuck things up. By his build and the way he carries himself I'd bet he's ex-military or something and used to winning. Just go along with him. Give him his kiddie time and we'll ring back when the half hour is up," Richards said trying to placate him.

"Twenty-seven minutes now," Lombardi said, looking at his expensive Bulgari Italia gold watch.

"Whatever. Just cool it," Richards said angrily.

A few minutes before the half hour timeline had elapsed, Tom Cole placed himself, coffee cup in hand, in the same position in which he had listened to his captor the night before. Same expression, same crossed legged seated appearance. When the phone rang, he didn't even look at it but just picked it up and remained silent. Seconds passed before Lombardi spoke.

"Cole. This morning, your mobile rang. A woman left a voice message wanting you to ring back. It showed a private number. Who would that be?"

As a trained army negotiator, Cole could read people's voices. He knew how far to push people and then reel them back in for his own benefit. He still had some wiggle room left, he thought.

"You've got my phone pal. Not me. How would I know, genius?"

Before Richards could grab the phone away, Lombardi exploded like a bucket full of fireworks.

"Don't be a fucking smartarse. It won't be good for your kid's health," he screamed down the line.

Cole immediately hung up the phone as Richards spun on Lombardi.

"Let me fucking talk to him. Your hot Italian temper is making things worse," he said loudly.

When the phone rang again next to Cole, he picked it up, but this time spoke first with a steely voice.

"I will not talk to you at all when you threaten my family. Keep talking like that and I will keep hanging up."

"Okay. Understood. But you are going to text this woman back," Richards said.

Cole knew that the text must have come from Jill Norton because of two things. First, he hadn't brought Summer in for breakfast and secondly it was a private number. Even as a retired copper, she wasn't giving her number out to anyone.

Good old Jill. On my case straight away.

He also realised immediately that he was now dealing with someone else on the phone.

Good. Pissed the other bloke right off.

Richards continued talking. "Just tell them you've gone away with the kid for the long weekend and you'll be back late Monday night. Do you have a relative up country that you can say you have gone to visit?"

"Yeah, I've got a sister up Yarrawonga way," Cole lied and continued quickly. "That's a better tone of voice. The other dickhead obviously can't control his temper. I wouldn't work for someone like that. You can't trust that type to stay on an even keel."

"What about the voicemail? You know you have no choice but to text her back. Tell her you are up country and out of signal range for a call," Richards replied without mention to the 'dickhead' comment.

"I won't know who it is until I listen to it," Cole lied again, knowing it could only be Jill Norton.

"No," Richards said emphatically. You can listen through your phone when I hold up the mobile and I will reply with your text from here."

Cole looked directly at the camera and spoke.

"Might work for that, but I've got to tell you that me and my daughter are expected at a birthday party tonight. If we don't turn up, we will be missed."

Richards thought for a moment.

"Give me the number and you can give them the same reply."

"My daughter was scared stiff by you lot last night. The only one she wasn't terrified of was the guy that had her in the car. The one that promised no one would hurt her. To save a lot of trouble, why don't you send him in here with my phone. I'll show him my contacts and he can make sure I only text them."

Think quick, Tom.

"Even if I listen over this phone into my mobile, it won't work. You'll have to put the mobile to your phone and then it'll have to play through to this phone. It will be mobile to landline to another landline," Cole said, hoping the caller would go for it. His mind was forming a plan on the run.

He let the suggestion hang in the air, knowing the guy on the receiver would be discussing it with his boss. The caller had not corrected Cole when he had said that he shouldn't be working for someone he didn't trust. This guy wasn't the boss!

Cole could hear a muffled conversation on the other end.

"Might as well do it, Al. Even if we try the voicemail over the phones, he's just going to say he can't pick the voice. Let's just get Morelli to go in there, balaclava on, with the phone and he can check the texts before Cole sends them," Richards half whispered to Lombardi.

"Whatever!" an impatient Lombardi answered. "We have to keep his contacts bluffed till Monday night."

Richards took his hand off the receiver and spoke to Cole again.

"Okay. We'll be sending a guy in with the phone. You show him the contacts, type the texts and show him before you send them. All right?" Richards said.

"That'll work," Cole replied with quiet relief.

"It had better fucking work, or else. One more thing. Seeing you are the boss of your side of the operation your company has on Tuesday, what other calls or texts are you expecting before then?" Richards said.

"None," Cole replied truthfully. "As you said, I'm the boss. I run the show."

What you fucking think, Cole, Lombardi thought, listening in on another extension.

"We'll send our man in soon," Richards said and then hung up.

Cole got up and walked over to Summer, smiling as he turned away from the camera.

Forward planning, boys. Forward planning. It's what keeps you alive!

Chapter Fifty-Three

Angelo Morelli thought about saying no to any demands from either Lombardi or Richards. He knew he was in a no-win situation with the kidnapping and what was being planned for Tuesday. It was either gaol or elimination. Simple as that.

Only himself, Joey and Feb had been witnesses to the brutal execution of Leo Carbone at the Brunswick safe house. From that moment on, he knew he had a use by date. He no longer cared about Joey or Feb. Their chance had come and gone the day before when they blindly followed instructions and kidnapped Cole and his daughter.

If either of them truly believed they would be saved, or even for that matter helped, by being 'patched' members of the Black Rats motorcycle gang, then they were dead wrong. Dead wrong. Three witnessed the horrendous slaying. Three witnesses would die. Even Richards wouldn't care as long as he was going to get a cut of the profits, because he certainly wasn't doing this for nothing. Lombardi would see to it that before the firearms got to their final destination, all of them would be given the 'Lygon Street kiss.'

Morelli didn't know why Richards had called him, but he was honestly at the point where he didn't care anymore. His life was coming to a sudden end no matter what Lombardi promised him. The only thing he was truly sorry for was the situation he had put the little girl in. This was doing his head in. He stood and stared at Lombardi and his offsider.

Richards suddenly picked up a balaclava from the desk and threw it at him.

"Got a small job for you, Angelo. About time you earned your keep. Get that on," he said, indicating the balaclava that Morelli was clutching in his hand.

"Our man in there is going to send a couple of text messages from his phone. I want you to check the numbers and contacts he shows you and what he types before he sends them. One should be going to some bitch that left a voicemail this morning. He reckons he won't be able to tell who it is from relaying it through the phones here. The other one is to get out of some party he is meant to be going to tonight. Check what he sends."

"Why am I going in there?" Morelli said slowly, fearing some type of trap. "You have his mobile. Why can't you do it from here?"

"We want him to keep that kid of his under control. He reckons she is shit scared of everyone but you for some fucking reason. You must have played nice guy to her in the car. Take the phone in there and then bring it back. Is that too hard to understand?" Richards said, with a menacing voice as he stepped within inches of Morelli and handed him Cole's phone along with his fetid breath nearly making Angelo gag. Morelli didn't blink. If there was one thing he could do to help this kid, he would. The consequences didn't matter to him anymore. What little conscience he had left was telling him to salvage some of the situation.

He was putting the balaclava on slowly when Lombardi spoke.

"Remember Leo, won't you, my friend? Stick with us and your life will be a bed of roses. Al Lombardi will make sure of it."

A six-foot-deep bed of earth covered in roses more likely, you lying son of a bitch, Angelo thought.

"The camera will be on you both just to be sure," Richards piped in, with a sneer on his stubbled covered face.

Morelli picked up the key to the 'cell' and walked out.

"Why the fuck is Morelli in this?" Richards said angrily, turning on Lombardi. "Is it just some sort of control thing with you, mate? King of Carlton and all that bullshit. You like to keep people under house arrest or something. I know all about you and the house at Brunswick. Joey and Feb might be getting paid by you, but they are Black Rats and I know about what went on there. Two went in and only one came out. It's not that I give a fuck, but this prick has no cajones mate. None at all. He's a fucking dead set liability."

Lombardi couldn't do anything but absorb the abuse. His mind was only concentrating on the job and Italy. In one way, he was glad Richards knew about what happened. It would make it simpler to eradicate him also.

"He tried to steal my Maserati. He got caught and I thought he and his friend would be okay on this job. I used Morelli to track Cole from work to his house rather than use your thugs. Don't worry. I'll take care of things after Tuesday. It's not a problem," Lombardi said.

Richards looked at Lombardi and spoke with a voice as cold as ice.

"He doesn't leave here, Al. If you haven't put a bullet in him straight after he loads the truck on Tuesday morning, I'll whack him myself. There's too much at stake here. This has to be down to us Black Rats and you. End of story. Cole and his kid won't know who we are, but that Morelli is nothing but dead weight. We can get rid of him on the highway, bit by bit. I've got a chainsaw in the truck."

Even he, the King of Carlton, Big Al Lombardi, felt a shiver travel up his spine with the mention of the chainsaw.

Chapter Fifty-Four

Tom Cole heard the door unlock. He immediately placed Summer behind him as the balaclava clad Morelli entered the room and spoke with a shaky voice, while inadvertently smiling at the little girl from under his disguise.

"You know what you have to do. Here is the phone," he said, handing it to Cole, while at the same time squeezing the hand of the kidnap victim three times.

Cole immediately stared into the slit in Morelli's balaclava and could see the pleading look he was getting back.

You don't want any part of this, do you? How do I tell him to help us?

Turning to Summer, Cole indicated to her to go into the other room where the television was. She disappeared very quickly.

"Are you the one that said nothing would happen to my daughter?" Cole said in a hushed voice.

Morelli replied with a faltering voice as he nodded, "She's just a kid."

Cole knew how to read the movements of both eye and body in his opponents. It was what had kept him alive in close quarter combat. He knew this person's heart wasn't in the battle.

"Thanks," he said quietly, noticing the man's throat constricting as he could almost see tears in his eyes. He waited for his captor to make the next move.

Morelli's voice came out, first as a croak and then after a cough, in a very strained manner.

"They want you to show me the numbers and the texts. Then you send them. Listen to the voicemail and then show me the numbers."

Cole did as he was instructed, and after listening to the voicemail knew he was correct. It was Jill Norton's voice. He immediately scrolled through his contacts. This was where his plan would either work or fail.

Tom Cole had always made a habit of never putting the real name of a contact in his phone for security reasons. He had shortcuts and monikers for every person. He knew them all including Jill Norton. Hers was Val. To Cole it was an honour to refer to Jill Norton as Val, which signified the Valour Award she had been presented with. Showing Morelli the contact Val, he spoke.

"This is the one in the voicemail. Val's her name. I'll send her a text if that's okay?"

"Show me before you send it," Morelli said, eyes flicking between Cole and the camera in the ceiling.

Cole nodded and proceeded to type the text into the phone.

Hey. Summer here has been playing up a bit. In Yarrawonga with my sister for a break. Be back late Monday night. Out of range on the farm up here. See ya.

He could see that when he showed his captor the phone contact that he looked scared and worried—even through the balaclava. Morelli nodded and Cole hit send.

The next text was the important one. He scrolled down to the entry 'Sig S.' This was the entry for Kate McLaren. He had it under that as a reference to the pistol Kate used at the range, a Sig Sauer nine millimetre. He showed it to Morelli.

"Who's this?" He said, qualifying it by adding. "They'll ask."

Crunch time. Cole thought.

"Her name's Sigrid. It's her party tonight," Cole lied, as seconds passed.

"Type the text and show me," Morelli replied.

Cole nodded and started to text. After this he had to delete both the 'Sig S' and the next one down which was 'Sig'. "That stood for Senior Sergeant Tony Signorotto. If either of those contacts were opened up it would show their details as both police officers at the Carlton Police Station. He typed quickly.

Not really into Lonsdale Street Greek food. Would have been there if it was Lygon Street Italian. Pass on my apologies to Rock. In Yarrawonga at the moment at my sisters. Out of call range.

Cole held the phone to Morelli's face, and after getting a quick nod back, he hit the send button to 'Sig S'. As Morelli turned around slightly to where Summer was sitting watching television, Cole quickly deleted both of the contacts for Kate and Tony, after manoeuvring himself so his back was to the camera. There was one last thing to do.

Handing the phone back to his captor, after also flicking it to silent, Cole dropped it onto the ground near himself. Both he and Morelli bent to pick it up with Cole feigning a stumble, landing his shoe on the face of the phone with enough force to completely shatter the screen. Picking it up, he looked at it quickly making sure the screen was so cracked you couldn't read a thing on it. He gave it back to Morelli.

"Don't think they'll let me use it again, anyway," Cole said, as he took a huge gamble and winked at Morelli.

Angelo Morelli looked at Cole and again squeezed his hand three times. As Morelli turned and walked past Cole, he whispered.

"Anything she needs."

Nothing else need be said.

There are three captives here. Not two. Cole thought.

Back outside, Morelli handed the damaged phone back to Richards.

"What did he send?" Richards said.

"Two messages. One to a Val and one to a Sigrid. Told Val that he was up country and the other one that he couldn't go to a party in Lonsdale Street tonight because he was up country. That's all," Morelli said honestly.

"He has two more calls to make. One tomorrow morning and one on Monday about lunchtime," Lombardi said to Richards at the same time as indicating to Morelli to leave.

"To his company?" Richards said, looking back at Lombardi.

"Absolutely. He might be the boss of this operation, but he's not the owner of the company. I've checked that out through the Business Registration Directory. Someone named Ian Kent is registered as the owner and general manager of National Security Services. This is a government contract and he will be all over it looking for more secure contracts and will expect calls from Cole. He can use a burner phone and call him tomorrow and Monday telling him that he is away but will be back late Monday night. He just needs to tell him that he will see the security crew at seven on Tuesday morning at the loading dock. I want you to go in and listen both times, Tony. Enough of this fucking around with phones. I'll feel a lot better when it's our rules and our way. That goes with everything from now on. Agreed?"

"Agreed. Should keep the big boss satisfied and off his case," Richards said, while looking at Cole through the monitor.

Richards had seen Cole's phone being stood on, and looked at it without saying anything, before throwing it into the bin nearby.

"If he still has a job with his company after losing three thousand shooters, they'll have to give him a new one," he said with a laugh.

Chapter Fifty-Five

Kate McLaren had been working with Task Force Calibre till late Saturday afternoon.

Along with Tony Signorotto, Phil Stone, Max Tyler and Chloe Schaeffer moving around the cramped upstairs office at the Carlton Police Station, there were also police from the Brunswick Highway Patrol and the Special Operations Group who had come in to receive their latest briefing and pick up a copy of the Operation Order pertaining to the firearms shipment, which Kate was just doing the final check of. Any further last-minute changes would not be in print: They would be done 'on the run.'

The one omission to the resources that was of concern to Phil Stone and his team was that the Police helicopter would not be available. It had been a toss up at a much higher Command level as to whether to send the Air Wing to the firearms convoy or a previously booked priority with a drug raid up on the border with New South Wales at Mildura. Politics won out and they would have to go without the chopper in Melbourne.

It was just before five o'clock when the Highway Patrol and the Special Operations Group had been given their instructions and left the Task Force office, when Stone called a halt to the day's work.

"Listen up. We are pretty sure we have covered all our bases. We know that John Moore has told Lombardi about the date and time of the firearms shipment into Tullamarine. That happened at that Vietnamese restaurant. Moore will be arrested, one way or the other, once these pistols are safely tucked in bed at the Police Armoury. That will be the first and last time he sees them. Superintendent Archer is drooling at the prospect of slapping a set of cuffs on him there and then. He will be handed over to the C.I.U. and has a lot of explaining to do with the videos we have of him at the Crown Casino, along with his bank account statements. No doubt Moore has passed on the convoy route also. Senior Sergeant Signorotto and I have had a long discussion with the Highway Patrol and the S.O.G. and decided not to change it. We want the heavy hitters right in front of the truck, not blocked by the National Security Services car at the rear.

"At the pointy end, the S.O.G. will head the convoy. The second vehicle will be a Brunswick Highway Patrol BMW sedan from Dawson Street Traffic Headquarters. A Sergeant from there will be driving. Senior Sergeant Signorotto will be in the front seat and I will be in the back monitoring the convoy comms. The S.O.G. Toyota Land Cruiser with four of their finest on board and armed to the teeth will have enough firepower to fight a small war. Behind us will be the white five-ton Hino truck that the Armoury left there yesterday. It will have a National Security Services driver and in the passenger seat will be Tom Cole, who you know, is the Operations Manager for them. There will be one hundred and fifty black Pelikan brand gun cases, each with twenty Smith and Wesson Police and Military nine-millimetre pistols. In addition, there will be approximately fifteen further Pelikan cases carrying the empty magazines and what adds up to thirty rounds of ammo for each pistol. All the cases will be padlocked, and the master key will be with me in our car. The barrel torches for the firearms will be coming next week. We don't have to worry about those."

"Are the shooters able to be used straight away boss?" Max Tyler chipped in.

"Good question Max. The answer is no, basically. Each of these pistols need to be stripped down, checked, oiled and put back together before they can be fired. There is a small metal block in the breech of each one. You can actually put the full magazine in and then rack the slide so that there is one round up the spout, but when you pull the trigger, that little block prevents the firing pin from hitting the back of the round. It sounds like a misfire, but it won't do any good until that block is removed. You can keep pulling the trigger until you are blue in the face, but it won't fire. A big job for the boys and girls at the Armoury to set them all up before they fire their first rounds in the hands of recruits at the Academy. Anyway, back to the convoy."

"We will have two wingmen from the Dawson Street Special Solos Section riding shotgun for us. They will be zipping up and down the convoy constantly and are used to escorting V.I. P's from Tullamarine airport, where they facilitate non-stop runs to their destination. Hopefully they will get us out of any traffic issues that arise. There shouldn't be much traffic around though because it is a rostered day off for the tradies."

"We've distributed the Operation Order to all relevant departments including D.24. All comms will go through them and they have given us a dedicated channel for the Operation. Call signs will all be prefixed by 'Calibre.' The list of all call signs is under Appendix 'C' at the rear of the Operation Order, and if I may give a big thanks to Chloe for compiling all of this.

"I've taught her well," Phil said with a dead pan face while all the others in the Task Force gave him the Bronx cheer.

"It's a pity that we can't have Air 490 hovering over us, but as a lowly Superintendent, I was outweighed by a Deputy Commissioner, who is obviously under the pump from some member of Parliament regarding a drug bust in his electorate up near Mildura. Apparently that job will go all day and the headlines should help both the D.C. and the politician in the Herald-Sun on Wednesday."

Sergeant McLaren, yourself, Max and Chloe will be outside the Police Armoury in Cambridge Street from seven in the morning along with quite a few local Highway Patrol crew and units from Collingwood, Carlton and Richmond. Kate, you've put together a good traffic plan which is Appendix 'D'. Your job will be to co-ordinate traffic flow so that when we come south along Wellington Street from Alexandra Avenue, we don't get held up. We will turn right into Peel Street and then immediate left into Cambridge Street and swing left into the loading bay Our car will go in with the truck right behind. The S.O.G. and the N.S.S. car will remain outside. If Lombardi and Richards want a piece of the action there, then I'm sure our S.O.G. boys will be more than willing to entertain them."

"I think we are all in agreement, that if Lombardi tries anything, it will be somewhere at that end. It's strange that Max and Chloe have been past his place in Lygon Street earlier today and it appears that it is closed for renovations. There is definitely something going on, because I've had Mick York and Johnny Petran from the Melbourne Divisional Response Unit looking everywhere for him. The word on the street is that he and his flash Maserati have gone to ground. They will keep looking for him over the weekend and Monday. Let's hope they come up with a sighting."

"Everyone will carry full operational equipment in case we have to go 'hands on'. Okay with you, Tony?" Stone said looking at his Senior Sergeant who appeared to be as happy as the proverbial cat in the cream factory.

Signorotto replied calmly, with steel in his voice and a glint in his eye.

"Sir, I could still roll over the bonnet of a police car if I had to. Don't you worry about that. It'll be good to get some fresh air on Tuesday. You know me, sir. Always lead from the front. If Lombardi wants to upset my apple cart, he'll be one very sorry King of Carlton."

You are still the hard man, aren't you, Tony. Just itching for action and only need the S.O.G. as back up rather than you backing them up. Times change: Hard men don't, Stone thought, smiling inwardly as he turned and kept speaking.

"Kate. Any questions?"

"No, boss. We'll get you into the Armoury A.S.A.P."

Stone looked around the faces of his small Task Force.

"Okay. All back for a final briefing on Monday morning. Now that we are all seeing each other at Susie's party tonight, let's get out of here, put on some glad rags and look forward to a good night. What time at Dom's again, Tony?"

Tony Signorotto looked at the wall clock which was showing just shy of five-fifteen. "Seven onwards, you lot. Susie's looking forward to it and so am I. No doubt Dom will put on a good night as per usual. We have the upstairs room to ourselves. See you all there."

With that, the Task Force Calibre personnel dispersed and headed off downstairs.

Chapter Fifty-Six

After throwing a plain jacket on over her uniform shirt to drive home, Kate headed downstairs, grabbed her phone and went straight to her car.

Supermarket, home, shower, change and wait for Tom and Summer. Get a move on, Kate.

During the afternoon with the Task Force, she had deliberately left her mobile phone on her desk downstairs so as not to be disturbed. She didn't even think to look at it, which would have told her she had two text messages from earlier in the day. One from Tom and another from Jill Norton.

Stepping out of a quick shower about six o'clock, she suddenly realised she had not checked her mobile in hours. Drying her hair one handed with a towel, she picked up the phone and saw the messages, realising they had arrived some hours before.

Upon opening the one from Tom, she felt at first deflated then confused.

Greek food. Lonsdale Street. Rock. Yarrawonga. What on earth's this about?

She stood there, dripping water onto the floor, thinking about what she should do. Besides the feeling of being stood up, she really didn't feel like going to the party by herself.

Bloody men. Who does he think he is. Out of range. Bullshit.

Staring at her phone, she suddenly recalled there was another message. Opening it, she saw Jill Norton's name come up in the display. It said to ring her A.S.A.P. Thinking it may be something to do with Tom, she called her immediately.

"Jill. Sorry. Just saw your message. Been flat out all day. Haven't been near my phone," Kate said.

Jill Norton got straight to the point.

"Kate. Have you heard from Tom? I got this strange text hours ago about Summer playing up and they've gone to Yarrawonga to stay with his sister. Did he call you at all? Told me yesterday he was picking you up for the party."

Kate cut in quickly with her reply.

"Jill, I got some weird text about tonight being Greek food in Lonsdale Street and apologising to whoever Rock is. Also, from what he told me one day, he doesn't even have a sister let alone one in Yarrawonga. I don't know what to think, especially now he's not picking me up for the party," Kate said worriedly.

"Is he working on anything that's giving him grief at the moment?"

"I can't really say anything, Jill, but he's on a subcommittee for a police job that Tony and Phil have had to form a Task Force for. That's why I've been working all day. It's all hush hush stuff, if you know what I mean. Not allowed to talk about it Jill. Sorry."

"That's okay, luv. Know all about secret squirrel stuff from when I was in. This is all too closely connected, Kate. What worries me the most though, is that little Summer is not around. Tom is big enough and ugly enough to take care of himself. We both know his background. How about we pick you up and take you to Dom's?" Jill said quietly.

"Don't really feel like going now to be honest, Jill," Kate replied.

"Kate. Think about the two texts. We need to get Phil and Tony aside tonight and tell them. See what they think."

"Know what you mean, but I don't know what they can do on a Saturday night. I'll try and track down someone from National Security Services tomorrow and see what I can find out."

"How about we swing past your place in about thirty minutes and then we can all get our heads together. Sound good?" Jill said insistently.

"Yeah. Okay. I'll be ready. I'll text you my address in Flemington. Thanks Jill."

"See you soon. Don't worry, We'll sort it out," Jill said finishing the call.

Very strange. He's a big boy, though. If he's in trouble, I'm sure he will know how to handle himself, Jill thought.

Chapter Fifty-Seven

Dom was in his element. The top floor of his bistro was crowded with the type of people that he loved: Family and friends and lots of children. You just had to have the young ones to make the occasion. If you left them out when they were young, you would never get them back in the family fold.

The birthday lady, Susie Signorotto, was sitting at one of the long tables, deep in laughter and conversation with his wife, Maria. The Santino and Signorotto families had been friends for a long time, and he was as proud as could be that Susie and Tony had chosen him and Maria to be Godparents to their beautiful little daughter, Gracie.

There were quite a few police at the party from Carlton and the surrounding stations of Collingwood, Fitzroy and Richmond. Tony Signorotto had been a respected cop around the traps for years. The sight of the big man with three stripes grasping some drugged out cretin by the neck and lifting them off you was a life changing moment. Respect was one thing a cop held in high regard, so when an invitation came from the man himself to attend at Dom's, it was treated as gold. You were there. Simple. Of course, the other advantage was the attendance of Dom's beautiful daughters. It was always a great night because you knew that there would never be anyone there to give you aggro about being in 'The Job.'

One of Dom's favourite people, Jill Norton, had also just sat down with Susie and Maria. She had just finished a long and sometimes animated conversation on the other side of the crowded room with Phil, Tony and the new Sergeant at Carlton, Kate McLaren. Dom was a bit disappointed for Kate, because it looked as though her new friend had either not been able to come to the party or had stood her up. He hoped it was the former. When he waved to Kate, he only received a half-hearted gesture in return. As he moved around the tables replenishing drinks and motioning the waiters to keep the pasta platters coming, he could overhear bits and pieces of what Kate was saying to the group.

"I've shown you the text that I got from Tom, and Jill had shown you the one she got. They are both weird, don't you think?"

"You are saying he doesn't have a sister at all, Kate?" Tony Signorotto said.

"One time at the shooting range he said it was just himself and Summer. No other relatives."

Both Signorotto and Stone looked at her with puzzled expressions.

"He knew that it was Italian at Dom's tonight. There are no Greek restaurants in the city called Dom's. I can't see how he could muck that up," Stone queried the other two.

"That's for sure, Phil. Also, this Rock business. What's with that?" Tony said.

Max Tyler had been privy to the very first words of the conversation before he had been sidelined by Silvana Santino for a dance. When a Santino daughter held you by the arm you had to move heaven and earth to make sure you weren't taken for the night. They were all beautiful girls, but Max was feeling himself more than attracted to Chloe Schaeffer as the days went by, especially when she had walked in by herself wearing a bright red dress that she had poured herself into. When he untangled himself from Silvana, he went back to the police huddle.

"Sorry. I overheard what Kate and Jill told you about the texts. I've got another angle on it," he said to his fellow Task Force Calibre colleagues.

Tony Signorotto smiled at Max before he spoke.

"Okay Mr. Detective. Let's hear your suited-up explanation."

"I think Tom's trying to tell you something. That bullshit about Greek food. He knows it's Italian at Dom's. Absolutely. Also, I'm thinking outside the square here, but I reckon the reference to passing on apologies to the Rock is double talk aimed at you, boss," Max said, pointing at Phil Stone.

"Me! How do you figure that one, Max?" Stone said.

"Rock. Stone. It's got to be a heads up to Tony with the crap about the Greek food and a further heads up to you, sir, to get your attention about the Rock bit," Max said.

"Interesting and plausible, Max," Phil Stone replied. "However, there's not much else we can go on at the moment. Kate said she's tried ringing him, but the call's not even going through. I nipped out just before and called Ian Kent, the owner of National Security Services and he told me that he's not expecting Tom to call him until tomorrow, and then, with a final call about the transport job to come in on Monday. He said that Tom's has been working flat out to make this first job as Ops Manager come off like clockwork. He even told him to slow down a bit and rest up over the weekend and enjoy his time with Summer. Ian's going to keep in contact with me, but I can tell you, he's not overly concerned. He says Tom's a big boy, and with his background can handle things. Ian should know, because he's ex S.A.S. also."

"I hope that's the case. Either that, or I have been absolutely stood up for the night," a glum sounding Kate McLaren said as she turned to see Dom beckoning Tony over, away from the centre of the room. "Dom wants you, Tony."

Tony strode over with a smile on his face.

"Thanks for the upstairs room, Dom. It's fabulous."

"I always keep up here for family, my friend. It's where everyone knows everyone and there's never any trouble. If ever there is then it stays within family, the way it should. Besides that, it gives Maria and me the night off to enjoy it with you. I have good staff downstairs who will make sure everything runs smoothly."

"You and your family have looked after generations of Police here. This is our second home and Dom's is what Carlton is all about. Good friends, family and great celebrations. I hate to mention it, Dom, but Phil and I are a bit concerned about Tom

Cole, the friend of Kate's. He's meant to be here tonight but hasn't shown up," Tony said.

"Yes, I have seen that he isn't here. The lovely Kate is looking a bit sad. She is a Carlton girl now, so if he has done the wrong thing about her, I expect you to do something about it," the old restauranteur said excitedly.

"Easy my friend. I don't want any of my boys having to give you mouth to mouth after you collapse on the floor," Tony said with a laugh.

"I get Susie to do it, thanks so much," Dom said, with a grin and a wink. "Anyhow, what troubles you really my friend. I know that look in your eye. Not everything is hunky dory?" the wise Italian whispered.

"Well, between you and me, he is in charge of the civilian side of a Police operation at the moment. Unfortunately, we are pretty sure that your lowlife neighbour down the road, Al Lombardi is involved with this job too, but not in a good way," Tony said.

With the mention of Lombardi's name, Dom Santino's eyes lit up.

"Ah. I knew there was something I had to tell you about that no-good gangster," he said.

"Not your favourite Lygon Street trader?" Tony said, smiling.

"He is a trader. A trader of drugs and prostitutes. A black mark on the whole street," Dom said, almost spitting the words.

"Agreed my friend. Max and Chloe went past his place late last night and said it was closed for renovations."

"That's what I was going to tell you about. A very good friend of mine who owns Sergio's Pasta Paradise, which is next door to that filthy Club Maximus, came in for an espresso earlier today and said there had been a lot of activity in the back alley behind his place last night. He saw Lombardi giving orders to some thugs. No arguments, but they were putting a lot of food and stuff into a black van. When Sergio looked at the men, one of them told him to mind his own business and to piss off. As he was turning to go back inside, Lombardi just stared at him. Sergio was going to ask him a question about what was going on and that is when that gangster pulled back his coat to show a pistol tucked into his belt."

"Did he pull the gun on him?" an anxious Signorotto said.

"No. Lombardi just stared him down as the others drove off in the van and an old car. Sergio went back inside and quickly locked his door. He said he could hear Lombardi laughing like a madman in the alley. This morning though, he said that filthy den is locked up tight with a handwritten sign in the front window saying it is closed for renovations. That cannot be, Tony," a gesticulating Dom Santino said.

"Why not, Dom? Could be legit," Tony replied.

Dom Santino came closer to Tony and spoke quietly as he waved a finger in his face.

"Two reasons. First is money. Money is everything to that piece of slime. Why close it down at the start of a long weekend when all the labourers have been paid from the big construction jobs in the city and have a couple of itches they want scratched. Booze and sex. They pack out Club Maximus every weekend when they don't have the money. This weekend they do, and they have more time to spend it. Booze, drugs and whores across four nights. If Lombardi was serious about his club, he would have waited till next week to close it. Something is wrong with this."

"Also," he continued, "for renovations inside or out to any of these historic buildings, you need permission from the Melbourne City Council. Before they even consider giving anyone a permit, your next-door shops have to have their signatures on the application, so the council know there has been discussion along the strip. Sergio never received anything from Lombardi and neither did the bookstore on the other side. The sign in the window is just a handwritten note. Nothing to do with any application or council permit. This is all bullshit, Tony. He is up to something, this no-good son of a whore!"

Tony Signorotto knew only too well not to doubt Dom on anything to do with the heritage side of Carlton and its famous old buildings. He knew Dom was the President of the Lygon Street Traders Association.

Dom Santino changed the subject away from the darkness of crime when he spoke next.

"It is time for us to raise a glass of Chianti to the beautiful Susie, eh?"

"Mate. You and Phil got me back on the Coca Cola a few years ago. I'll leave the Chianti to you," Tony said, putting his arm around the shoulder of his Italian brother, as they walked through the room crowded with friends and family.

Chapter Fifty-Eight

Phil Stone waited until all of Task Force Calibre were in the office, before addressing them.

"Okay, folks" he said, looking around at each of them before continuing. "Hope you've all had a quiet Sunday. Don't know about you, but I'm finding it harder and harder to recover from any sort of event at Dom's. Must admit though, Susie's birthday bash was one to remember. Think I'll be giving the Chianti and pasta a rest for a week or two, though. Thank God for the taxi industry. Once we hit one o'clock, I knew it was time to leave the car keys behind in his safe. How'd you pull up, Senior Sergeant?"

The Officer in Charge of Carlton smiled from deep within his dark eyes before speaking.

"That was one good night, all right. I'm glad everyone had a great time, and I want to thank you all for coming along. Susie really appreciated it. As a tee-totaller, I can see another side of you all from the outside of a can of Jim Beam. Be assured, some of it isn't pretty. I videoed enough of you lot to keep me in bribe money for years."

Finishing on that note, he found himself being bombarded by balled up paper and a few other desk items that had been thrown by all around him. Laughter and jeers echoed around the room.

"Right you lot. Down to business," Phil Stone called over their heads.

"Chloe. I want you to do a final phone check with the Melbourne Highway Patrol and make sure we have a driver and two solos here ready to go at five-thirty in the morning. Make sure the Sergeant driving and the two riders have read the Operation Order, Kate. You can do the same with the Special Operations Group. Max, I want you to do the ring around with Collingwood, Fitzroy and Richmond and speak to their Senior

Sergeants to make sure you have the troops in place for your part of the operation if needed. They are to take up their positions and be ready by seven. Tell their bosses you are ringing on my behalf. I have to get into town and give the Deputy Commissioner a final briefing face to face. If you have any problems on the phones, Tony here can run interference for you. I don't think he'll have any trouble sorting his counterparts out. Let's get to it. It's now eleven-thirty and I should be back from holding hands with the tenth floor by one. You know the old saying about rank and marijuana. The more you suck, the higher you get. I should know. I've done my fair share. I want everyone finished by the time I get back because you are going home early, because I want you all to be fresh for tomorrow at five- thirty."

"Mick York and Johnny Petran got back to me about an hour ago. They have been constantly checking all known haunts for Lombardi, and the Bikie Task Force mob have been doing the same with the Black Rats. Zip, nil, none on Lombardi. Not to be found anywhere and all lights out at Club Maximus. We don't think Lombardi knows that we have Superintendent Bob Archer keeping an eye on John Moore. In regard to the Black Rats, it looks to be business as usual over the weekend at their clubhouse, a.k.a. A.R.D. Holdings. A few in and out and a long running barbeque for every leather clad dick head that wanted to attend. Interestingly enough, no sign though of their President or Sergeant-at-Arms. They may be away for a ride or something, but our boys weren't about to barge in and ask."

"I suppose what I'm trying to say is that we have to be very careful. These handguns are worth huge money on the black-market and the Dark Web. Safety first people. I just need a quick word with you Kate before I head off," Stone said in conclusion.

Tony Signorotto looked at Kate as she walked towards them.

"How are you feeling today, Kate?" he said with a note of concern in his voice.

"Yeah, boss. I'm okay. Still haven't heard from Tom though. It'll sort itself out in the wash, I suppose. Jill and her husband ran me home from the party reasonably early. I spent yesterday afternoon at the pistol range," Kate said.

"Tom's a member too, isn't he?" Stone queried.

"Yes, he is. That's where I first met him. I spoke to the range controller and he said he hasn't seen him for a couple of weeks. Understandable with this job on and looking after Summer."

Nodding his head, Stone continued.

"Just to keep you up to speed, Kate. Ian Kent rang this morning. Tom's been in contact by phone with him yesterday and again today just before this briefing. He asked him where he was, and Tom told him he was in Yarrawonga. Said he would be there on time for the job tomorrow."

Kate McLaren looked at her Superintendent with a quizzical expression before speaking.

"Did he say how he sounded? What he'd been doing? Anything like that."

"No, nothing. He just double checked that the truck driver and back up car from N.S.S. would be at Tullamarine tomorrow ready to go."

Tony Signorotto looked at Phil Stone.

"Strange that he got into Yarrawonga twice. Once yesterday and again this morning, and hasn't phoned either Kate, me or you, Phil," Signorotto said.

"He'll have phone coverage down here. I'll speak to him then," an angry Kate Maclaren stated.

"Yeah. I can understand your frustration Kate, but I think Lombardi is the person we should all be concentrating on here, don't you think?". Phil Stone spoke to her in a voice that was telling her to get on with her job and forget about her personal life for the time being.

Chapter Fifty-Nine

The Task Force crew weren't the only ones up early on Tuesday.

Tony Richards had given instructions to his Black Rats Melbourne Chapter to dump the body of Billy Stevens, which they had kept on ice, over the reinforced high metal gate of the Carnivores clubhouse late on Monday night. When they opened the body bag, they would see the attached toe tag telling them the Black Rats wanted retribution for the murder of their probationary member, and for them to be at the car park of the Brunswick Italian Social Club at seven forty-five Tuesday morning. It was an offer the Carnivores could not and would not refuse.

Richards had confirmed the set up with a phone call at four o'clock on the Tuesday morning. The Black Rats faithful asked no questions about the body dump. They had simply taken it from one of their freezers at their headquarters and followed the orders of their President. To make sure the Carnivores had got the idea, one of the Black Rats parked down the road and watched as Harley Davidsons arrived one after the other. They were all clad in their colours and most had firearms of one sort or another protruding from their panniers. It was time to settle some scores.

Richards was thinking to himself that this day was certainly going to be one to remember. Not only was he going to have a big pay day once they had gotten the stolen Police firearms to Sydney after the heist, but also, he would be the President of the most powerful Outlaw Motorcycle Gang in the land. Those idiot Carnivores would be no match for those S.O.G. arseholes. He was mentally naming it the Battle of Brunswick when the voice of Big Al Lombardi derailed his train of thought.

"The body dump go off all right?"

"All done. The Carnivores should be on their way in a couple of hours. The message said seven forty-five, so they will probably turn up a bit early trying to get the jump on us. Timings should be okay. When the shooters come off the freeway the Carnivores will either be letting off their first rounds or starting to get pumped by the cops," Richards said, with a grin on his stubbled face.

"I'll be on the Moreland Road overpass in plenty of time and I want you in Fleming Street then. Call me as soon as you get there. I've got one bit of insurance to deal with before we start. Get Morelli and your two boys in here."

Richards didn't bother to question him as to why he needed the long-time house guest and his two associates.

Angelo Morelli's brain had been turning somersaults as he scanned the old building. He suddenly had an idea and turned quickly, heading toward the toilet area. It was situated on the other side of the factory. Walking behind the toilet entrance he looked around desperately for what he wanted. He hoped the others had thought he was just going for a piss.

In the corner of the old tyre factory there was a mound of rubbish that had collected over the years. He looked down and could see that there were a lot of the old lead weight brackets that the tyre fitters attached to the wheel rims to balance them. A glimmer of a chance presented itself.

Morelli grabbed one from the dusty pile and walked into the toilet. He pulled the lead weight from its bracket, which left him with a flat piece of steel about four centimetres in length with flat ends which could be used as a screwdriver of sorts. Putting the small piece of metal in his pocket, he flushed the toilet and re appeared back into the factory area as Richards waved him over to the group to listen to Lombardi.

"Morelli. You and Tony's boys are going in to see Cole and his brat. I don't care if she screams, but I want Cole up against a wall while you, Angelo, cut a piece of hair from the kid and bring it back to me. Tell him nothing. He's not stupid. He'll know it's for insurance, so he does his job this morning. We'll be watching on the camera, so just do it quick. No fucking big man shit from you two, "pointing towards Richard's Sergeant-at -Arms and his offsider. "No threats, no bullshit. The more I watch Cole, the more I think he enjoys being threatened."

The two bikies didn't bat an eyelid. The Sergeant-at-Arms removed a large black revolver from his belt and held it loosely by his side. Angelo took a pair of scissors handed to him by Lombardi.

Morelli hadn't slept all night. He had wandered around every inch of the old tyre factory thinking of how he could help Cole and his daughter. He had walked lap after lap, even after being threatened by Joey and Feb to get some sleep. It was only after he stopped to sit down that he looked at the office prison that held the two kidnap victims.

Morelli had seen that it was a room that had been built inside the old factory and had a ceiling that was about five metres below the factory roof. Running from the outside factory wall along the roof of the office was a large steel air conditioning duct. It did a downturn of only about a metre into the office ceiling. He had got up and kept pacing, working his way over to the dirty window near where the duct joined the wall. He saw, after wiping some of the grime off the filthy window, that the duct came out into the wall in a side street off Brunswick Road and only had a drop of about two metres or so down to the footpath. Directly opposite on the other side was the beer garden of the old Sarah Sands hotel with a gate in the low Perspex fence which led to the back door. There was a chance, a small chance, but nevertheless, a chance. His plan, now that he had the piece of scrap metal, needed him to have access to the room where Cole and Summer were being held. This bizarre order from Lombardi gave him that opportunity. He took it immediately.

Banging loudly on the wooden door, one of the bikies yelled, "Get yourself and the kid away from the door now. We're coming in."

Chapter Sixty

Tom Cole had done what was asked of him over the past few days. He knew it was pointless aggravating an already bad situation while they were locked in the room.

The hardest part of the preceding days was keeping Summer from being too scared. She had tossed and turned in her sleep and was old enough to realise that they were being treated as prisoners. There was only so much he could do for her and kept reassuring her that everything would be all right.

He had gone along with the two phone calls that he was made to make to Ian Kent because he knew that his captors were listening. He had to play it straight, all the while hoping that his earlier text messages had at least raised a few eyebrows with Kate and Jill in regard to the situation that he and Summer were in. He had to keep planning though.

When the demand came for them to get back from the door, he grabbed Summer and backed away while watching the ceiling camera. The look he gave whoever was viewing would have left them in no doubt as to the outcome if and when Cole got hold of them.

The door flew open and the three balaclava clad figures stepped into the room. As one of them raised a revolver towards the now crying Summer, Cole pulled her towards him, turning her around so she was clutching his legs with her face buried in his stomach. The third hood stepped in front of the gun toting menace and spoke.

"All they want is for me to cut off a piece of her hair. Only a small piece. I won't hurt her, I promise."

The Sergeant-at-Arms pushed Morelli aside, raised the revolver again at Cole and smiled.

"Do what we want, or you will eat a bullet. Let her go and turn around."

Tom Cole had fought many battles before and plenty of them involved scum holding guns at him. He was not fazed by this individual. This time though, his daughter was involved.

Take it easy, Tom. This scum will get his.

He decided to take a chance when he looked at the pleading eyes of the hood holding the scissors. He was the weak link.

"You're not going to shoot anyone, pal. Your bosses out there won't allow it. Without me this job won't come off," Cole made the statement with a cool, controlled voice while holding Summer against him.

"Maybe so, big man, but I can blow her away," the Sergeant-at-Arms said, lowering the revolver about half a metre and aiming it at the back of Summer's head.

"You shoot her and then you will have to shoot me you ballless prick, because then there will be no need for me to live, so I won't be helping you or your gutless mates with anything. You really are dumb, aren't you? You won't make it back out the door. Someone will blow your head clean off your skinny little shoulders because you stuffed up the whole operation," Cole said with quiet menace.

The now sweating Sergeant-at-Arms swapped his handgun from hand to hand as he looked at Cole with confusion before being dragged away by his offsider towards the door.

Morelli stepped up to Cole and surreptitiously, away from the camera winked at him as he gently cut a small lock of Summer's golden hair from her head with the scissors in his left hand. Cole followed Morelli's eyes, catching on to the almost desperate plea from behind the mask.

He reached down and grabbed Morelli's wrist in what looked like an attempt to stop him cutting any more hair from Summer.

"You've got what you want, now get out."

As he slowly let go of Angelo's wrist, Cole watched Morelli's eyes as they kept flicking up to the air vent in the ceiling. The distraction of the two bikies arguing over by the door continued as the Sergeant-at-Arms suddenly broke away, stepping toward Cole and yelling at the same time.

"You control nothing here, big man. Understand?"

The phone on the wall rang suddenly. Cole picked up the receiver quickly as he could see trouble brewing with the revolver wielding fool. A voice screamed into the receiver.

"Put the one with the fucking gun on."

Cole held the receiver in front of the agitated gunman's face. It was snatched away immediately.

"We fucking need them. Get out of there now. Morelli's got what Lombardi wanted and what we don't need is you trying to be a bigger fuckwit than what you are. Now get out," Richards spat into the phone.

The balaclava bikie dropped the phone so that the receiver just swung against the wall. As he backed away, he spoke in Cole's direction.

"You'll keep, big man."

The three intruders backed towards the door as Cole noticed the one who had cut Summer's hair kept looking up and down towards the large air conditioning vent.

Chapter Sixty-One

Tom Cole knew that someone would be back for him very soon.

It was Tuesday morning, and the firearms shipment from the Smith and Wesson factory in the United States had most likely already landed at Tullamarine airport.

He was wondering how these hoods would run this operation. One thing was certain and that was his little daughter would unknowingly play a major role in their heist. He had spoken to Summer and told her that morning that he would most likely be missing for a couple of hours and for her to be brave until his return.

Cole knew that he would have to make his appearance as the Operations Manager for National Security Services at the airport. The phone that he had used to contact Ian Kent had been left on a table directly under the surveillance camera so there was no hope of him using it. When the wall phone rang again, he picked it up and just listened. There was no point in trying to bargain with these fools.

Lombardi spoke slowly and without fuss.

"Cole. This is what will take place now. First off, I guarantee that nothing will happen to your kid as long as you follow instructions. I will leave the man who cut her hair here with her. You will be back within a couple of hours max with the shipment. Just go along with everything. If I had wanted to eliminate you or your daughter, none of us would be wearing balaclavas. When my associates and I have gone after the job is done, you will be back with your daughter. Both of you will be alive and well. You will just have to figure a way out of your prison. We will be long gone by then."

"You will be driven out of here, blindfolded, in your company car and taken via back streets to where you will be left. After five minutes, you can take the blindfold off. The driver will be gone, and you will drive onto the freeway and continue on to Terminal Four at the airport and do the job. You tell your offsider that you are driving the truck. The loading should be almost complete by the time you get there. Get in and drive out slowly. No hanging around. Remember, we have your kid. There is only one way to play this and that is our way.

When the lead police car is taken out of the situation, that's when you tell your offsider to get out and reverse into your back up car as hard as you can and take off down Brunswick Road."

"Where will I go then?" Cole said.

"When you pass the old West Brunswick hotel on the corner of Grantham Street, you will see a Maserati pull in front of you. Just follow it to the end."

"Where's the end?" A calm Cole asked.

"You just follow my turn signal. I'll only do one turn to the left and you will pull in behind me. Are you clear on this? If you don't follow me, God help your kid. Clear?"

"Clear."

God will be on my side you prick because he won't be able to help a sick idiot like you. You'll need a lot more than God.

"Take the phone near the camera but you won't use it. If they ring you for any reason, give nothing away. The phone has a very sophisticated bugging and tracking device. I will know where you are at all times and if you use it, my man will look after your kid till you get back," Cole played down his anger when he replied.

"Yes. I understand it all and I will go along with it. Touch another hair of her head though and I assure you that you won't see the sun go down. You haven't done your homework about who you're dealing with," he said, staring at the camera with a look of ice.

"I do not want you or your kid. I want that shipment of firearms. The sooner we get this done, the better for you. It's simple. The guns for the girl. When you get back here you will be locked in with her again. Your door will open in a minute and I want you to step outside and I will send my man in."

Cole gave the frightened Summer a hug and said goodbye, reassuring her that he would soon be back. Stepping outside the office for the first time, he watched a man in a balaclava approach. He spoke slowly to him as they began to pass each other.

"That child is too young to give evidence against any of you in the kidnapping case you are going to face. Take that fucking mask off when you go in or you will scare her to death."

Morelli nodded but stood outside the door by about one metre and made sure he was out of range of the office microphone, which he knew Lombardi and Richards were monitoring. Looking at Cole he whispered quietly.

"A.C. vent. Ceiling. When you return. I'll fix the screws. She's okay with me."

The professional soldier in Cole forced him to remember the words but not to react in any way. He knew immediately there was a small window of hope as he walked to his car. He had already changed into a new shirt and tie which had been placed in the room obviously to make his appearance at the airport more professional.

A balaclava clad Feb Felagi indicated for him to get into the rear seat. As Cole did, he was blindfolded and pushed face down and told to stay in that position. Felagi got into the driver's seat, started the car and slowly exited the factory building, at first heading west along Brunswick Road before making several detours and U-turns, all the aim of not letting Cole know where they had come from.

Tom Cole had no intention of raising himself off the seat until the car had stopped and the five minutes were up. It was not time for heroics. He had to win the end game, not just part of it.

The vehicle came to a halt after ten minutes or so and Cole heard the driver's door open and close. He counted to sixty slowly five times then raised himself up and removed the blindfold. Looking around he knew he was in a side road off Brunswick Road. Getting behind the wheel he looked down and saw a clear plastic pouch on the passenger seat. It contained the lock of Summer's hair that had been cut from her. Grabbing the pouch in one hand, he reached into the glove compartment and took out a small note pad and a biro. He scribbled a short note on it and then put it in the plastic pouch after which he put it into his jacket pocket. He wasn't going to waste time looking for the driver as he started the car and drove towards the entrance to the freeway. Standing in a front yard some distance away, Feb Felagi phoned in to Lombardi and told him that Cole was following instructions and was headed towards the freeway entrance.

Minutes later, Lombardi exited the old *Sam's Tyre factory* in his Maserati, followed by the Ford sedan piloted by Richards. Behind the Ford was the black van with the Sergeant-at-Arms of the Black Rats driving, together with his bikie offsider. By the time Cole had turned onto the Tullamarine Freeway, Lombardi was on the way to his Moreland Road overpass vantage point and Richards would soon be parked and waiting in Fleming Street, Brunswick.

The President of the Black Rats smiled to himself as he pictured the van, Black Rats flag hanging out of the window for the Carnivores to see as they approached down the driveway of the Brunswick Social Club.

It would send those fucking Carnivores bat shit crazy.

Chapter Sixty-Two

Task Force Calibre was now in operational mode.

Phil Stone and Tony Signorotto were seated in the Melbourne Highway Patrol BMW sedan, which was parked directly outside the goods arrival bay behind Terminal Four at Tullamarine airport. Behind the wheel was Sergeant Eddie Downes, one of the most experienced Highway Patrol officers in the Victoria Police Force.

Ready to go was the Special Operations Group vehicle with its four occupants in full paramilitary gear. Behind their vehicle were the two hand-picked solo riders on their BMW motorcycles.

Stone had already made contact with the two National Security Services armed guards who were waiting in their vehicle behind the five-ton Hino truck that would transport the firearms.

Tony Signorotto turned to Stone.

"They're just starting to load the first pallet of the guns and accessories. No sign of Tom Cole yet," he said.

Just as Stone was about to reply, the Toyota sedan of Tom Cole's drove in from the other side and parked away from National Security Services vehicle. He got out slowly and started to walk towards the two guards. Stone and Signorotto approached him.

"Tom. Haven't been able to get hold of you. Is everything all right?" Signorotto said questioningly.

Cole turned toward them. "Yeah. All okay. Been up country. Bit of a break. Let's get this done and dusted," he said flatly.

Phil Stone replied quickly.

"Tom, Kate hasn't heard from you and you were a no show at the party on Saturday night at Dom's. What's going on?"

Cole gave his answer in a very brusque and rude manner.

"Fellas. I'm not going to stand here and be questioned by you two in regard to my social life. Besides, I think Senior Constable Catherine Maclean can look after herself. The only thing I need to tell you is that there is a small change to the running arrangements and that is that I'll be driving the truck. The rostered driver is going to be the observer. They've given me a guard who has basically nil background in escorts and very little firearms experience. He hasn't seen an angry man his whole life. Anyhow, let's go," Cole said, stepping away from the two police officers to give instructions to the driver.

Phil Stone and Tony Signorotto looked nonplussed at each other as did the convoy driver when he was told to move into the passenger seat of the five-ton truck. Cole got into the driver's seat and looked anywhere but back at the two police.

"There's something not right here, Phil," Signorotto said. "He's basically just told us to piss off and in the same breath referred to Sergeant Kate McLaren as Senior Constable Catherine Maclean. This is bullshit."

"I know," Stone replied. "Also, he is now driving the truck because he reckons the rostered driver's wet behind the ears. He told me at the latest security meeting that he was only using ex-military guys on this. Experienced in weaponry and tactics. Said all their team are from one of the services and with experience in high level security. Give Jill Norton a quick ring and find out if Tom turned up at his house last night with his daughter."

"Will do," Signorotto said.

Phil Stone waited by the Highway Patrol vehicle which Sergeant Downes had idling in preparation for the convoy start. Just as Signorotto got off the phone, Cole started up the firearms laden truck and swung out from the loading dock, as did the back up security car. He stopped next to the S.O.G. vehicle and motioned one of the black clad Police over to him. Looking down on him from the driver's seat, he handed him the small plastic pouch containing Summer's hair and a folded note.

"Give that to Superintendent Stone straight away."

The officer walked quickly to Stone and handed him the package then got quickly into the black Toyota Landcruiser which was at the head of the convoy. Cole began to inch the truck forward and hit the air horn at the same time.

Stone jumped in the Highway Patrol BMW as did Tony Signorotto. Taking up a position behind the S.O.G. vehicle, the convoy slowly drove out from the Terminal Four loading dock and headed towards the Tullamarine freeway on route to the Police Armoury in Collingwood.

Stone quickly undid the plastic pouch, staring with a look of disbelief on his face. In one hand he held the precious lock of hair and in the other, the note. Tony Signorotto had seen the S.O.G. member hand Phil Stone the packet but before he could ask what it was, Stone read the note out loud.

They have her. Go along with me. Don't know full plans or destination. Trust me. Insider helping.

Phil Stone jumped on the radio to the rest of the convoy and informed them to be extremely vigilant. He didn't mention the kidnapping of the child because he didn't want to divert the crews involved away from their concentration on the job in hand. He wanted them totally focussed.

"Jill said there is no sign of movement at Tom's house. It's starting to fall into place now, Phil. Do you want me to ring Kate?"

"Yes, mate. Tell her the full situation and be prepared for all those units to move quickly. Something is going to go down here and I don't think it is planned for the Collingwood end of this trip. Get onto D.24 to get some back up from the Highway Patrol here A.S.A.P. Let's lock this down quickly Tony. It's useless trying to stop Tom at this point. He has his daughter uppermost in his mind and even if we did stop him, I guarantee you someone is expecting him to complete this trip. There will be eyes and even ears on him."

After a quick and angry phone call to Police Communications, Tony Signorotto turned to Stone.

"Big petrol tanker crash in Mt. Alexander Road in Flemington. Evacuations in progress. They actually wanted our solos but I told them to get stuffed."

The two old friends looked at each other before Tony Signorotto spoke with a grin on his face.

"Hope you can still roll over the bonnet of a Police car, mate.?"

Chapter Sixty-Three

Sergeant Kate McLaren was seated in a police sedan alongside Max Tyler and Chloe Schaeffer. They were parked in Cambridge Street, Collingwood directly outside the roller door entrance to the Victoria Police Armoury.

The Operation Order had been checked and re-checked with the various police units that she had at her disposal and in position for the arrival of the firearms delivery. She was just closing the folder of paperwork when Max Tyler spoke.

"Kate. That's Superintendent Archer running this way."

Kate looked up in alarm and saw Archer beckoning towards them from about fifty metres away. They immediately jumped out of the car and met him about halfway down the footpath.

"What's wrong, sir?" Kate said urgently.

"John Moore. He's dead. Shot himself downstairs in the toilet block."

"Fuck," Max Tyler said in disbelief.

"I was going to his workstation just to check on him and see how he was reacting, seeing as this is the delivery date for the pistols. He wasn't there, and one of his co-workers said he had taken one of the service pistols to test in the Safe Loading Unloading Device. It had come back from one of the stations with a slide mechanism problem. I went through to the safe room, but he wasn't there. That's when I heard the gunshot from downstairs. You'd better come in quickly," Archer said in an agitated voice.

"You stay with the car, Chloe. Any questions from the troops, you answer them. You're all over the Operation Order," Kate said as she headed off with Max Tyler and the visibly shaken Superintendent. Chloe threw Max a roll of crime scene tape as he left.

Upon entering the area just outside the toilet and shower block, Max instructed one of the Police Forensic Senior Constables to stand guard at the doorway and start a log of anyone who need to be down there. He knew there would be a lot more people over the next hour or so. Being the only detective there he knew it would be treated as a crime scene no matter even if it was a suicide. There was a Police firearm involved so the Ethical Standard Division would have to attend along with the local Yarra C.I.U. crew on duty.

The three officers entered the crime scene area. Their senses were immediately assaulted with the gagging, overpowering smell of gunpowder, urine and excrement. Looking at the body of John Moore, it was obvious that it had rid itself of bodily fluids when, in his nervous and frightened state, he had pulled the trigger of the nine-millimetre pistol which was now lying beside his body. The back of his head had been blown away.

An obviously upset Bob Archer stood with his hand over his mouth. Tears were forming in his eyes. Max Tyler bent down and looked closely at the body which was dressed in black slacks, white shirt and the standard police departmental issue grey dustcoat. In the top outside pocket, Tyler could see an envelope protruding. Carefully removing it, he handed it behind him to Kate McLaren who looked at the unaddressed and unsealed envelope before she looked at Archer and spoke.

"Sir. Is it all right with you, as his boss, if I open this? I think we all know that it will most likely be some form of suicide note."

"Yes Sergeant," a visibly shaken Archer replied. "Poor bastard. Read it."

Kate did as she was instructed. Once she had read the half page note to herself, she turned to make sure everyone else but herself, Archer and Max were out of hearing range before she read it out loud.

Can't live with this. I've sold myself and all my workmates out. Lombardi will sell these guns to the highest bidder and innocent people will die. He has owned me for too long. Can't take the pressure and the disgrace any longer. I'm sorry, Bob. My time is up. It's the only way out.

The initials JM were scrawled at the bottom of the note. Kate turned to Max Tyler.

"Max. I'll leave you in charge of this. I'm taking the Superintendent upstairs. I'll call the Yarra C.I.U. and the Ethical Standards Division as well as Phil Stone."

"Yeah, thanks Kate," Max said as he tied crime scene tape across the doorway to preserve the area. The gunshot wound was obviously self-inflicted but until the local C.I.U. wrote it up as such, it was still regarded as a crime scene.

Kate McLaren walked slowly with Bob Archer up to the office area where she saw several employees standing around in groups engaged in quiet chatter. She addressed them.

"There has been a firearms incident downstairs in the male toilet block. It is now a crime scene, so please ensure you use the bathrooms at the other end of the building."

Some of the nervous workers who were standing around with their arms folded, nodded and headed back to their workplaces. Most of them stared at the empty desk where John Moore had last sat.

Kate began making a coffee for Bob Archer when her mobile phone rang.

"Tony here, Kate. There's been an update on Tom Cole which I have to tell you about, so listen up."

"Go on," Kate replied. "I've got one here for you, too. You go first."

Signorotto explained what had happened with the note and hair without any interruption from his Sergeant.

"Just better let you know we presume Lombardi will try something on the way rather than at your end. Be prepared to get yourselves and the other units back over here quick if we call. Got that?"

"Understand fully, boss. Now for what's happened here."

"Go on," Tony said. "What's happened?"

"John Moore has committed suicide in the toilet block here at the Armoury," Kate said in a matter of fact voice.

"Oh shit, Kate. What happened with him?"

"Took one of the pistols that had come in for servicing, put it in his mouth and, well, you can imagine the rest."

"How's Bob Archer taking it?"

"He's okay. I've got Max in charge of the scene, but I'm calling in Yarra C.I.U. to take over. It's their patch."

"Definite suicide?"

"Yep. This is what you need to hear though. He left a note naming Lombardi. It says he'll sell the guns to the highest bidder."

"Lombardi's disappeared. Club Maximus is closed. Little Summer has been kidnapped and now John Moore has topped himself. We know he was definitely tied in with Lombardi. Safe to say the piece of slime is going to make a play this morning. Thanks, Kate. Get your troops ready and over here when and if I ring. We have to play it safe from here to Collingwood at the moment. Make sure Max hands the crime scene over as quick as possible."

"On it, boss," Kate replied and put her phone down.

Tony Signorotto was just finishing the call as the convoy exited from the airport road onto the Tullamarine freeway.

"Phil. Proof positive. Lombardi's our man," Signorotto said after relaying the news of Moore's suicide.

Chapter Sixty-Four

The Sergeant-at-Arms of the Black Rats, together with his brother bikie, had placed the black van in the empty car park of the Brunswick Italian Social Club. They had made sure the colours of the Outlaw Motorcycle Gang were hanging from the darkened side window and were easily visible to anyone approaching across the open expanse of bitumen. To give the Carnivores an added incentive, they had parked the van far enough out from the fence so the approaching riders could encircle it in true wagon train style.

Leaving the car park by climbing the back fence, they made their way back along Park Street rather than returning via Brunswick Road. They knew they could get back to their base at the old tyre factory by turning onto the bicycle path that crossed Brunswick Road at the railway line.

They made good time, and once there, the Sergeant-at-Arms rang his President, Tony Richards, who he knew would be in position further west along Brunswick Road at Fleming Street.

"Van's in place, Tony."

"Okay. Where are you now?" Richards replied from behind the wheel of the parked Ford he was soon going to use as a battering ram against the lead police vehicle.

"We're on the bike path at Brunswick Road, just near the factory."

"Stay there and tell me when the Carnivores have come over the railway line. It's the most direct route from their clubhouse and I don't see them weaving in and out of any backstreets on their way here. They will be fired up and ready to take no prisoners. They'll have their colours on and think they are on a mission from God."

"Gotcha. We'll head back then and be ready to transfer the guns."

It wasn't long before they heard the overpowering and familiar rumble of what sounded like a huge gathering of Harley Davidson motorbikes coming from the east in Brunswick Road. The Sergeant-at-Arms peered out cautiously from his observation position and saw a phalanx of motorbikes, all with headlights blazing. They were stationary at the traffic lights at Sydney Road. The riders were wringing the necks of the throttles. The noise was not only deafening but also threatening. It looked the starting grid of the Australian Grand Prix at Philip Island—except there was nothing European or Japanese about it. It was all chrome and steel American muscle!

When the traffic lights changed, there was an explosion of noise as the riders launched themselves and their steeds westward along Brunswick Road toward the Brunswick Italian Social Club car park.

"Need to get a bit of a count as they go by," the Sergeant-at-Arms said as he stepped back towards his concealment. "Looks like their Melbourne Chapter is all here," he said to his gob-smacked offsider.

The motor bikes went through the railway crossing in pairs, with their President at the head of the phalanx. The Sergeant-at-Arms of the Black Rats, despite having nothing but hatred and contempt for the Carnivores, was impressed nonetheless with the sight.

They got as far as counting thirty-eight Harleys as they passed on their way to their destination. The two Black Rats gave it about thirty seconds after the last duo crossed the railway gates before they stepped out from their secluded position. They saw that most of them were carrying some sort of firearm in their panniers, with the obvious intent of wiping out the Black Rats down the road.

The mistake that the two Black Rats made was something that all children had been taught from the age of letting go of their parents' hands. Look right, look left and then look right again when you cross the road. Simple stuff. The two bikies had unknowingly signed their own death certificates. Their eyes had followed the departing motorbikes and had forgotten about the four Carnivores that had been running 'Tail Gun Charlie'. It was a job that was delegated to members on all 'runs'. The aim was no different to that given to a fighter pilot in World War Two. Keep an eye on the pack and watch their backs!

One of the tailing riders saw the two Black Rats crossing the road just as the bells and lights of the railway crossing came into operation, signalling an approaching train.

The Black Rats moved out of the way of the descending boom gates and as they turned towards the factory, they saw the stationary Carnivores. They had not even heard the last four Harleys. One Carnivore slapped his co-rider on the shoulder as he recognised one of the Black Rats.

"That's the Black Rats' Sergeant-at-Arms," he screamed, at the same time as he pulled a Colt Magnum revolver from his belt and aimed it at his enemy. Two others pulled a Russian twelve-gauge coach gun and a Mossberg pump action shotgun from their panniers. The fourth rider had a pistol holster strapped to his handlebars and proceeded to remove an old handgun for the inevitable confrontation. As a car came to a halt at the railway gates on the other side of the railway tracks, the booming sound of the .357 magnum revolver superseded the clanging warning bells at the crossing. The Black Rats Sergeant-at-Arms heard the crack of the handgun and was immediately covered in blood and gore as his offsiders head exploded like an over ripe watermelon. The bikie was stone motherless dead before he could touch his own weapon.

As he saw his comrade fall, one of the Harleys Davidsons came around the end of the boom gates, onto the railway tracks, and drove straight towards him with the rider brandishing a pump action shotgun whose blackened barrel end was getting bigger and bigger the closer he came.

The Black Rats Sergeant-at-Arms pulled his Blackhawk revolver, and kneeling on one knee with a two-handed grip, pumped two shots at the steel horse and rider. The first shot ricocheted off the shotgun's barrel and straight up into the open-faced German styled military helmet the rider was wearing and tore a path through his face, forcing the Carnivore to be blown backwards off his bike.

The second slug punctured the petrol tank and caused the riderless bike to explode in a ball of fire and grind to a flaming halt in the middle of the railway tracks.

Several people in cars on either side of the railway gates had abandoned their vehicles and run in any direction, as long as it was away from the chaos that was unfolding around them.

The Sergeant-at-Arms rolled sideways and fired more shots at the three remaining Carnivores. One spun off his motor bike still holding what looked like a Nazi style military pistol. As he fell with a wound to his shoulder, the machine pistol racked off a quick-fire spray of bullets, one of them severing the throat of the Carnivore next to him. The bikie staggered off his Harley and let it fall to the bitumen. He fell first to his knees, clutching desperately with his leather gloved hands, uselessly trying to stem the pumping river of blood from his severed carotid artery.

The one uninjured Carnivore grabbed hold of his comrade with the bullet wounded shoulder. Both advanced slowly on the Black Rats Sergeant-at-Arms, who was crouched next to his dead brother rider.

It was the Sergeant-at-Arms who realised that neither he nor his sworn enemies were about to die in a shootout. The steel that was coming his way wasn't from a pistol or a shotgun. It was from a fast approaching Brunswick bound train.

The terrified bikie went to jump over his dead comrade-in-arms, but his boot caught on the railway track. As he fell to the ground screaming, the last thing that went through his brain was the front undercarriage bogey, which by this time, had smoke pouring from it due to the train driver slamming the brakes on.

A witness who actually saw the train strike the Outlaw Motor Cycle Gang members would later testify that even over the sound of the screeching metal brakes, he still heard the terrified scream of the two about to be crushed Carnivores staring like stunned rabbits at the unstoppable one hundred and fifty ton steel behemoth bearing down on them. Motorbikes were pulped to scrap metal and bodies disappeared under the train.

The severed head of the Black Rats Sergeant-at-Arms rolled open-eyed into the grass verge at the side of the track.

Chapter Sixty-Five

From his vantage point standing on the Moreland Road overpass crossing the Tullamarine Freeway, Big Al Lombardi felt like a general about to put his war plans into action.

The only thing he was looking for was what he could see approaching in the city bound lane. A smile came to his face when he observed the speed limit obeying convoy coming towards him.

Everything looked like it should. The lead vehicle loomed like a big black porcupine with its mass of communications aerials, both big and small, covering the black Toyota Landcruiser from front to rear. The second vehicle in line was the Highway Patrol BMW followed by the white Hino truck with the National Security Service car bringing up the rear. Moving up and then slowly dropping back along the convoy's length like protective sheep dogs were the two Highway Patrol BMW motorcycles.

Elimination of Tony Richards and others would be even easier. He would take Richards, Feb and Joey with him to Sydney where he had arranged a little greeting ceremony for them when they took a lunch break at Gundagai. His Calabrian brothers from the Goulburn Valley had been contracted some time ago. They had their instructions from their Melbourne *fratello* and would carry them out. From Gundagai to Sydney there would be only be himself and the truck driven by a member of the Goulburn mafia. His former passengers were set to go on a permanent diving trip in the Blowering reservoir in the Kosciusko National Park-with some very heavy lead weights to help them on their way.

He had seen enough. Walking quickly to his Maserati he drove off along Moreland Road before turning right into Melville Road, Brunswick. From there it was a left turn into

Dawson Street before heading along Grantham Street. He pushed the speed limit at times but still knew he could arrive at Brunswick Road in enough time to be able to turn in front of the white Hino truck driven by Cole. When that happened without any Police vehicles around it, he would know that he was more than halfway to perfecting the heist.

What he didn't expect to encounter was the heavy build-up of traffic along Brunswick Road heading towards the city at this early time in the morning of a long weekend. The strange thing added to that was that there was no traffic coming the other way.

Pulling to a halt in Grantham Street, he stepped out of his luxury ride and looked along Brunswick Road. Traffic was only crawling. Reaching for his phone, he quickly rang Feb back at the factory.

"What the fuck is happening up there? Traffic is hardly moving down where I am," he said angrily as if to say it was Feb's fault.

Feb and Joey had heard the train crash. They hadn't come out of the factory, but Feb had asked Joey to go up to the mezzanine window to have a look.

"Boss. There's a train stopped across Brunswick Road. Been some type of accident. That's why the traffic is fucked up your way. An ambulance and a fire truck have just pulled up. Looks pretty bad. Traffic back your way is pretty stuffed," Feb said.

Lombardi's brain went into semi-controlled overdrive.

This isn't happening. Think. Think.

Disconnecting from the call without saying another word to Feb, he jumped into his car and spun right at Brunswick Road before doing a quick U-turn. He'd have to get Cole to follow him around back streets to the factory. All the time he was thinking of an alternative route he feared one thing, and it wasn't the ambos or the fire trucks. It was that whatever had happened would attract local police. Carlton police. There was a back alley to the factory, so he'd have to get Cole to follow him there and get inside via the back-roller door.

As he sat with the Maserati's 4.7 litre dual overhead cam V8 idling wildly, he rang Feb back.

"Yes, boss. What's going on?"

"Feb. We won't be coming in the front way off Brunswick Road. It'll be through the back-roller door off the laneway. Make sure you keep an eye out for us. The cops will be everywhere by the time we get back if that train crash is bad. Any chance the train would be moved soon?"

"No way, boss. Looks from here like a couple of bikies have been hit. Bodies and motors all over the place."

Lombardi didn't say anything. Putting the phone down he made himself concentrate on what he could control, and that was just getting the shipment back to the factory—hopefully!

Chapter Sixty-Six

The roar of over thirty Harley Davidsons turning off Brunswick Road, down the long driveway into the carpark of the Brunswick Italian Social Club, was deafening. The intimidation factor was in the extreme and was exactly what the President of the Carnivores wanted to achieve: The only trouble was that there was no one in the carpark to intimidate.

Riding directly across the open bitumen space, the Carnivores could see the banner of the Black Rats hanging outside of the black van, waving in the light breeze like a red rag at a bull. Or in this case to a herd of bulls.

The Carnivores either didn't know if there were people inside the van, or their opposition, the Black Rats hadn't arrived at the location. It simply didn't worry any of them as they pulled out their weapons and slowly started to circle around the taunting van and its emblem of opposition.

The first round fired in anger was always going to come from their leader and it came out of the barrel of a nine-millimetre Glock semi-automatic pistol. The shot pierced the Black Rats head on the flapping emblem and shattered the side window of the van. From then on it was a free for all target practice.

One by one, the circling bikies began to pepper the stationary vehicle with everything from pistol rounds to solid shot gun slugs. Bit by bit the van began to look like a colander.

Inside the Social Club, the live-in caretaker had seen the progressive destruction of the vehicle which he had noticed parked outside when he had woken up. He hadn't felt like going out to inspect it until after he had read the paper and had eaten his breakfast. He was thanking God at that moment for his choice of food over curiosity.

He had seen quite a few brawls both inside and outside the club after the vino had taken effect on the Italian membership, with many waving arms and loud voices, but nothing as cold and calculating and downright dangerous as what was happening now. This was complete mayhem.

He immediately dialled triple zero and was put through to the police operator at D.24. The first and most important things he said were two words. *Help and guns!*

Outside in the carpark, the President of the Carnivores was diverting his troops from the all-out assault on the van to take up positions so they could cover the driveway for what they all presumed was the imminent arrival of their sworn enemy, the Black Rats Motorcycle Club.

Chapter Sixty-Seven

The Police radio burst into life, startling Tony Signorotto and Phil Stone.

They had been talking car to car with the other units in the convoy, but the authoritative and concerned voice of a D.24 operator was very different . They had been issued their own radio channel for Operation Calibre, so they realised immediately there must be something urgent for the cross over from the normal operational channel for the area.

"V.K.C. to Calibre 110," the voice said clearly, using the designated call sign of the Superintendent in charge of the Operation. Even though the caller had a copy of Operation Calibre in front of him on his radio console and would have known that the call sign was linked to Phil Stone, the professional in him would only ever refer to call signs rather than names.

"Calibre 110 receiving," Stone replied immediately.

"Your exact location please?"

"Tullamarine freeway, citybound about two kilometres from the Brunswick Road turnoff."

"Calibre 110, I need to relieve you of your S.O.G. escort immediately. Calibre 400 are you monitoring this?" The D.24 operator said to the Sergeant in charge of the S.O.G. vehicle travelling directly in front of Calibre 110.

"Affirmative. Monitoring same," came the crisp but understanding response from the S.O.G. leader.

"Thankyou. Saves two calls," the operator replied. "Calibre 110 and 400, we have an unfolding situation in the car park of the Brunswick Italian Social Club in Brunswick Road, east side at the Tullamarine freeway overpass. 400. Are you familiar with the location?"

"Yes. Familiar with location."

"Caller states that a large number of what look like 'patched' motorcycle gang members have been circling a vehicle in the empty car park and appear to have been, and I quote the caller. *'Blowing the shit out of the vehicle with firearms of all descriptions.'* The caller is the live-in caretaker and is bunkering down inside the club."

"We have no closer S.O.G. or Critical Incident Response Units. Deputy Commissioner Operations has directed Calibre 400 attend. Copy that 110 and 400?"

"400 received. Sorry 110 but we will have to leave you to it. Safe travels and may the Force be with you," the S.O.G. Sergeant said as Stone and Signorotto watched the black Toyota Landcruiser in front emit a puff of grey smoke as the driver accelerated quickly away from in front of their vehicle.

"Calibre 110 received and understood," Stone replied knowing it was useless to put up a case for the S.O.G. to stay. The Deputy Commissioner Operations had spoken, so that was that.

Sergeant Eddie Downes, the driver of the now lead vehicle, the Melbourne Highway Patrol Series 5 BMW sedan, slowly accelerated to give themselves a bit more space back to the Hino truck, at the same time as constantly checking everything around him. The experienced driver was not about to have his hard-earned reputation as a Highway Patrol member of over twenty years stature taken without a fight. He knew as much as his two on board colleagues did, that something untoward could happen any second, now that their main firepower unit had been taken from them.

"Gents. Get set for some quick reactionary driving if needs be," Downes said, as he settled into a relaxed but totally controlled driving position behind the sports steering wheel.

"Whatever it takes to keep us mobile, Eddie. We're in your hands," Tony Signorotto said calmly from the front passenger seat.

Phil Stone got straight back onto the operator who he knew had not signed back off their channel.

Chapter Sixty-Seven

"V.K.C. Calibre 110."

"Go ahead 110."

"I want you to call Carlton 255, Sergeant McLaren and the following call signs and get them heading in our direction."

"Go ahead with the call signs, 110."

"Along with Carlton 255, I want Yarra 210, Collingwood 210 and Melbourne 210. Get them mobile and tell them to keep vigilant. I want them spread over the distance between the Collingwood Armoury and Brunswick Road up to Sydney Road."

"Received that. Carlton 255, Sergeant McLaren, Yarra 210, Collingwood 210 and Melbourne 210. Did you receive the last?" the calm operator said.

Being on the same Operational channel along with the convoy units, Kate McLaren answered immediately.

"Carlton 255 received. All those nominated units meet me at Wellington Street and Alexandra Parade A.S.A.P. for instructions."

The replies came back crisply with all units acknowledging.

Tony Signorotto turned around and faced Phil Stone.

"This looks like the old divide and conquer tactic, mate. S.O.G. gone and us in front," he said.

"Absolutely," Stone replied coldly. "I think we may be coming to the pointy end of this ride. We know Lombardi's connected with bikies. This is all starting to fit into some sort of pattern I'm afraid. The freeway looks okay but I'm more concerned for when we get off. Contact Vic Roads and see if we can get a green light all the way down Brunswick Road. No time to phone them. You'll have to go straight to their Channel 26."

"Doing it now," Signorotto said, picking up the Motorola portable radio and turning the dial to the Vic Roads channel.

Christ. I hope there's no one scanning this, Signorotto thought.

Parked in the old battering ram Ford in Fleming Street, Tony Richards was intently listening to his illegal police scanner and heard the request Signorotto asked for.

Chapter Sixty-Eight

The two Carnivores that their President had placed at the bottom of the driveway of the Brunswick Italian Social Club made their decision. Unfortunately, it was not a wise one.

They could see a black vehicle slowly approaching down the ramp to the car park and, without speaking to each other, immediately presumed it was just another black van much the same as the one that they had help shoot to pieces earlier. The combined thought process just meant more Black Rats.

Both bikies stepped into view of the Toyota Landcruiser. What they couldn't see was that two of the four-man S.O.G. crew had gotten out of the vehicle and taken up positions on the specially installed standing platform that had been added to the rear of the Police four-wheel drive. Both were armed with Remington twelve-gauge pump action shotguns as well as their standard issue nine-millimetre Smith and Wesson Police and Military Special automatic pistols. They were itching to go to war.

If the first Carnivore to raise his sawn-off shotgun had only realised he wasn't facing a van load of tribal bikies, but instead, some of the most highly trained fighters in the land, the police equivalent of the famed S.A.S., then he would never have turned the business end of his shotgun towards the approaching vehicle.

From a distance of about thirty metres, the second bikie turned to look at his offsider, thinking that he had dropped to one knee to take up a combat stance in preparation to shoot. When he fell backwards almost at the same time as a small arms calibre weapon discharged, he saw the red stain spreading quickly across the black leather of the Carnivore's emblazoned vest.

The second Carnivore did not hear or see the two police jump off the back of the Toyota. By the time he turned around, both of them had crossed the ground between themselves and the wide-eyed bikie. He was suddenly looking into the up-close business end of a pump action shotgun.

With every intention of dropping his weapon to ground in front of the black helmeted robot-like creatures, he twitched his firearm hand a fraction too much and immediately became the target of a face full of capsicum spray. Lying on the ground looking upwards, screaming and weaponless, the bikie was immediately tethered to a traffic pole bearing a yellow sign displaying the words *'proceed with caution'*.

A voice boomed from the speakers under the bonnet of the S.O.G. vehicle, calling for the occupants of the mostly destroyed black van to show themselves. The Sergeant could see there was no person in the driver's or passenger areas, and one of his crew had stealthily got a look in the open rear area where one door was hanging off its hinges.

"Nil occupants, 400."

"Received," came the reply with the following words of warning coming over the speakers.

"In ten seconds, I will fire upon the vehicle. If there is anyone inside, show yourselves immediately with your arms raised."

The S.O.G. troops, minus their Sergeant were now all out of the vehicle and had taken up positions behind bullet proof shields. They had covered off on all angles and areas of the car park but were concentrating on a group of approximately twenty motorbikes by the far fence.

The President of the Carnivores and his heavily armed offsiders stood from behind their cover near the motorbikes with weapons raised, thinking that if a shot was fired, by whoever this enemy was, at the destroyed van, it would be the perfect diversion for them to take the opportunity to fire on the now still Toyota. Bad choices abounded.

Behind the darkened, bullet proof five millimetre thick glass of the Landcruiser, the Sergeant slid back the metal roof and immediately appeared and fired their police issued forty millimetre grenade launcher, not at the vehicle, but what, at a later Coroners Court hearing, he would calmly describe as their major threat, that being the pack of heavily armed offenders. The fact they offered themselves up on a platter was inconsequential to the Sergeant.

The group of bikies were immediately engulfed in pieces of scorching metal, petrol and rubber as the grenade exploded into the first of the pristine Harley Davidsons.

What a waste of good motorbikes, the Sergeant thought.

A second grenade was fired toward a smaller group of bikes, turning the car park into an inferno of flame and burning fuel.

It was later revealed that the President of the Carnivores died from being struck by a set of chrome handlebars being cut loose from one of the Harleys. It decapitated him where he stood. Several others lost an arm or leg and a one hundred and ninety-centimetre-tall bikie would be forever be nicknamed 'Stumpy' after the infamous day, as both of his legs were severed at the knees.

When the smoke cleared, the Carnivores who were not injured lay prostrate on the bitumen staring wide eyed at each other at what had just taken place. The time frame from the moment the S.O.G. had entered the driveway until the second grenade had been launched had been no longer than five or six minutes.

To ensure no more riders could escape, two S.O.G. walked quickly around the remaining upright motorbikes and took to their tyres with razor sharp Commando knives.

The Sergeant stepped out of his vehicle looking like a modern-day Mad Max and strode over to one of the living Carnivores and rolled him over onto his back. He pulled his automatic pistol from its holster, aimed it at the head of the Carnivore and spoke.

"Why on earth did you try and take us on?"

The bikie looked up at the black clad police officer and with a stuttering voice replied.

Chapter Sixty-Eight

"You're not a Black Rat!"

The Sergeant replied. "Don't insult me. We are the Special Operations Group."

The body count would reveal two dead Carnivores along with eight with missing limbs and nearly all with burns from the exploding petrol tanks. None of the Harley Davidsons would ever go on a 'patched' run again. The Melbourne Chapter of the Carnivores had been decimated.

Chapter Sixty-Nine

Tony Richards had been listening intently to all the calls coming across his police scanner when he heard the request put out by Tony Signorotto via the Calibre 110 call sign for them to be given a 'green' all the way down Brunswick Road. On hearing the answer come back saying yes, he started up the old Ford and moved to the opposite side of Fleming Street where he could get a better view of traffic coming up Brunswick Road towards him.

He knew that his target would be in the form of the latest black Police Highway Patrol decaled BMW Series 5 sedan. His aim was to hit the driver's door of the police vehicle with as much speed and force as the old Ford could muster. It wasn't just about heisting the pistols, it was also about revenge on police in general. He had an inborn hatred of all forms of law and order. When the bull bar adorned old Ford hit the German machine, all he wanted to see was destruction.

Sergeant Eddie Downes, the driver of the now leading police car, was an experienced officer and although there was no immediate proof of it, he made himself think and drive as though he was driving into some sort of trap. He knew also that his two passengers had the same thought on their minds.

Looking straight ahead but at the same time speaking to Tony Signorotto he spoke.

"Boss, we are just about on the turnoff. Can you ask the truck and the back-up vehicle to space out a bit? If something goes down, we all need a bit of wriggle room."

"Good idea, Eddie," Tony said immediately, making a grab for the radio handset. Before he could though, the voice of the same D.24 operator as before broke in.

"Calibre 110?"

"Calibre 110 receiving," Phil Stone replied immediately through his portable radio.

"Calibre 110. Please be aware that it appears Calibre 400 have reported shots have been fired at the job I sent them to at the Brunswick Italian Social Club car park. We know you will be near that point very soon so be on alert. 400 has the situation under control but has called for multiple ambulances to assist. Copy that 110?"

"Copy that V.K.C. We are just coming up the exit ramp from the freeway at Brunswick Road. We will be past there in one minute," Phil Stone replied quickly.

"Add to that 110, there is a situation at Brunswick Road and the railway boom gates near Sydney Road. Looks like a fatal between a train and motorcycle at this stage. No prizes for guessing who came off second best in that one."

"Roger that V.K.C. If we have to divert, I will get back to you. We also have a possible hostage situation at another unknown location connected with this convoy, which at this stage we have to handle from this end. I will call the Deputy Commissioner Crime as soon as I can. Over and out."

"Thanks Calibre 110," the unflappable operator said calmly.

"Christ, Tony, This might come down to the wire. Let's hope we can get through this. We want to look after both the shipment and Tom, but I can't go along with him forever. I'll have to get onto the big bosses at headquarters now," a very worried Phil Stone said as he scanned the roadway around him while reaching for his phone. As he did, Eddie Downes chipped in.

"Just because we have a green traffic control signal all the way down Brunswick Road, I still want time to look at every little thing around us, so I am not doing this fast. If I have to take evasive action, I want room to manoeuvre. Can you two please keep an eye out for anything that looks out of the ordinary?"

"Okay," Signorotto said as the convoy swung left onto Brunswick Road, passing the entrance located on the opposite side of the road leading down to the Brunswick Italian Social Club. "Don't know what's happened with the S.O.G., but you can smell burning fuel coming through the vents." Two hundred metres further east, the experienced Highway Patrol driver would have his expertise in the handling of his pursuit vehicle tested to the extreme.

Three sets of eyes were peeled for danger around them but mostly on anything coming towards them or from behind.

Eddie Downes was not treating the green traffic control situation as a right of passage. Too many occasions on night shift over the years had given him mental scars regarding the number of police vehicles who had treated both green and red traffic lights with flagrant disregard.

The old Highway Patrol moto of a red light being treated as 'nightshift green' had brought many a police officer bad karma and, in some cases, death. The opposite was just as bad with civilian drivers, where some fool had driven straight through a red light into an opposing vehicle. Sometimes it was just that 'Red meant Dead'.

All eyes were searching when Eddie Downes, just about on the intersection with Fleming Street, yelled loudly.

"Look Out. Hold on qui...!"

Chapter Seventy

Eddie Downes's steady right foot on the accelerator of the police vehicle, combined with his split-second warning, not only saved himself from being killed but also saved the lives of Phil Stone and Tony Signorotto.

The balaclava clad Richards had seen his quarry and driven at it like an Exocet missile. The one possible thing that he hadn't accounted for, was the fact that when Downes had sighted the Ford battering ram coming towards him at warp speed, the police driver's slow speed meant that the patrol car was able to be turned quickly to the left. If Downes had been going any faster, the turn would have been too late, and the impact would have been directly into the driver's door.

The fraction less speed by Downes didn't however avoid the Ford hitting them like a runaway train, but it meant the extensive damage was caused between the front of the police vehicle and the windscreen.

The old Ford, courtesy of the attached bull bar, sheared the front section of the BMW halfway off the remainder of the car. The three occupants were immediately enveloped by the front and side air bags as their bodies were rag-dolled around the cabin.

Tony Signorotto's head was slammed into the passenger side window frame whilst Eddie Downes was virtually thrown sideways onto his front seat passenger. In the rear seat behind Signorotto, Phil Stone had heard the quick warning from Downes and the fact that he was sitting on the opposite side to the impact gave him a split second to brace himself.

Time seemed to stand still in the aftermath of the horrific collision. There was the sound of crunching, grinding metal combined with shattering glass one second and then the absolute silence as the combined worlds of the police officers whirled before their eyes. Seconds passed in disbelief.

As the officers reached for each other in survival mode, the voice of Tony Signorotto cut through the air. "Whatever is on top of us is now backing up from on the bonnet."

Shaken but still alive, they turned their attention to what they could see out the front of their crushed vehicle. The view consisted of a car with a huge chrome bull bar reversing off them. The sound of crunching glass and scraping metal was now combined with the crash of the vehicle falling from the bonnet of the police car to the roadway. It then drove across in front of them and disappeared at a rapid rate north along Fleming Street.

The truck driven by Tom Cole had braked heavily as had the National Security Services car behind him. Only the two flanking Highway Patrol solos kept moving. They accelerated up both sides of the truck to the rear of the wrecked Highway Patrol car where the two Leading Senior Constable riders jumped off their mounts and ran to either side of the BMW police car to give their fellow officers what assistance they could.

One solo rider pulled out a multi-tool from his equipment belt and slashed at the air bags. What they were left with were three dazed but uninjured officers.

Tony Signorotto pushed Eddie Downes off him, speaking quietly.

"You saved our lives, mate."

"I could just feel something was about to happen," Downes replied. "Too much of a coincidence with the S.O.G. being called away."

"You okay?" Signorotto said to Phil Stone who was pushing the now deflated air bag away from himself.

"All good. Where's that car gone? The one that hit us." An angry Stone said.

One of the solo riders who was off his motorbike and helping spoke up.

"He's just rammed you and taken off. Got to be deliberate." He said as the sound of a revving engine overcame any further conversation.

The two solo riders looked back at the firearms truck only to see it reversing quickly before smashing into the front of the National Security Services car, completely crushing the front of it, causing the radiator to explode and spray a vertical stream of hot water.

Tony Signorotto was halfway out of the damaged police car and looking at the Hino truck.

"What the hell is going on?" he said with a disbelieving voice of what he was witnessing, before realising that the truck was now accelerating towards the two BMW police motor bikes parked next to the offside of the wrecked Highway Patrol car.

"Look out!" A solo rider near the driver's side door yelled at the same time as leaping backwards out of the way of the five-ton vehicle that was now coming back towards them.

Tony Signorotto realised immediately that the driver was not aiming at any of them, but at the two motor bikes. He looked up at Tom Cole and could see the expression of anguish on his face and he knew that what was about to happen was to do with the kidnapping of Cole's daughter.

The two BMW 1200 c.c. motor bikes disappeared under the front of the Hino as Cole veered past the crash scene. One of them was pushed up against the wrecked police car and the other was dragged under the truck as it accelerated along Brunswick Road. The expensive piece of police machinery was spat out from under the departing vehicle soon after.

Phil Stone and Eddie Downes had managed to extricate themselves from the wreckage of the pursuit vehicle and together with Signorotto and the two solo riders looked at the damaged National Security Services car and the two crushed motor bikes.

Stone slammed his fists into the roof of the BMW and screamed.

"Christ. That's the pistols gone!"

Tony Signorotto looked at his long-time workmate before speaking.

"Maybe. Maybe not. Tom's done this for a reason. I could see it in his face, and I know he won't go down without a fight. This is all to do with Summer being kidnapped. I'll get on the radio and get Kate and her crew over here quick. Eddie, you'd better get onto Traffic Headquarters and get us another car if you can real quick and get some assistance for those two stranded National Security guards."

Both of the police officers got on with their respective jobs as Phil Stone rang into D.24 communications while he thought to himself how he was going to explain losing track of three thousand pistols.

Chapter Seventy-One

Big Al Lombardi knew that Cole had to come along Brunswick Road towards him. The thing that was concerning him was the amount of traffic that was building up from the area of the blocked railway line near Sydney Road.

With his eyes glued to the driver's mirror of his Maserati, he breathed a sigh of relief when the white Hino appeared from behind. He immediately pulled out in front of the truck and at the same time put his arm out the window frantically pointing to Cole to follow him left into Grantham Street. He saw Cole raise his two hands from the steering wheel in a questioning manner, but he followed him anyway.

Lombardi then drove via a series of side and back streets until he finally turned right into Sydney Road and then right again into Barkly Street. Having already phoned Feb at the factory to have the rear roller door open, he pulled into the dark interior with the Hino behind him. The roller door came down quickly as Cole jumped out of the cab, walking quickly towards the office where his daughter was being held.

As he did, he passed the old wreck of the Ford which had made it back only minutes before Lombardi and himself. Tony Richards went to step in front of Cole, speaking as he did so.

"Get over there and start to load the other truck. I want the..."

Richards never got to finish his sentence as Cole picked him up bodily off the ground and slammed him against the Ford. He held the long haired bikie in position with one hand as he whipped the large revolver out from Richards grimy jeans and flicked open the pistol's chamber, causing the six rounds of ammunition to clatter onto the concrete floor before he threw it into the open window of the car and barked at the stunned Richards.

"Get out of my way, you pathetic piece of shit. I'm not unloading anything. I want to see my daughter," Cole said angrily as he ripped the balaclava off Richards face before dropping him onto the floor.

Lombardi could see that Richards was about to attack Cole from behind but jumped between them.

"Later. Not now. Let's just get these guns transferred," Lombardi said.

"He's seen my face and he's seen yours. He's going to be knocked," Richards spat back at Lombardi.

"He's yours to deal with later," Lombardi said.

"You're fucking dead meat, pal. No one does that to a Black Rat and gets away with it," Richards screamed at Cole's back as Lombardi blocked his path.

All he got from Cole was a raised middle finger in return as he burst into the office area and found Summer sitting on the couch with Angelo Morelli not far away in a chair. Before he could speak, Morelli got up and passed by him heading towards the door, whispering to him as he did.

"You've probably got ten minutes max to get out through the vent. I've removed the screws and I'll lock the door on the way out," the nervous kidnapper said with a shaky voice. "I'll keep them from here as long as I can. With all of us unloading it won't take that long to transfer the guns though."

As he was about to get to the door, Cole spoke.

"Why are you helping us?"

Morelli replied quietly.

"I'm not one of them. That prick Lombardi executed my mate with a bullet through the mouth. The two that were with me when we grabbed you are witnesses to it. Being an extra in this was one thing I had no choice in. You're not the only kidnap victim here. He's totally fucking mad and don't believe for a second he won't kill you and your kid. It's him that told us to take your daughter as well." Pointing up at the vent he continued. "Get yourselves up and out of here. It leads to the side street. Hurry up."

"You're not wearing a balaclava either. I know what two of the others look like and now you," Cole said quietly.

"I don't care," Morelli said in reply. "I'll do time for kidnapping no matter what happens from here on in. I want your kid out of this, but Lombardi won't care. He killed my mate over a stupid comment. Just get out of here while you can."

Morelli closed the door quietly. Cole heard the lock turn and immediately dragged the table over, jumped up on it and set to work. He lowered the vent cover down onto the table. He had just got down onto the floor when he heard someone trying the door handle.

"Come and help load this truck, you prick. Who locked this fucking door?" The agitated voice of Tony Richards cursed from outside.

Cole immediately began to think of what to do. He knew he had to grab Summer and get her up into the vent but daren't make a sound at the moment. The situation was saved when a second voice called out.

"Leave them. You and I will take care of them before we go. Just get back here. I don't want a kid screaming when I wave a gun at her." The door handle was released a moment later.

Cole waited a few seconds before he picked Summer up. She immediately grabbed her father around the neck, hugging him tightly.

"Sweetheart. We are getting out of here right now," he said, explaining that he would lift her into the duct and would follow right behind her. "Were you okay while I was gone?"

"Yes, daddy. The man was nice. We played. His name is Angelo."

Lifting his daughter up quietly into the ceiling vent, Cole tried to think of ways to pay back Angelo. After what this Angelo had told him, he thought grimly to himself that the only pay back would come in the form of a bullet from one of his associates.

Chapter Seventy-Two

An agitated Tony Richards had just finished manhandling several boxes of pistols from a pallet in the Hino onto the floor of the dark blue Hyundai rental truck that would transport their heist to Sydney.

Together with Feb, Joey and Angelo, they had done the bulk of the work and he wasn't in the mood to entertain anyone who wasn't putting their back into it.

"Lombardi. Where are you? Get over here and help," he screamed at the gangster who was hurrying down from looking out the mezzanine window onto Brunswick Road.

Lombardi yelled back.

"Have you thought about where your other two mates have gone? They should have been back here before we got back. I've been up at the window looking at that mess by the railway line and there are tarps over at least two bodies and motor bike parts everywhere. There's also a shotgun lying on the road with a chalk circle around it. What does that tell you, eh?"

"What are you fucking saying ?" Richards shot back as the others listened on.

"Somethings obviously gone down out there and I reckon your two goons are probably lying under those tarps. Because of them we are going to be stuck in here. That's what I'm fucking saying, you idiot. I should never have got you lot in on this," a now screaming Lombardi said to Richards with the distance between them closing rapidly.

The rest of the crew looked nervously at each other, realising that tensions between the two were at boiling point.

Richards turned away from Lombardi and quickly ran up the stairs to the mezzanine floor window and looked at the carnage fifty metres down Brunswick Road. While he and the others had been transferring the stolen guns, the nagging feeling had been eating away in his gut about what had happened to his two missing bikie brothers. Now he knew.

Despondency didn't stay with Richards for too long after he returned downstairs and confronted Lombardi. He looked him in the eye before speaking.

"They were never going to get anything out of this anyway. I'm the President and they died fighting for the Black Rats. They will always be my brothers."

Lombardi stared back, thinking to himself.

It's more money for yourself that you're thinking about. You couldn't give a fuck about your so-called brothers!

Lombardi's mind was racing trying to keep up with the constantly changing situation. He cut open one of the padlocked boxes with a set of bolt cutters and removed two of the brand new pistols. He then cut open another case and took out a box of ammunition and four magazines for the guns. Walking quickly to the Maserati, he sat in the passenger seat and loaded sixty rounds of bullets into the four magazines and then slammed both of the mags into the firearms. He racked each pistol so they were ready to fire. He didn't know that the temporary blockages in both pistols meant nothing would happen when you pulled their triggers. He put one of the pistols between the expensive leather driver's seat and the console and the other into the tray in front of the automatic gear shift.

I will always be the King.

By the time he returned to the truck he could see the transfer of the weapons had been completed. Richards, Feb, Joey and Angelo were sitting down and taking a breather. They were sweating and tired. Angelo managed to raise himself and walk up to the mezzanine window, taking in the scene just up the road. He had done this, not to see what was happening but as a diversion. Walking back down to the floor area, he deliberately went past the small steel door that was inset into the larger roller door which faced onto Brunswick Road. The smaller door was closed but he could see the lock cylinder was missing. It could be closed but was not able to be locked. He realised this could be his escape route if he thought what would happen with Cole's escape happened soon.

His courage returned and his attitude was beginning to turn into survival mode. He took another chance immediately and spoke to the others.

"If we are going to get out of here, I wouldn't do it for a good hour or so. The cops are everywhere out there."

Everyone, including Lombardi, looked at the usually quiet Morelli. Silence reigned. Suddenly the gangster walked up to him and poked a finger in his chest before he spoke. Morelli froze.

"He's right. I want us out of here soon, but an hour won't hurt."

The others nodded their heads in collective weariness.

Slipping his balaclava back on to continue the subterfuge, Morelli pushed the boundaries even further as he walked towards the office.

"I'll check on Cole and his kid."

Entering the locked room, Morelli lent up against the inside of the door and stared up at the open vent. After staying for about fifteen seconds he left the room, locked the door and before Lombardi or Richards could speak, he gave them a thumbs up sign and nodded his head.

Outside the tyre factory, Cole had lowered Summer to the ground and run across the narrow street and straight through the back door of the old Sarah Sands hotel.

Due to Brunswick Road being blocked off at Sydney Road because of the now crime scene that existed at the railway line, the pub was completely empty. Cole dragged Summer through to the front of the hotel where he grabbed a bartender by the arm.

"Quick. I've got to phone the police. Where's a phone? Give me your mobile, will you?" he said with a steely voice.

The bartender replied with a grin on his face.

"No need to mate. Just look outside," he said.

Cole pushed open the bar door onto Sydney Road and saw police vehicles on each of the four corners of the intersection with Brunswick Road. There were blue and red flashing lights everywhere. He picked up Summer and ran to the nearest vehicle, grabbing open the front passenger door, nearly causing the police officer to fall out.

Cole looked at the officer and stammered, "Kate?"

Chapter Seventy-Three

With a look of relief, Kate McLaren pushed Tom Cole and Summer into the rear of the police car and immediately told Chloe Schaeffer, who was driving, to head to the nearby Traffic Branch headquarters where she knew that Phil Stone and Tony Signorotto were located.

Having been told via a phone call from Tony Signorotto of the near fatal ramming of their Highway Patrol car, she was not going to waste time. Tom Cole had a story to tell and little Summer needed looking after.

Within minutes they were pulling into the building. Tony Signorotto and Phil Stone came straight out to the car. Signorotto could see the look on Tom's face and spoke first.

"First things first, Tom. Is Summer okay?" he said looking at the little girl who was chatting animatedly with Chloe Schaeffer.

"She's fine, Tony," Cole said with relief in his voice. "I'm so sorry, mate. I couldn't do anything about before. It was all planned days ago after they grabbed us at our house. I had to go along with it all because of Summer. That's why I slipped you that note. The guy with the Maserati is in charge of it, but right now I don't think he knows we've got out."

"All that other shit can wait, Tom. Number one priority is Summer. Young Chloe here will take care of her. We'll get her over to Jill Norton's place and keep her right out of this. Now we know it is Lombardi with his Maserati. Where were they holding you?" Signorotto said.

"It's that old tyre place next to the pub where Kate was parked. Down from the railway line. I've been past there before for work. Think it's called Sam's Tyres. It's been there for years but now it's empty. You know it?" Cole queried.

"Yeah, we know it," Stone said to a nodding Signorotto. What's he got in there? Is the truck with the pistols inside? How many with him?"

Tom's mind quickly dissected all the questions in a flash.

"There's Lombardi and his main helper. Some dude and two others who have all the hallmark of being bikies. There's one other by the name of Angelo, who I think is some sort of kidnap victim also. Don't know the full story but he told me Lombardi shot one of his mates in the head. He looked after Summer when I drove the truck."

Kate McLaren stepped in with a police folder containing Operation Calibre. At the rear of the folder were several pages of colour photos which she showed to Cole. They were photos of Lombardi and his crew including Richards which had been taken by the surveillance crews over several days outside Lombardi's Club Maximus in Lygon Street. Cole ticked off on all of them immediately.

"That's them. You'll want to get your hands on this Richards character. He's the one that rammed you. No injuries to you lot or the bike riders?" Cole asked with dread in his voice.

"No. Everyone survived. About a hundred grand's worth of police vehicle damage, but that's for the bean counters to figure out. You won't be looking at charges seeing that it was a kidnap situation. Not if I've got anything to do with it," Phil Stone said.

Tony Signorotto turned back to the others and spoke.

"Got hold of Jill Norton. She'll take care of Summer. Tom, if you want to tell Summer she has not only Jill to look forward too but also a new batch of strawberry pancakes, I'll get Chloe to drive her over there. I think we need you at the factory scene. I've got a bit of a plan for our hero kidnappers."

"Let's get all our cars over to the area and in position," Stone said urgently.

Cole walked over to his now smiling daughter who was delighted to be getting a ride in a real police car and going home to see Jill Norton.

Signorotto leant in the driver's window and spoke to the young Constable and Summer.

"A very precious cargo, Chloe. See you back at Sydney Road as soon as you can."

"No worries, boss. See you soon."

Chloe drove out the concrete chute that led into Dawson Street.

Phil Stone called Tony and Kate over to where he was talking to Tom before speaking to them all as a group.

"Whatever plan you have, Tony, it has to be done by the uniforms. The S.O.G. will be tied up with that shootout at the Brunswick Italian Social Club and as sure as God made little green apples, I'll bet that and the railway line scene are both connected to the gun heist.

Apparently, we can get a couple of Critical Incident Response Units heading our way, but they are way down the peninsula finishing up a job right now. Whatever is going to be done I want the uniforms to resolve it. We're not looking too good in the eyes of the Crime Department right now for losing the guns. Let's hear your plan, Tony."

"Okay. There's five of them, but really there's only four from what Tom said about this Angelo character. We know none of the guns are able to be fired until they have those blocks removed and have been serviced, so as far as I can see we have them inside the factory, and like Phil said, we aren't looking too flash with the big brass. Time to reclaim some respect. If they're in there, they probably won't want to make a break for it until the scene clears at the railway line. All these crime scenes are connected and we could wrap up some wannabe gangster and some bikies if we move now. You agree, Phil?"

"Think I know where you're going with this, Tony. We need to get this scene clear at the railway line or at least make it look as though as though all the coppers have gone," Stone said with a malicious grin on his face.

"The boss and I will talk to Command now and get them to gradually get everyone away from the railway scene over the next forty-five minutes or so, but we'll have cars out of sight on either side of that factory. This will give those hold up inside some hope for an exit plan," Signorotto said.

Tom Cole chipped in. "When they find that Summer and I have got out, they will make a break for it straight away. I think we need to move now."

"That's all fine, but I want it stopped inside or before they hit the street. I don't want bloodshed on Brunswick Road unless we can help it and I certainly don't want it to be our blood. I want them surrounded and certain that they don't have a choice but to give up when they try to exit," Stone said emphatically.

"It will be their choice all right, Phil. It will be either give up or go down fighting. To my way of thinking, the average little Italian gangster and a few bikies won't be that brave. If we get everyone clear of the area it should work and I think we can do it with just uniforms. If it comes off, we've got a bag of crooks and our shooters back. What do you say, Phil?" Tony Signorotto said as everyone looked at the Superintendent.

"We've got some face saving to do, people. Let's get cracking."

Chapter Seventy-Four

Big Al Lombardi was a thug and a gangster, but he was no fool.

When he took another look out of the mezzanine window and saw the same scene as before, he had a growing fear in his gut that the timing for their exit from the hideaway was now being far too controlled by outside factors: And those outside factors were in turn being controlled by the police. It was time to shift the goal posts and re-arrange his own playing field.

There was no way in hell that the scene outside would be clear for hours and by that time even the dumbest Police Force would tie the car park shoot out and the railway incidents together, and every police car would be looking for the white Hino truck. Even with the new truck, Lombardi figured that there would be roadblocks on all major highways within hours with zealous cops opening up every tailgate as if they were working on the Dover crossing in England looking for illegal immigrants. He had to move now and take a huge punt. If it came off, nothing would change as far as the pistol sale went. If it didn't, survival became paramount. Just his survival though. He laid the blame for the railway line mess squarely at the feet of Tony Richards.

Even with a worst-case scenario of Richards not showing at Gundagai or being caught, Lombardi knew he could still get out of the country without using commercial flights or shipping. He would be able to live on money that was wire transferred to wherever he went. It galled him though that he may have to give up on the firearms deal. All he had to do was use one of his contacts to give him safe haven in the Calabrian infested city of Griffith in New South Wales. They would see to it that he got back to the mother country of Italy.

With all these thoughts criss-crossing his spiderweb-like mind, he finally made a decision. It was time for him to get out, and to do that he had to dangle some sort of carrot in front of Tony Richards. That carrot would be leaving Richards to his own devices with Cole and Morelli. Lombardi called out to him.

"Tony. Come over here."

Richards rose tiredly from his seat and walked over to Lombardi.

"Tony. I'm leaving now to get up to our overnight stop at Gundagai. I want to make sure everything is okay with the plan. Give me an hour and you leave also by the back door. Whoever you want to bring, or not bring, just manage it. I don't care who you knock, but I'd suggest you take care of Cole. He knows too much. His kid is too young to legally give evidence against us so maybe just tie her up and leave her. If you want, jam up her memory a bit and blow her father away in front of her. Angelo is a liability also. Just bring Feb and Joey," Lombardi said like a father talking to his son.

"Yeah, sounds okay. I'll take care of things here and we'll meet tonight in Gundagai," Richards replied to a nodding Lombardi.

"Fuck you. What you are is a pathetic gangster," Richards thought as excitement grew inside him with the idea of leaving the factory with the firearms and just Joey and Feb, but never heading to the rendezvous.

I've got plans of my own, Lombardi. Three thousand of them to be precise.

Lombardi patted Richards on the shoulder then walked over to the others to explain the slight change in plans. Lombardi did not care about the bloodshed that Richards was about to bring down on them like a red curtain. With that sorted, a relieved Lombardi climbed behind the wood grained wheel of his Maserati, indicated for Feb to raise the roller door and drove out, turning left into Sydney Road. Looking in the rear-view mirror he could see the blue and red flashing lights of the police cars at Brunswick Road lighting up like a hundred Christmas trees.

Driving north along Sydney Road, Brunswick, he knew the odds of Richards getting to Gundagai were slim at best. When he weighed up the risks and benefits, he might lose out on the deal and could be betrayed, but by that time he would be far away and able to run his businesses from overseas. If the deal came off, great. If Richards survived, he wouldn't survive for long. Lombardi would make sure of that.

Chapter Seventy-Five

With Lombardi gone, Richards looked intently at the railway scene in Brunswick Road from his position on the mezzanine floor, at the same time as he was racking his brain regarding the possibilities of a distribution network for the stolen firearms.

The first thought was that it was the opportunity of a lifetime. The money he could get would set himself up for life, if only he knew where to off load them. He didn't have the contacts like Lombardi did, he realised.

It dawned on him slowly that it would have been better if he was trying to get rid of three hundred pistols instead of three thousand. Even hiding that many would be a nightmare because they would have to be able to be moved at a minute's notice. The O.M.C.G. headquarters of the Black Rats was certainly big enough, but it could be raided for other reasons at any time of the day or night. The other choice was to divide them up into smaller batches, but even then, he still had to get them out of their present location.

The thought of actually meeting up again with Lombardi and just taking his share of the profits in Sydney still had appeal. His bikie persona though kept thinking of other areas of sale. He wouldn't sell to any other bike gangs because the possibility that any future firefight in a turf war could come down to himself or some of the Black Rats catching a bullet from their own on-sold weapons cache.

His attention was diverted from his distribution problem when he noticed that the train that had been stationary across the railway crossing was being backed up away from the boom gates. Together with that, the surrounding police cars had their crews back in them and looked ready to leave.

It had been a few hours since the incident had taken place and Richards, although he had also seen a shotgun on the roadway, was really none the wiser if his obviously dead or injured brother bikies had been taken down in a shootout or hit by the train. At some stage the road had to be re-opened and train services restored and there were only so many photographs and measurements that needed to be taken.

He bounded down from the mezzanine level and yelled to his three remaining accomplices who were gathered around the blue Hyundai.

"We're going soon, so get fucking ready. It looks like they are finishing up outside. Make sure everything is tied up and secure in the truck. Angelo, I want you to come with me. It's time we dealt with that prick Cole. Grab some rope from the truck. "

Morelli's radar turned to high alert. "What's the rope for?" He questioned.

Richards spun around, holding his large revolver loosely in his right hand.

"Just do what you're fucking told. I need it for the kid. Get some and bring it to the room now," he said with anger in his voice.

Morelli walked quickly over to the far side of the Hyundai truck and started to panic when he saw Richards try the door handle of the room where Cole and his daughter were supposed to be.

"Bring the fucking key over here, Morelli. And get that rope quick," Richards growled in his direction.

Angelo Morelli's brain went into overdrive as he got a length of thick rope from the truck and walked slowly back, stopping between Richards and the front roller door. Taking a further two short steps towards Richards, he called out.

"Here's the key," he said as he threw it in the air towards the right hand of Richards, forcing him to swap the revolver to his left hand. At the same time, Angelo dropped the rope to the floor to minimise himself for what was about to happen.

Unlocking the door with his right hand, Richards yelled back as he began to enter the room.

"Hurry up. I've got to take…." he said, his voice fading and then rising to a crescendo.

"What the fuck. Where are…? He said rushing back into the factory only to see Morelli kicking open the small insert hatch in the big roller door and starting to bend down to get through to freedom.

Richards had to swap his revolver back to his right hand before he fired off two shots in quick succession before Angelo had made it fully through the door. One shot punched a hole through the steel roller door centimetres from the terrified Morelli's head. The second shot hit him in the left shoulder blade taking out two ribs before exiting through his chest. Falling to the ground half in and out of the small door, Angelo watched his blood pool on the ground beneath him before his eyes slowly closed and he lay still.

Richards screamed back to Feb and Joey.

"Get the back door up and let's get out of here now," he said running to the blue Hyundai and jumping into the driver's seat. Firing up the motor, he turned to see Feb half in the passenger door but looking back at the body of Angelo Morelli.

Richards yelled, "He's fucking dead, Feb. Forget him. I was going to knock him anyway, the fucking prick. He let Cole and his kid out somehow and now we have to get out before the cops swarm over here. We'll grab Joey and get back to our clubhouse."

Feb said nothing but finished getting in as Richards exited the door and stopped to get Joey, who was standing in the alley with hands raised.

"Fucking get in, Joey," Richards yelled through the open drivers' window at his statue like brother-in-arms, before suddenly noticing the feeling of cold steel as Max Tyler pressed his service pistol against the bikie's right temple.

"Both hands on the steering wheel, Richards," Max said with his gun partially through the open window.

"I'm not done yet, copper," Richards said quietly as he suddenly accelerated away down the alley knocking Max's pistol back out of the window. Tyler dropped to one knee and fired two rounds into the drivers' side rear dual tyres, hitting both.

As he accelerated, Richards looked to his left only to see the body of Feb Felagi being dragged from the open passenger door by a female cop. A crazy thought flashed through the bikie's mind.

It's all mine now. All mine.

With the air gone from the rear tyres and his panicked acceleration, Richards couldn't fight the Hyundai's steering as it slammed into the brick wall that formed the left of the alleyway. His head pitched forward and hit the steering wheel. With a bleeding forehead he jumped out of the truck and looked at the two police that were standing some two or so metres in front of him. One of them was a cop in uniform who was pointing his pistol directly at him. The other he recognised as Tom Cole.

Blood from the cut was running down his cheek as he tried to focus on a grinning Tony Signorotto, the face behind the pistol, who was separating him from his escape into Sydney Road. Without thinking of the consequences, Richards started to raise his revolver and take aim at Signorotto. It was always going to end badly.

Tony Signorotto knew he had justification to shoot. He fired one shot only. Richards' right knee exploded instantly from the nine-millimetre round causing him to scream and slump up against the truck, his knee wobbling around inside his tattered jeans, blood pumping down his leg and onto his black boots.

Tom Cole went into S.A.S. mode as he took three quick steps towards their quarry, grabbing the wounded bikie's revolver hand with both of his and twisting the firearm backwards causing Richards to keep screaming in pain as the pressure from Cole rotating his hand and keeping the bikie's wrist still caused a loud popping sound as Richards' radius bone separated from the scaphoid bone in his right hand.

Richards dropped the firearm as he slumped to his knees.

Chapter Seventy-Five

"Not so big now, eh, little fella," Cole said menacingly down at his foe.

Tony Signorotto looked back up the laneway and could see Phil Stone holding his pistol at the back of Feb Felagi's head as Kate McLaren slapped a pair of handcuffs on his wrists as she held them behind him. The form of Joey Salessa was on his knees nearby with his hands cuffed behind him and the slim form of Chloe Schaeffer with one foot jammed down on his crossed-over ankles to prevent him from standing.

"Where's King Rat?" Tony thought quickly.

Signorotto bent down on one knee in front of Richards and grabbed him around the throat with one meaty hand, squeezing hard and speaking with venom in his voice.

"Where's Lombardi?"

Even in his semi-conscious state, Richards pulled back slightly as Cole still gripped his broken hand. Seconds went by before a raspy voice emitted from the throat of the defeated bikie.

"Get fucked, pig."

Tom Cole made a slight adjustment to his stance and dragged Richards' useless hand ever so slightly to one side, causing an ear-piercing scream from the offender. Signorotto took no notice as he spoke quietly into the ear of the sweating, pale bikie.

"You can try giving the correct answer this time, little man. At this point in time, your wrist will heal, but with one more incorrect reply, you will for evermore only be able to wipe your arse with your left hand. Up to you though, my friend. I would seriously consider telling the truth now, because if you don't you will have to get very up close and personal with your future cell mate when you want to take a dump down at Barwon prison. You will have to employ your own toilet paper boy."

Tony Richards' head nodded slowly as he spoke haltingly.

"He's gone. Sydney. Maserati." He then fell face down into the dog faeces smeared bluestone pitches at his feet.

"He obviously wants a cell to himself," Tony Signorotto said quietly to Tom Cole as he placed his Smith and Wesson pistol back in his holster.

Chapter Seventy-Six

"V.K.C. to all units. Keep a lookout for a late model Maserati sedan, grey in colour. This vehicle is wanted in connection with the attempted theft of a shipment of police firearms. It is being driven by one Alessio Lombardi. Vehicle was last seen in the Brunswick area and is reported to be heading to Sydney in the last hour. Units have now been made aware of several firearm related incidents in the vicinity of Brunswick Road, Brunswick and West Brunswick involving Outlaw Motorcycle Gangs. This Maserati is believed to be connected to these incidents and if seen is to be approached with extreme caution. The male occupant is said to be armed and dangerous. Any sightings are to be called in before permission for any interception is given. Senior Sergeant Tony Signorotto, call sign of Calibre 250, is the principal in this search. V.K.C. out."

The lookout had been broadcast to all units on the police radio channel that covered a wide area that included Sydney Road, Brunswick North through Coburg, Fawkner, Broadmeadows and continued up along the Hume Highway to Wallan.

While Superintendent Phil Stone had taken charge of the Brunswick scene where Tony Richards, Feb Felagi and Joey Salessa were all apprehended, he had dispatched several other units under the overall command of Tony Signorotto to conduct the search for Lombardi. Kate McLaren was on board with him whilst a second vehicle contained Max Tyler and Chloe Schaeffer.

The complete crime scene at the railway line and Sam's Tyre factory had been sealed off and re-established after the successful ruse to flush out the hijackers. The other person who had been taken into custody was the severely injured Angelo Morelli who had been transferred to the Alfred hospital by Air

Ambulance after being re-located to parkland in Royal Parade. He was listed as critical.

As Kate McLaren drove quickly through the northern suburb of Fawkner toward the start of the Hume Highway at Broadmeadows, Tony Signorotto spoke to her.

"Kate. I know we have to find Lombardi, but I am so glad Tom and his daughter are safe. You must be relieved too?"

"Yeah, I am boss. The whole situation is bad but could have been a lot worse. A bunch of dead and shot-up bikies just means less work for us in the long run. I reckon that Morelli character is another victim of all this and has been for a while."

"I managed to talk to the detective who escorted him in the Air Ambulance on the way to the Alfred hospital. I think Tom and Summers' survival is in a fair way down to him. If he survives and is willing to testify against Lombardi, Roberts and the other two, we will have to get him into the Witness Protection Program and buy him a whole new life," Signorotto said in a serious tone.

"Absolutely. Honestly though, after all the shit that it looks like Lombardi has caused, I'm not too fussy if he gives up of his own accord or if he takes us and our friends on."

Tony Signorotto looked across at his driver with a puzzled expression.

"Us and our friends? Not with you, Kate."

The ardent pistol club member in her came out in her reply.

"You, me, Smith and Wesson," Kate said with steel in her voice.

The new breed. Only the time and places change. Never the attitude! Tony Signorotto thought as his mind flashed back to days gone by.

"Let's hope all the units around have picked up on the seriousness of that D.24 broadcast before," he said as Kate pulled the unmarked police vehicle to a stop at the red traffic control signal at Mahoneys Road where Sydney Road became the Hume Highway. Sitting at the lights, he noticed a police solo turn left from Mahoney's Road and accelerate northwards along the highway.

"Scares me when you see these solos doing traffic stops. By the time they get off their bikes, someone can have the drop on them before they can do anything about it," he said.

Kate had been deliberately travelling about ten kilometres per hour under any speed zone she entered just in case they had missed Lombardi on their way north. He could have pulled off the road for a number of reasons. The only thing that seemed definite was his Sydney destination.

Minutes later as they drove through Campbellfield, the police radio burst into life.

"All units. All units. We have a report of a solo down. Location is the Hume Highway approximately five kilometres south of the Kal Kallo Roadhouse on the outbound lanes. Has been called in by a motorist in what looks like a traffic stop gone wrong. Ambulance is en route from Wallan. Only description of the fleeing vehicle is what looks like our suspect from the earlier call. A grey Maserati. Witness says the member has let some shots go at the vehicle but has then been backed over. Any unit please, any unit to deal? This is one of ours."

Kate McLaren immediately switched on the electronic siren located under the bonnet and activated he blue and red flashing lights in the rear parcel shelf and behind the grille of the unmarked Holden Commodore. She hit the accelerator hard as Tony Signorotto jumped on the handset of the radio just before several other units responded.

"Calibre 250. Show us about two minutes away."

"Thanks 250. Sit rep A.S.A.P. on arrival. Looking critical at this stage according to an incoming call from a doctor at the scene. Member has been knocked off his solo and then reversed over after firing shots."

"Roger that," came the reply from Signorotto who felt as though someone had 'walked over his grave' as the saying went, remembering what he had said minutes before to Kate.

Neither Kate nor Tony spoke as the police vehicle hurtled north. The voice of Max Tyler came over the radio.

"Calibre 550. Shows us dealing also. "

"Roger that 550. We will need the C.I.U. at the scene. Anything else, just get back to us."

"Roger that," Tyler said as Chloe Schaeffer accelerated past the Fawkner cemetery some five or six kilometre behind Signorotto and McLaren.

As Calibre 250 flashed past Mount Ridley, they could see the road up ahead was completely blocked. A semi-trailer looked as though it had deliberately put itself across both north bound lanes to stop any further vehicles passing. Kate slowed but kept the emergency 'lights and bells' going as she pulled to the left and drove slowly up the left-hand grass verge until she came to a complete stop just back from the scene itself. They jumped from the vehicle and ran the last few metres with dread in their hearts as they saw the prone body of the solo rider lying motionless on the grass. A man walked towards them shaking his head.

"I couldn't save him. I'm so sorry. That car just reversed over him and crushed his chest. There wasn't anything I could do. I'm so sorry."

Just beyond the dead police officer, Tony could see a police motor bike lying on its side, the front wheel rotating slowly. Turning to Kate, he went into crime scene control mode which stopped him from becoming emotional about the dead officer.

"Make sure no vehicles come through. Block the whole highway off both sides if you have to. Max and Chloe will be here soon," he said as the high-pitched sounds of multiple emergency vehicle sirens could be heard approaching. The professional police officer in Kate forced her to turn way from the death scene and take up her duties as directed. Signorotto turned back and spoke to the doctor as two paramedics stood up from the body after covering it with a tarpaulin that was handed to them by a crying motorist.

Chapter Seventy-Six

"Were you a witness. Did you see everything that happened?"

"My wife and I were headed on holidays and were travelling behind a Maserati in the left lane when the policeman came by us and levelled off next to the driver's window of the car. Whoever was driving the Maserati started to slow but pulled out so that he was in the centre of two lanes and forced the police officer across also. Suddenly the driver just moved over right on top of him and hit him. Everyone behind just came to a stop and watched. It was like a horror show. After the officer hit the ground, he pulled out his revolver slowly and pointed it at the Maserati. He was on his knees. No one knew what was happening. It was like it was all in slow motion."

Signorotto guessed what was going to be said next but had to ask the question anyhow.

"I know it's hard, but I need you to tell me exactly what happened after that."

"I think the police officer was actually holding back from shooting, but then the Maserati's back wheels started to screech on the road as it just flew backwards towards him. He fired two or three shots which sounded as though they hit the car but then he was knocked over and the Maserati went up and over him. He was just squashed under the back wheels. People were screaming at the driver to stop the car, but he wouldn't. Next thing he just went forward over him again and took off up the highway. It's all just so shocking. The poor police officer didn't stand a chance."

The investigator in Signorotto then asked the most important question of all.

"How far was the Maserati from the policeman when he started to back up? What I'm saying is, could it have been accidental, and the driver didn't see the officer?"

The witness replied slowly.

"No way. He backed up about three or four metres. That driver deliberately drove over him. He knew what he was doing.

He then just drove forward and took off. He was trying to kill the police officer—and he succeeded."

Tony Signorotto comforted the doctor and his wife, who was sitting on the ground sobbing. He turned to Max Tyler and indicated for him to come over to him.

"Max. I'm going to have to leave all of this with you and Chloe but I'm sure there is a lot of help on the way. Get D.24 to get the Homicide Squad up here. This is now a murder scene."

"Right on it, Tony. What are you and Kate going to do?"

"We are going to get up the highway and find this piece of scum. Never know your luck, Max. One of those zingers might have struck him or his car."

Chapter Seventy-Seven

Lombardi sat slumped behind the wheel of his Maserati. The problem with his luxury ride was that it was not going anywhere.

In a strange way he was glad it was all coming to an end. All the plans for the hijacking and sale of the firearms had been compromised since shooting up the Carlton Police Station. That was the start of the downhill ride and now the ride was over— or so he thought.

He never once though blamed himself. It was the fault of the police turning up and arresting Ivan Volkov and subsequently forcing him to quickly relocate everything to the Brunswick factory. Little by little there were roadblocks preventing him from achieving greatness. No, the blame was not down to him and that was exactly what made him kill that police officer by backing over him. If he was going to bow out it would be with the S.O.G. or the Armed Robbers or someone or some group that was worthy of his capture. Not some lousy Highway Patrol officer on a motorbike. After all, Al Lombardi was a crime boss. He deserved respect from the Police. His mind had exploded with the disrespect of being pulled over by some country cop like he was an ordinary motorist.

His world had caved in at that point in time, so he just went for broke and backed over that pig. The thought that some bike rider had put two bullets into his Italian chariot infuriated him. Two fucking shots. One which ripped a hole through one of the three hundred-dollar Pirelli Pilot Super Sport tyres and the other shattering one of the taillight assemblies.

Serve the prick right. That light alone is worth a thousand dollars.

The turn off to Beveridge was only a tantalisingly short distance away but it might as well have been a hundred kilometres. The tyre was shredded with the weight of the big sports saloon.

"Fuck that cop bikie," he screamed aloud with no one to hear his venting. "Outlaw bikies and cop bikies. They've all fucked me over."

Suddenly over the crest of the hill behind him, a Holden Commodore began to slow as it approached and began to pull very slowly in behind him, stopping some ten metres back.

A light bulb moment of madness formed in his mind as he saw two police officer get out of the front doors. Without putting a lot of thought behind his next action, he leapt out of the driver's seat after first grabbing the two fully loaded pistols that he had taken from the shipment. He pointed them directly at each of the officers as they stood impassively behind each door. They did not reach for their own weapons.

"Both of you put your hands on your head and move away from that car," Lombardi screamed. "Leave the car running."

Tony Signorotto looked across at Kate McLaren with a smile on his face.

"You think this is fucking funny, big man?" Lombardi screamed again. "Keep it up and I'll blow you both away."

"What do you think you are going to do Lombardi? You're finished. Besides all the firearms offences, you have kidnapping and the murder of a police officer on your hands."

"It'll be two more in a minute if you don't get out of my way. Ironic, isn't it? A pig and his piglet blown away with their own pistols," Lombardi said as he waved Kate McLaren over to stand beside Tony Signorotto. "Now very gently, remove those guns with your opposite hand and drop them to the ground."

To his complete surprise, both police officers answered in unison with an emphatic '*No.*'

Lombardi grinned at Signorotto.

"You've got one last chance before I kill the bitch next to you," he said as he pointed one of the stolen nine-millimetre pistols at her.

What happened next would go down in Police folklore and be brought up at many a boozy police function for years to come wherever Signorotto or McLaren attended.

Kate stepped forward, still with her hands in the air, until the barrel of Lombardi's pistol was pressing hard against her blue police shirt directly between her breasts.

"Pull the trigger, fat boy. Go for it," McLaren said defiantly at Lombardi.

The colour drained from his face.

"I'm taking your car. Now unless you want to die here bitch, you'd better step aside."

Kate didn't move. Lombardi took a step to his right to go to the police vehicle. The Sergeant kept leaning in against the muzzle of the pistol and took a step to her left. To infuriate Lombardi, she smiled at him as she spoke.

"That would be the hardest thing you've ever held against a girl's tits, eh, little man? That pistol would be five times the size of your dick on a good day. What do you reckon, Senior Sergeant?"

Before the astonished Tony Signorotto could muster an answer to the unfolding situation, Lombardi took a step back, aimed at the smiling policewoman and pulled the trigger.

The only sound that came from the firearm was a resounding click. Lombardi aimed the second pistol at Signorotto and pulled the trigger with the same result. Looking down at his hands as they held the two useless pistols, he didn't see the vicious kick that Kate delivered between his legs. A scream and a rush of air burst from his lungs as he dropped both weapons and clutched at his balls.

Lombardi lay on the ground in a foetal position.

Signorotto looked at his Sergeant in amazement.

"Glad you remembered about those pistols needing to be stripped and serviced before they could be made operative, Sergeant. You had me worried there."

She replied over what was now a high-pitched moan bubbling from Lombardi's mouth.

"He's going to be somebody's bitch in gaol. Lowlife prick. Wants to kidnap little girls, so as far as I'm concerned, he gets whatever they want to lay on him in the can."

Signorotto sucked in a large gulp of air as he looked down on the pathetic, twitching form of Alessio Big Al Lombardi lying next to his damaged Maserati.

"Next time you want to snatch little girls, Alessio, you'd better think about what some big girls can do to you."

Lombardi's eyes rolled back in his head.

Chapter Seventy-Eight

In the life and times of those working at the Carlton Police Station, the previous six months had gone extremely quickly. Not had there only been a lot of interviews and paperwork to get done for the just finalised criminal trials of Alessio Big Al Lombardi and his fellow partners in crime, namely Tony Richards, Feb Felagi and Joey Salessa, but the presentation of the briefs of evidence that were compiled in assistance with the Homicide Squad on charges of murder in relation to the Highway Patrol officer killed and the execution of Leo Carbone together with a plethora of kidnapping, theft and firearms offences had to be meticulous to gain the convictions.

Lombardi had pleaded not guilty to all the charges and demanded a separate trial from the other defendants. This was basically so he could lay blame for everything on Tony Richards, especially when it came to the kidnapping of Summer Cole. Lombardi claimed that he didn't know that he had run over the police officer even though he had to reverse up to do it. As for Leo Carbone, he categorically denied that he knew there was a round in the gun when he pulled the trigger, splattering Carbone's brains and skull all over the kitchen walls of the safe house where he had Felagi and Salessa keep both Carbone and Morelli captive. On the attempted murder charges regarding the unsuccessful firing of the pistols at Signorotto and Mclean, well, that was a case of him never wanting to kill them. Or so he claimed.

Lombardi sacked his legal team in the end, stating that he could defend himself and present his case in a much better light. It all ended when the presiding judge commented that he would need all the lights from the Melbourne Cricket Ground to get himself out of his dark place. His defences were brushed aside one after one. He went down on every charge.

Big Al Lombardi was sentenced to life without parole on the murder charges. The attempted murder, kidnapping and firearms charges were part of his package. When he argued that the judge, by law, must state a minimum sentence, His Worship asked him how old he was. A bemused Lombardi stated he was forty-six years of age. The judge told him to remember that number. Lombardi did not see the irony.

Tony Richards was sentenced to a combined twenty years for the kidnapping of Tom Cole and his daughter, while Feb Felagi and Joey Salessa were given the same. Richards earned himself an extra five years after he was convicted of assault with intent to cause serious bodily harm for the car ram on the Highway Patrol vehicle that was escorting the firearms. When all the other charges relating to the firearms themselves were rolled into the evidence, even the defendants had stopped counting at twenty. By that stage it was irrelevant. They would all be old men when they eventually walked out of Barwon State Prison. Happier times had now descended on the Carlton Police Station as they had two events they were all talking about.

The first had taken place two weeks previously at the Victoria Police Academy at which the entire crew from the Carlton Police Station had attended. It was the presentation of the Victoria Police Valour medal to their own Sergeant Kate McLaren for her stance on the Hume Highway at Beveridge in staring down Lombardi and enabling his capture by herself and Senior Sergeant Tony Signorotto.

The second was the one that was taking place at Dom Santino's Lygon Street restaurant. What a night it was. The engagement party for Kate McLaren and Tom Cole.

Dom and his wife Maria were over the moon not only for them both but also for little Summer who over the last few months had recovered completely from the trauma of the kidnap with the help of the Santino girls, Gina, Silvana and Rosa. She had been basically adopted by the family to the point where there was a very friendly tug of war rivalry being waged as to before and after school minding duties between Maria and her girls and Jill Norton. There was never a time when due to the vagaries of Tom's work as the now Managing Director of National Security Services and Kate's busy work as a Sergeant at Carlton that Summer would go without her extended family.

The party had all the trappings of a big Italian affair of which Dom and Maria insisted was their engagement present to the young couple. Kate and Tom had even approached Tony Signorotto trying to get him to convince the Santino family that they wanted to pay. He just shrugged his shoulders at them in a gesture meaning that it would have been easier to get blood out of a stone than convince Dom and Maria to give them a bill for the night. This was the Italian way and only God knew what they would do for the wedding.

Everyone from Kate and Tom's work was there including Max Tyler and Chloe Schaeffer, who, a lot of people were saying would be the centrepiece of the next big Santino celebration.

Tony looked around the crowd and still couldn't believe how some of these great people had helped him turn his own life around. He hadn't had a drink for a few years now and with his gorgeous wife Susie, who was on the other side of the room chatting with Phil Stone's wife Mandy and Tony's little daughter Gracie, life couldn't have been better. As Dom would say, there are only two things in life. Family and friends.

Phil Stone made his way over to Tony. No matter when or where they got together it always ended up in shop talk. Stone started off the conversation with the Angelo Morelli situation.

"Got the word back from Command. After Morelli's evidence went a long way to get the convictions on all the others and considering he nearly died from that bullet, the Department approached the Police Minister's office and they thought it would be better all-round if he was offered a new life under the Witness Protection Program. If he had to stand trial himself, he wouldn't last five minutes at Barwon prison. There are quite a few bikies in there including Tony Richards. It would be a death sentence."

Signorotto smiled at Stone as Max Tyler made his way over after untangling himself from Chloe Schaeffer on the dance floor.

"Where's he picked for the rest of his life?" Tony said to Phil.

"Would you believe Guadeloupe in the Caribbean. Seems he's a big fan of that television show *Death in Paradise.* He's going through all the paperwork and passport stuff next week.

"I don't think anyone of us, especially Tom, would want to put him out as roadkill for the Black Rats after helping get Tony Richards twenty-five years in the can."

"Good luck to him I say. Lombardi executed his best mate in front of his eyes which will affect him mentally for years. A rum at sunset in the Caribbean is a good way to recover. I don't have a problem with it at all, do you, Phil?"

"No. Wouldn't mind joining him there, actually," Stone said with laughter as Max Tyler interrupted the conversation.

"Sorry gents. Just remembered something I had to tell Tony. When I was up at the County Court yesterday interviewing a crook in the cells, I ran into a prison officer who is an old mate of yours, Tony. He was on escort duties up from Barwon State Prison."

"Who was that?" Tony Signorotto said, feigning surprise.

"A bloke by the name of Bob Chesterfield. Old Highway Patrolman. He was the guy who gave us the first tip ages ago on the possible gun heist when he overheard that Carnivore having a go at a Black Rat in the holding cells. Remember?"

"Oh, yeah. I do remember. I actually rang him a couple of weeks ago down at Barwon so he could remind Lombardi mid trial that his precious Maserati was being sold off as proceeds of crime. We had a great chat about that and a few other things. There's a young Vietnamese restaurant owner by the name of Binh Le who's been waiting to pick it up for a bargain price. I told Bob to mention it to Lombardi that he should have been a lot nicer to Binh Le's sister that night he had dinner in Richmond with the late John Moore. Binh is going to sell it off and use the money to get his uncle and aunt over to Australia. Dom is helping him with the visa side of things. Apparently, Lombardi nearly had a stroke when he heard that an Asian would be buying it," Signorotto said.

The three hard-nosed police officers burst out laughing before Max could continue.

As he walked away into party central where Dom and Maria were hosting one of the best evenings that Santino's had seen in a long time, Phil Stone looked at Tony, smiled, winked and raised a glass of red to his Senior Sergeant who was nursing his usual Lemon, Lime and Bitters. Stone spoke quietly.

Tony clinked his glass against Phil's. "Cin Cin." It was all that was needed to be said.

Chapter Seventy-Nine

Bob Chesterfield might have been retired from the Victoria Police Force for some years now, but he didn't mind working three days a week as a Prison Officer at Barwon State Prison.

Because he was part time he was used mainly as transport guard for whenever a prisoner had to be taken up to Melbourne for a trial or a hearing. His job was to make sure they got on the bus at each end of the journey and when he had to wait for one of them at a court, he stayed downstairs near the cells. Having had police experience, a calm head on his shoulders, and a steady demeanour with the harder of the criminals, he usually attended the higher County or Supreme Courts.

Everybody trusted Bob and considered him to be just another retired, burnt out cop. But Bob, like most, might leave 'The Job' physically, but never spiritually—and never in their hearts. People said there was nothing more ex than an ex-cop, but the loyalty always remained to the boys and girls on the Thin Blue Line. The one thing they would never forgive was a cop killer. And Lombardi had murdered one of Bob's fellow Highway Patrolman. When cops needed cops in a hurry, they prayed for the Highway Patrol to be around. They had the fastest cars and the best drivers and would break their necks to get to a police in trouble call as quick as they could. There was many a hardened detective who would shout a beer at a later date for a lifesaving moment from the Highway Patrol.

Bob Chesterfield was never going to let Alessio Lombardi get away with killing a brother Highway Patrolman. He had no intention of killing or harming him himself though. He would leave that to Lombardi's fellow inmates. All Bob had to do was to 'put a flea' in someone's ear. It would roll from there.

Lombardi had dropped Richards' name continually in his own trial, stating that it was Richards who was the one responsible for the kidnapping of Summer Cole and that he, Lombardi was against it completely, so it was obvious that Richards would want to have words with his friend Alessio when they both got to Barwon Prison.

Days later when Lombardi was arranging his bunk and spreading out his meagre belongings after being taken to his cell, a familiar voice spoke from the door.

"Hello Al. Good to see you've made yourself at home," Tony Richards said as he limped over to the visibly shaking Lombardi. Make sure you don't spread yourself out too much. Don't get too comfortable. Your new cell mate probably will want some space, too."

A terrified sounding Lombardi replied.

"Are you my cell mate?"

"No, Al. Not me, but I believe he has been waiting for you to arrive. Says he knows you real well. He's just outside. I'll bring him in."

The large bear like figure of Ivan Volkov stepped around and filled the doorway.

Leaning down, he picked Lombardi up by his shirt until his feet were almost off the ground.

"So nice to see you, Little Al."

Lombardi's bladder gave way at that point and warm urine flowed down his legs onto his prison issue shoes. Looking back at Richards, he saw the shiv being passed backwards to the waiting hand of Volkov.

About the Author

Phil Copsey served with Victoria State Police Force, Australia, for forty years. His hard-earned experience fighting crime on the streets of multicultural Melbourne compelled him to write his debut novel, Blue Justice. His depictions of characters and crimes are infused with authentic operational details, told through the eyes of his composite character, Sergeant Tony Signorotto. Phil is a natural storyteller who returned to study towards the end of his career to begin his Tony Signorotto crime series.

*

You are welcome to email the author at *philipcopsey@gmail.com*

By the same Author

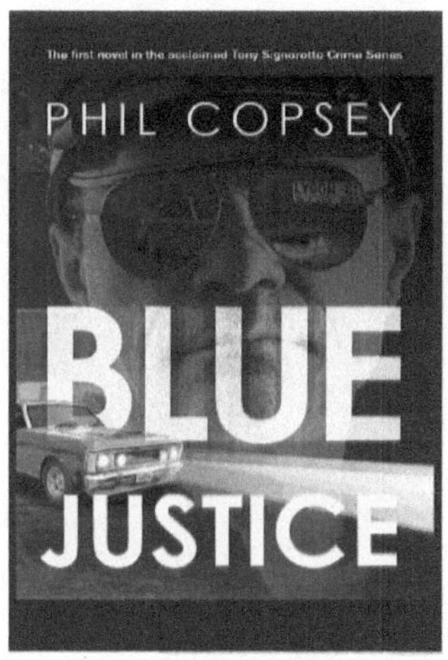

Blue Justice is the first of a gritty new crime series published by in case of emergency press.

Don't look for puzzling cases, corpses in locked rooms, ingenious criminal masterminds, this is a novel about police on the beat: ugly, raw, and morally uncertain. It's not about solving crime. It's about solving problems.

Sergeant Tony Signorotto has good friends, plenty of enemies, and the sort of family connections that just might get him killed.

Buy **Blue Justice** from
https://icoe.com.au/bluejustice.html